SNAKE OIL:
TOO GOOD TO BE TRUE

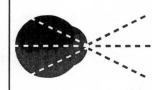

This Large Print Book carries the
Seal of Approval of N.A.V.H.

SNAKE OIL: TOO GOOD TO BE TRUE

BOOK TWO

MARCUS GALLOWAY

THORNDIKE PRESS
A part of Gale, a Cengage Company

Farmington Hills, Mich • San Francisco • New York • Waterville, Maine
Meriden, Conn • Mason, Ohio • Chicago

GALE
A Cengage Company

LIBRARY OF CONGRESS CIP DATA ON FILE.
CATALOGUING IN PUBLICATION FOR THIS BOOK
IS AVAILABLE FROM THE LIBRARY OF CONGRESS

ISBN-13: 978-1-4104-8564-9 (hardcover)

Published in 2018 by arrangement with Cherry Weiner Literary Agency

Printed in the United States of America
1 2 3 4 5 6 7 22 21 20 19 18

Snake Oil:
Too Good to Be True

Chapter One

Montana
1878

Life was mostly made of small things. Big things, more often than not, were nothing more than window dressing or outright lies. Certainly, there were plenty of natural wonders that were every bit as impressive as their size or appearance might suggest. Most of those, however, were created by the one who'd created most everything under the sun and for that omnipresent being to pull off an impressive trick was largely to be expected. Mortal men had two choices. They could devote themselves to crafting large spectacles or hone their skills enough to make the smaller ones count for more than they were worth.

A prime example of the latter was the little circle of clay resting atop the second knuckle of Professor Henry Whiteoak's left hand. Strictly speaking, it was nothing more a small sliver of thick mud that had been baked and painted after being fashioned into a common shape. Once the first coat of coloring had been applied, a second brush had swiped across its surface to add a filigree design around a single letter. That letter was an M which stood for Minstrelerro; the saloon in which that chip could be redeemed for ten dollars.

It certainly wasn't the only one of its kind. There were stacks of similar chips piled on top of the professor's table along with more stacks of chips that were worth less. The smaller stacks of black chips were guarded most ferociously, further proving the value of lesser things. But the chip on top of the professor's hand wasn't like the others stacked in front of him. That one jumped and flipped with subtle movements of its owner's fingers, journeying from one side of his hand and back to the other. It captivated some of the men sitting at the round table where Whiteoak had taken residence for the last several hours, but didn't have any discernable effect on the rest. Whiteoak himself didn't so much as glance down at it.

"What the hell are you waitin' for?" sneered one of the men who'd been watching Whiteoak closely. Since the professor hadn't moved much in the last several seconds, the fellow's impatient eyes darted back and forth between Whiteoak's face and the chip he so casually manipulated.

"I'm thinking," Whiteoak replied.

"Thinkin' about what? A three-dollar raise?"

"Apparently."

"That ain't a fortune, Silky Britches. Either push the money forward or fold, goddammit."

Whiteoak's britches weren't made from silk, but they were a somewhat expensive cut of cotton. Compared to the rags wrapped around the impatient man's malodorous body, however, the professor's finely tailored suit might as well have been the robes of a king. He tapped his chin with one hand while using his other to put the clay chip on its edge upon the table and set it to spinning. Though he knew what he meant to do, he furrowed his brow in a show of contemplation while continuing to fidget in a way that he knew would aggravate his impatient audience. "Three dollars can buy a lot in this saloon. Several drinks. A few turns of the roulette wheel."

"Call or fold!"

"It could buy you a fairly good time with Alice over there," Whiteoak added as he pointed to a pleasantly plump working girl sitting in a gambler's lap at another table. "With some sweet talk, it might even grant you several memorable minutes with Stormy."

Hearing that name caused the impatient man to look away for a moment. Considering Stormy's curving hips, slender waist and ample bosom, it was surprising that not all of the men took the opportunity to look in her direction whenever they had the chance.

When he looked back again, the impatient man slammed his hand against the table. "Call or fold!"

"Take it easy, Jorgens," Wade muttered. "He's just trying to get a rise out of you."

"Well he's about to get more of a rise than he'd like if he don't make his play."

"Why are you trying to rush me?" Whiteoak asked. "Is your hand that good?"

"Maybe you're just holding up the fucking game," snapped the man who sat to Jorgens's left. So far, every one of the professor's attempts to engage him in conversation had been met with slack-jawed silence. Since Whiteoak hadn't been able to catch his name, all he knew was that he was bald.

Whiteoak looked over to his right. "What do you think, Wade?"

Wade was a slender man a few years younger than Whiteoak. He was an amicable fellow who laughed at the others' jokes without making any of his own. When it came to betting, he was a bit too cautious for his own good but had made a small profit in the course of the night's game. To Whiteoak's question, he nodded and replied, "You are holding up the game a bit, Henry."

"So I am," Whiteoak said. "I'll raise. Three hundred and sixty dollars."

Jorgens narrowed his eyes and gritted his teeth. "I only got three fifty."

"Then you don't have enough to cover the bet."

"What about a side pot?"

"No."

"What did you say?"

The friendliness in Whiteoak's tone was barely enough to cover the surface of his words when he said, "No side pot. You can cover the bet or you're out."

"What kind of bullshit is that?"

"This isn't a house game, which means certain traditions don't need to be observed. Side pots are nothing more than a way to allow lesser players to sit at a table with serious gamesmen. If you don't have enough money to cover the bet, you fold. If you don't have enough to cover any of the bets, you get up and play somewhere else. I believe there's a penny ante game across the street, but it's not my responsibility to accommodate someone who wants to play above their means."

The table fell silent. Even the music that flowed through the air of the Minstrelerro wasn't enough to break the icy stillness that had enveloped the game. When Jorgens stood up and reached for the gun strapped around his waist, Whiteoak snapped his arm forward to point a silver-handled .38 at him. He'd drawn it from the holster buckled around his shoulders so quickly that the movement could barely be seen.

"Easy, now," grunted the bald man sitting next to Jorgens. "Ain't no reason for this to get bloody."

"However much blood is spilt will be on this asshole's hands," Jorgens said.

"I'm just trying to maintain the integrity of this game," Whiteoak said. "I didn't sit down at this table to indulge childish whims."

"Childish?" Jorgens bristled.

Wade scooted his chair away from the table to put some distance between himself and the two bulls that were locking horns, but wasn't about to spark anything worse by moving more than that. "You both have a point," he said. "This isn't a house game and we can conduct it as we see fit. But a side pot isn't unheard of and I, for one, don't have any problem with one."

"You're not in the hand," Whiteoak said in a steely voice.

"I am," said the greasy fellow to the professor's left. "And I don't have a problem with it, either."

Shifting his gaze in Greasy's direction, Whiteoak was careful not to let Jorgens out of his sight. Relaxing his fingers caused Whiteoak's .38 to dangle from his trigger finger. "Well, then," he said in a tone that was much more reminiscent of the banter he'd spewed all night long. "I suppose I'll have to abide by the table's wishes. I'm nothing if not a fair player."

"That's it?" Jorgens asked skeptically.

"It is," Whiteoak replied, "unless you'd rather it wasn't."

Jorgens dropped back down onto his chair. "I just wanna play a damn card game. You gonna accept my bet or not?"

"Of course I will."

Jorgens picked up his cards and asked, "I take it you call, then?"

"No. I fold."

"You what?"

Greasy started to chuckle. "He was winding you up, you damn fool. Pushing you to see how far you'd go to play them cards you're holding."

After anxiously glancing down at his hand, Jorgens said, "Yeah, well, maybe I knew that and was just playin' along."

"Maybe," Whiteoak said.

"Only way to find out is to call. What do ya say?" Jorgens grunted to the only one left in the hand.

Shaking his head, Greasy tossed his cards onto the stack of dead wood. "I'm out."

Jorgens placed his cards face down while scooping up the pot. It wasn't a bad haul, although a good portion of the money in it belonged to him at the start of the game. "Yer all a bunch of cryin' babies," he said.

Whiteoak pushed away from the table and tugged at his lapels to straighten the lines of his waistcoat. "If that's the case, then this baby needs his bottle. Anyone else care for a drink?"

"Nothing from you," Jorgens spat.

The others at the table nodded gratefully.

While most men would have been happy simply walking away from a table so soon after guns were drawn, Henry Whiteoak couldn't resist patting Jorgens on the shoulder. "Be sure to keep an eye on my chips, Wade. I don't trust this one."

Whatever peace may have been cobbled

together between Whiteoak and Jorgens was shattered by those words. Jorgens jumped back to his feet and spun around while swinging an arm back to hit the professor with an elbow. Whiteoak stepped aside, but couldn't evade the blow. He caught enough of Jorgens's elbow to send him staggering back and into the chair of someone playing at another table.

That gambler seemed large enough when he was seated. Standing up, he looked more like a wall than a man. Wide shoulders, a thick chest, and burly arms were coated in muscle and his meaty hands closed into fists as he turned around to glare at the insects that had bumped against his chair.

"What the *hell* is goin' on?!" the big man roared.

Whiteoak looked at the large fellow as his finely trimmed eyebrows flicked upward in a surprised expression. "I can explain. You see . . ."

But the big man was already riled up. Seeing Jorgens pick up his chair to take a swing with it was more than enough to push him all the way over the edge. Before Jorgens could bust his chair over Whiteoak's back, the big man dropped him with one clubbing blow to the face.

Turning to see Jorgens reel from the

punch and drop the chair he'd been holding, Whiteoak chuckled uneasily and said, "Thank you very much, good sir."

Those were the last words to escape his mouth before the big man's fist connected with his face.

It was always a strange thing being knocked off one's feet. The first time it happened, Whiteoak was very young and unable to appreciate the finer aspects of the brutal act. As he'd grown into a man and his skills with stringing words together was honed into an art, Henry Whiteoak found himself in many more fights.

Some he lost and others were soundly won. Every last one of them, however, provided opportunities even if it was just an opportunity to excuse himself from a bad situation or take his leave of reality for a short spell. This time, as he toppled toward the floor, Whiteoak angled his body so he could land on his side where one arm could protect his ribs. With the other arm, he reached out to snag Jorgens's ankle and give his leg a sharp pull.

Jorgens let out a surprised yelp as his balance was taken away. He caught himself before falling onto his face, but was unable to do so before knocking into the big muscular fellow once again.

16

Baring his teeth like a wild dog, the big man unleashed all of his fury in a storm of fists that thumped against Jorgens to send him straight back into the table where he and Whiteoak had been playing cards. Before that table was overturned and every last chip was sent to the floor, Greasy and Wade grabbed Jorgens to toss him in another direction. The big fellow was there to catch him and slammed a fist into Jorgens's gut.

"Don't got . . . a problem with you," Jorgens wheezed.

"That's where you're wrong, mister," the big fellow sneered.

Whiteoak listened to the exchange as he crawled away. As he struggled to escape the fight he'd started, Whiteoak was careful not to ruin his suit along the way. At the first opportunity, he got his feet beneath him and stood up to dust himself off. Almost immediately, he found himself looking directly into a face that could have been chiseled from clay by the hand of a drunk.

"If it ain't Henry goddamn Whiteoak," the ugly man said. "I been looking for you."

CHAPTER TWO

The fight didn't last much longer. Fortunately, Jorgens was smart enough to apologize profusely and accept a few more lumps from the big fellow before buying him a drink. Once it was clear that no more punches were going to be thrown, the saloon fell back to its normal degree of chaos.

The Minstrelerro was more than twice as long as it was wide. Its entrance was at one of the short ends of the rectangular building and a bar ran almost all the way from front to back. On the opposite side, situated against the other long wall, were two stages. The main stage was larger and closer to the front window so passersby could get a glimpse of the show being put on without being able to see too much. The smaller stage at the back of the main room usually had racier shows for its customers. The girls wore less, danced with more abandon and were available for private performances after the song died down.

Music was as much a part of the Minstrel-erro as the planks of the stages. A narrow box sectioned off from the rest of the room contained two pianos, several guitars, and a few other instruments along with chairs for the artists who played them. Depending on the time of day, one might hear selections from Brahms or Stephen Foster, inspirational or revolting, sublime or rambunctious. The musicians were so accustomed to their surroundings that none of them fretted when a fight broke out. They simply gave their instruments a rest and took a moment to refill their drinks. By the time Whiteoak and the ugly man who'd found him arrived at the bar, a violinist was launching into a soothing piece meant to calm frayed nerves. The song was received with a few bawdy shouts, but otherwise seemed to accomplish its task.

The man who accompanied Whiteoak to the bar had a round, lumpy head covered in hair that might have been hacked off with a machete. In some areas, the dark bristle was cut all the way down to the scalp. In others, it sprouted just tall enough to be flattened by a hard night's sleep. Toward the back of his head, two long scars prevented any hair from growing at all. His rumpled clothes and battered shoes added more to his disheveled appearance, though his eyes beamed like those of a king.

It had been a while since Whiteoak had seen Corey Maynard, but not a lot had changed. His eyes were still cheerful and sharp, although now they gazed out at the world through a pair of glass lenses framed in thin copper circles. Grinning as if to display the tooth he was missing, Corey said, "You never know when to quit, do ya?"

"I beg your pardon," Whiteoak replied in an overly dramatic tone.

Corey waved that off before gripping the edge of the bar with both hands. "You ain't never begged nobody for nothing and you ain't about to start now."

"Is that such a bad thing?"

"Not begging? Nah. Strutting about like a peacock to make sure everyone sees how much better you are than them . . . maybe."

"You think I'm better than most folks? How very kind, sir."

"Sorry," Corey chuckled. "I meant strutting like you *think* you're better than everyone else."

"Ah. I see."

Corey leaned with one elbow propped on the bar and a foot resting on the brass rail below so he could stand sideways and look straight at the professor. "Do you, Henry? Do you see what I'm getting at? Because this little scuffle tells me you don't."

"What's that supposed to mean?" Whiteoak asked while waving to catch the barkeep's attention.

"Remember New Orleans?"

A wistful smile drifted across Whiteoak's face, causing the sharp lines of his mouth and cheeks to curve upward as a contented sigh escaped his lips. "How could I forget New Orleans and all the lovelies residing therein?"

"That," Corey said while poking Whiteoak's chest with a single finger. "Right there. That's what got you into trouble and what nearly got us both dumped into the foulest corner of them bayous."

"How was I supposed to know Miss Tilly's brother was so large?" Whiteoak said meekly. "Or so easily offended."

"Because you did your level best to offend him, just like you did with them fellas over at that table," Corey replied as he nodded toward the card table where Jorgens, Wade, Greasy and the bald man were settling in for another hand.

"Strategy is what that was," Whiteoak replied slyly. "By testing a man's limits, it opens the workings of his mind like the gears of a pocket watch to a clock smith."

Corey didn't say anything to that. Instead, he locked a stern gaze onto the professor and scowled disapprovingly.

"All right," Whiteoak admitted. "Perhaps I just wanted to rattle him."

Still not responding to the professor's glib tone, Corey kept his scowl firmly in place. "And the fight?" he asked.

"Somewhat accidental, but also fun. Come on now! It hasn't been that long since we last worked together. Don't tell me you've stopped enjoying a good tussle in that short stretch of time."

"Sure I do. I just don't gussy it up with fancy talk and high notions."

Whiteoak waved his hand dismissively. "It's not worth all of this seriousness," he said. "No harm done. Just ask him."

It wasn't until that moment that either man took notice of the bartender who'd approached them and stood waiting. When Corey and Whiteoak looked over at him, the skinny barkeep told them, "I've seen a lot worse and so has nearly everyone in here. You should see what happens when someone's caught cheating. That's when things get rough. Disagreements between players aren't much of anything at all, so long as no shots are fired."

"There now," Whiteoak said. "You see? Nothing at all. For that bit of sobering sanity, I'll buy the first round of drinks for me and my friend here."

"So much for sober," Corey grumbled.

"What was that?"

"Nothing. Pour away, my good man."

Whiteoak pointed to a bottle on a shelf behind the bar. When the barkeep brought it over along with two glasses, the professor asked, "Do you know who I am?"

"Course I do," the barkeep replied. "You're that salesman who puts on the medicine show every other night."

"And twice on Sundays," Whiteoak chimed in. "Have you ever seen my shows?"

"Sure."

"Then you know the miracles I can perform." With every word he spoke, Whiteoak slipped deeper into the flowery pattern of speech used to captivate the hopeful crowds that gathered around his wagon every other day and twice on Sundays. "Are you aware that I possess a mixture that can heighten the flavor of your liquors to such a degree that you could charge triple your regular rate?"

"Henry," Corey warned. "Enough of that."

"Why?" Whiteoak asked.

Almost immediately, the barkeep said, "Yeah, why? Did you say triple the regular rate?"

Before Whiteoak could launch into his pitch, Corey asked, "Didn't you have a bit of trouble with that stuff recently?"

"Not at all!"

"What trouble?" the barkeep asked.

Despite the angry scowl Whiteoak showed him, Corey said, "That business in Kansas. Remember? I believe some of the folks there got a little sleepy when . . ."

"No sleepier than normal when consuming fine vintages," Whiteoak hastily said. "Besides, I am always refining my mixtures and perfecting every tonic. As it says on the side of my wagon, results are guaranteed."

The barkeep scratched his head while looking at the shelves of liquor behind him. "Guaranteed, huh?"

"Most assuredly."

After a short contemplation, the barkeep said, "Eh, maybe I'll just stick to what I've got. Haven't had any complaints yet."

"I'm sure you haven't. But think of the possibilities if you can offer a superior product at no extra cost to you. Well, apart from the nominal price of my mixture, that is." Sensing the barkeep's hesitance the way a predator could smell weakness from a lame animal, Whiteoak raised the glass of whiskey he'd purchased and said, "Next time you visit one of my demonstrations, I'll show you how I can raise the quality of your liquor to new heights with a free sample."

"Free, you say?"

"Indeed."

"All right. Enjoy the drinks, fellas." With that, the barkeep turned and walked away.

Whiteoak watched him while gnashing his teeth. "You may have cost me a very lucrative business opportunity," he said quietly.

"You told me about what happened in Barbrady," Corey replied. "Wasn't that more of a mess than you prefer?"

"Yes, but I handled it quite nicely."

"So you've said. Although I can't really say how much of what you told me on any matter was truth and how much was bullshit."

"I prefer to call it colorful embellishment for the sake of a good story," Whiteoak said.

"Yeah, well, us regular folks call it bullshit. Besides, I've learned a few things while I was away that you should know."

"Like what?" Whiteoak grunted before drinking his whiskey in a single gulp.

"First of all, there's a price on your head."

"That's nothing new. Every good businessman has competitors. The more ruthless those competitors are," the professor added, "the better it reflects on the businessman."

"Leave it to you to turn a bounty into yet another reason to puff out your chest."

"What's the other thing you needed to tell me?" Whiteoak asked.

Corey picked up his drink and took a sip. The whiskey had enough of a bite to put a temporary snarl on his face. Letting out a slow breath, he said, "We haven't finished talking about the first thing yet. The price that's been put on your head is ten thousand dollars."

"Impressive."

"To collect the reward, bringing you in alive ain't an option."

Whiteoak's eyebrow raised a bit when he heard that. "Funny. The folks who've been angry enough to send gunmen after me usually want me breathing so they could knock me around a bit before finishing the job themselves."

"It seems these fellows know better than to give you a chance to talk your way out of it," Corey explained.

"That does make some degree of sense. And how do you know so much about this? Have you stooped so low as to count bounty hunting among your varied professions?"

"No, although shooting you could be one job I might enjoy." After sending the remaining contents of his glass down his throat, Corey added, "The ten grand would be a mighty fine bonus, as well."

"Very funny."

"The men who put up the money for the reward are some of the ones who were on the losing end of that bank robbery in Barbrady. Those men have deep pockets and know a lot about you. They knew enough to come to me to ask for some help in setting you up for a fall."

Displaying a poker face that was as solid as the Rocky Mountains, Whiteoak asked, "Did you accept?"

"If I did, I'd be dragging your lily white hide out of town right now. But I sure as hell wasn't the only one who got that offer and those rich old men from Kansas are most likely gathering some very nasty killers to finish the job. Seeing as how I still think of you as something of a friend, I'll probably be in their sights as well."

"I see," Whiteoak sighed. "Now that isn't quite as funny."

CHAPTER THREE

Hannigan's Folly was a small town nestled in a very large mountain range in the wilds of Montana. It was named after the unwise decision of Daniel Hannigan to try and venture past those mountains when the rest of his party had been wiped out by the rigors of a long ride from Nebraska. While some may have commended such a bold move, others saw the futility in moving on without the benefit of partners, wagons or horses to pull them. Daniel Hannigan, as it turned out, was an idiot. So was the rail-thin young man who stood in front of Whiteoak's wagon later that evening.

"My good sir," Whiteoak said to the young man. "How long have your teeth been in such a state?"

The younger man had a crooked nose, pockmarked skin and mean eyes. Whenever he talked or drew a breath, he opened his mouth wide enough to show discolored teeth that were crooked, chipped and worn to nubs. "As far as I can remember," he said.

"And have you seen a dentist?"

"Sure I have. I saw that dentist right over there." Swinging his arm to point at the crowd behind him, he singled out the man standing across the street in front of a doctor's office. The man was dressed in a black suit and waved when Whiteoak and the rest of the crowd looked in his direction.

"And I'm sure he's done the best he could to treat his patient," Whiteoak said.

The young man in front of the professor said, "All he wants to do is yank the teeth outta my head!"

"That's all that's going to help you, Bill," the dentist shouted back.

Snapping his fingers and raising his voice to be heard above both of them, Whiteoak said, "There's nothing wrong with the good doctor's methods. The only problem is that he doesn't have the benefit of years of experience plying the trade of medicine across this vast, wonderful country of ours."

"I've practiced in three major cities, including New York," the dentist yelled. "You're nothing but a shyster."

"And that's your opinion, sir. What I'd like now is young Bill's opinion on this." As he spoke, Whiteoak reached for a small table that had been set up in front of his wagon and covered by a white handkerchief. Whiteoak pulled the handkerchief away with a flourish to reveal a squat bottle of murky white liquid.

"What the hell is that?" Bill asked.

Much to Whiteoak's delight, the dentist across the street had had enough. With a frustrated wave of his hand, he turned and walked back into his office.

"This," the professor announced, "is Whiteoak's Fresh and White! A patented brew of my own design, this will give you a mouth so clean that your tongue will thank you for the pleasure of living between your teeth. Your breath will be so fresh," he added with a playful nudge to Bill's arm, "that your wife or lady friend will be thanking me as well."

That got a mild chuckle from the crowd, which Whiteoak reacted to as if it was a standing ovation. Considering the wagon behind him, it wasn't much of a stretch for him to feel like he was performing on a stage. Less of a mode of transportation and more of an expression of Whiteoak's personality blown up and spread across a shack on wheels, the wagon was covered in brightly painted pictures, broadly enthusiastic slogans and testimonials that rose the professor and his wares to near godhood.

During his shows, the rear door of the wagon was propped open to grant the professor access thanks to a small set of steps. On either side of the door, hooks were screwed into the side of the wagon bearing chimes, measuring spoons, strips of rusted tin and anything else that might clatter together noisily whenever the wagon was in motion or a modest breeze came along. Some of those items were useful, but anything of value was either stored inside the wagon or within the many locked drawers on the wooden frame's exterior. Whiteoak approached one of those drawers now, pulled it open and removed a small bowl and a flask.

Grabbing for a spoon hanging nearby, he said, "Inside this flask is simple water," which, of course, was a lie. "All one needs to do is mix my Fresh and White with water and vigorously apply to your teeth for a smile that shall be as memorable as the stars in the sky." That part, at least, was mostly true. The effect lasted for a short while as did many of Whiteoak's beauty products. As long as the number of unsavory side effects was kept to a minimum for the duration of his stay, the product served its purpose.

"You," the professor said while pointing to Bill with one hand and stirring his mix with the other, "are not receiving any compensation from me to provide your assistance. Is that correct?"

Bill grunted in a confused manner.

"He's too dumb to be a shill for anyone!" someone from the crowd shouted, which was one of the most honest things spoken at Whiteoak's demonstration.

"And I'm sure you're not the only one who suffers from the affliction of regrettable dental hygiene," Whiteoak continued.

Since he'd gotten some laughs before, the man who'd spoken up a few moments ago said, "I know there's some dogs in the alley behind my shop that have teeth almost as bad as his!"

The laughs that came from that were a bit more enthusiastic, but didn't last as long. While he didn't have a smile worth mentioning, Bill's angry glare was truly memorable. Having plenty of experience in knowing when someone was about to throw a punch, Whiteoak pulled him closer to the table and handed him the tin cup he'd filled with the recently mixed concoction. "Here you go, Bill. Try some of this."

Bill sniffed the murky liquid and winced. "I ain't drinking this."

"It's not supposed to be drunk. You take some in your mouth, swirl it about and spit."

Lifting the cup to his mouth, Bill did as he was told and took some of it in. After less than a second, he spat it onto the ground. "That stuff was bubblin' something fierce!"

"That's the key to it working," Whiteoak said to him as well as the crowd. "The fizz helps wash off the grime and dissolve it safely away while the fresh tasting ingredient you surely experienced freshens your breath."

"I didn't taste much."

"That's because you didn't try enough. Go on. Take the rest and swirl it about."

If he was standing alone at that wagon, Bill wouldn't have let one more drop of the strange mixture cross his lips. That much was apparent from the look on his face. But when he shifted his eyes to his neighbors and friends watching from the audience, he couldn't bring himself to refuse the drink. He made the best of it by facing the crowd head-on, lifting the cup and pouring its contents into his mouth.

Whiteoak was impressed. Since he was the one to create the stuff, he knew how hard it was to bear. The soda water that gave it its bubbling effect did little to dull the flavor of the paint that was mixed into the drink. Granted, the stuff wasn't the same sort of paint one might use on a fence or the side of a house, but it was a kind of paint nonetheless. Whiteoak first encountered the stuff on a trip to a small fishing town in New England. Thanks to its acidic properties, it was used clean the bottom of ships and clear them of barnacles. When used for decorating fence posts that got a great deal of exposure to salt water, a clear varnish had been mixed in to help repel water and bond the color to wood. Whiteoak conceived the idea for his Fresh and White when he'd seen it applied to a picket fence with rounded slats resembling a long row of blunt teeth.

The first thing he'd done was test the paint on the fangs of a dead dog. It worked beautifully, although it colored the gums and lips as well. It hadn't taken long for him to notice the flesh being burnt away from the dead animal's mouth when too much of the paint had been used. He then bought a large supply of the chemical and started his experimentation. After months of making no progress whatsoever, Whiteoak happened upon a chemist who tinkered with the formula further. The two of them brewed a similar stain from scratch. But there was always the danger of poisoning anyone who might swallow it.

"It'll be fine," the chemist had told him when handing over the final batch he'd been paid to make, "just as long as it's not consumed in large doses."

"What'll happen if it's swallowed?" Whiteoak had asked.

Not knowing Whiteoak's full intention for producing the viscous substance, the chemist asked, "Why would anyone want to swallow paint?"

"Just answer my question."

Since the professor was the one paying for his services, the chemist replied, "Blindness, dizziness, perhaps death." Narrowing his eyes a bit, the chemist said, "It is paint, you realize, and acidic at that. Not fruit punch."

"I'm just cautious."

Shaking his head at the man in front of him, the chemist sighed and said, "Being cautious means not drinking paint or having it anywhere close to something that might be eaten."

"What if it got into someone's mouth?" Seeing the suspicion returning to the chemist's face in larger amounts than before, Whiteoak added, "My sister has two sons and they're both dumb as posts. I love them, of course, but they've tried to eat everything from dirt to bullet casings and I want to make sure this won't do any harm if the boys get any ideas in their heads."

"Ahh. I see. I've got a few young ones myself and they can be trying. Keep this away from them, that's for certain."

"Just so I know, if they ingest a small amount, like some that was diluted in water, would they perish?"

"They'd get mighty sick, that's for certain."

Sensing he wouldn't be able to get much more out of him, Whiteoak purchased the paint's formula and went about his business.

It took just over a year after that for the mixture to be mostly perfected. The process involved constant fiddling with varying amounts of dye, water, and eventually a brand of seltzer that diluted the paint further while preserving some of its coloring properties. Since the acidic component removed decay and food residue from even the filthiest of mouths, Whiteoak tempered it with mint leaves and some peppermint candy for the breath-freshening aspect. Finally, he managed to put together a mixture that colored teeth and stripped away yellowness without killing the small animals he fed it to during his experiments.

The first person to try the product was himself. That was a must for him, which went a long way in clearing his conscience whenever one of his customers experienced adverse effects from one of his products. After all, if it was good enough for him, it was good enough for the rest of the world. While the current formula for Fresh and White didn't make teeth as bright as some of the earlier versions, it proved to be much less nauseating for those who couldn't follow directions and swallowed it. There were also fewer instances of holes eaten through the occasional cheek.

Whiteoak had only started selling the dental tonic a few weeks ago in Montana. Judging by the expression on Bill's face, it wasn't exactly a glaring success.

"What do you think?" Whiteoak asked the young man in front of him.

Bill's head angled back and his neck muscles tightened.

"Don't swallow!" Whiteoak instructed. To the audience, he added, "As stated clearly on the label, the Fresh and White tonic functions best when swirled in the mouth and spit out. Besides, that also lets the true flavor shine through."

Stopping himself a heartbeat before swallowing, Bill sloshed the stuff around and spit it on the ground near Whiteoak's feet. "Tastes like candy after a while," he said.

"And I've never tasted bad candy," Whiteoak said to the crowd that had inched forward to get a better look at Bill's mouth.

"It's still bubblin'."

"That means it's working. Take a look for yourself." The professor handed him a small shaving mirror. Some time ago, he'd toyed with the notion of using a mirror that had been doctored in some way to make someone appear more attractive, but Whiteoak couldn't bend the laws of nature. Of course, that didn't mean he wouldn't stop trying.

Bill took the mirror and opened his mouth a bit. Everyone in front of the wagon leaned in and even Whiteoak craned his neck for a closer look. At first, Bill didn't seem to like what he saw. His expression shifted between curious and confused. Then again, that was a normal state for Bill's face. Eventually, he turned to the professor and opened wide.

"Is this a joke?" Bill wailed.

"A joke?" Whiteoak replied nervously. "I don't think so."

Facing the crowd directly, Bill peeled his lips back like a snarling dog and said, "Take a look at this! I ain't looked so good since I was a kid!"

Before Whiteoak could see much of his

handiwork, he proudly declared, "Of course it hasn't! But now that my Fresh and White is available for purchase, anyone can enjoy an improvement such as this."

Having stepped forward, Whiteoak now got an opportunity to examine his customer. Bill's teeth were definitely whiter. They were also foaming. Small bubbles could be seen across the surface of his teeth, spreading to Bill's lips and landing on his tongue as the acidic traces in the tonic ate away generous portions of fungus and week-old meals encrusted on his teeth. Whiteoak hoped that anyone farther away than he couldn't make out so much detail. To that end, he handed Bill a flask of water and encouraged him to drink.

"This stuff feels really good," Bill said enthusiastically. "The longer it's in there, I feel all clean and . . ."

"Please," Whiteoak said while forcing the flask into Bill's hand. "Have another rinse."

Bill took a big mouthful of water and spat it out. When he started talking again, the bubbles weren't nearly as prominent. That was good since several members of the audience were now stepping up for a closer look.

"It does look a little better," one of the women in the crowd admitted.

"The boy looked like he ate dirt before," a

skeptic pointed out. "Any dose of clean water would be an improvement."

The crowd contained about twenty people, most of which vied for a better spot from which to see Bill's teeth. A pair of men standing in the back remained where they were, however. They seemed content watching Professor Whiteoak instead.

"While our young friend informs you of the specifics regarding the miracle of effervescence he is currently experiencing," Whiteoak said, "feel free to purchase a bottle of my Fresh and White solution so you can bring that miracle into your very own homes."

Only a few pushed forward with money in their hands. Although Whiteoak reached out to take the payment from them, his eyes drifted nervously to the men who were working their way toward the garishly painted wagon. There was nothing distinctive about their faces or the manner in which they dressed. There wasn't anything distinctive about the guns strapped around their waists, either. Most men in Montana went about their daily lives heeled. What struck Whiteoak as troubling was the way those two men kept their hands less than an inch from their pistols, steady and prepared to put those guns to work at the first opportunity.

When he felt a hand drop onto his shoulder, Whiteoak tensed and nearly reached for the .38 kept discreetly under his suit coat.

"Nice show, Henry," Corey said.

"You really shouldn't sneak up on a man like that," Whiteoak warned.

"I'd like to have a word with you once you finish here."

"Sounds like a good idea. How about you stick around and wait for me to pack up?"

Chapter Four

Though the armed men still watched him from a distance, Whiteoak found time to perform one more demonstration before putting an end to his show. After that, he shook a few hands, took a few complaints and talked his way out of a few refunds before packing his supplies away and calling it a night. Once the last of the professor's customers wandered off, Corey stepped up to the wagon.

"I hope there's a good reason for making me wait through that, Henry."

"You're the one who came here and snuck up on me, remember?" Whiteoak pointed out.

"Yeah. I said I wanted to have a word with you. I was thinking we could meet over a drink somewhere. If I wanted to hear you bluster about your damn tonics, I would've arrived earlier."

"You see those two men standing there?"

"You'll have to be a little more specific."

"The two men wearing guns and a look on their faces like they're about to pull their triggers," Whiteoak said.

After taking a second to look for himself, Corey said, "Oh, I see the ones you mean. Friends of yours?"

"Hardly. I was thinking they might be the bounty killers you were mentioning a short while ago."

Corey looked again. "I don't recognize them, but that doesn't mean a lot. That kind of money turns an awful lot of men into threats."

"Perhaps you could ask them what they want?"

"You think I could do that?" Corey chuckled. "Now why would I stroll up to men with dead eyes like that and ask what they want?"

"To prevent any trouble that might spill over into a crowded street."

"Or, so you can put on the appearance that you have men like me watching out for your sorry hide?"

Whiteoak raised his eyebrows and recoiled. "I'm flabbergasted that you'd think I'd put you in a position like that!"

"Really? Flabbergasted?"

"Perhaps that was a bit of an exaggeration," Whiteoak said. "Just tell me where they are."

"Where they were the last time you mentioned them. What's got you so worked up? Did they threaten you?"

"Not in words, but a man in my business can smell danger and those fellows there reek of it!"

"A man in your business," Corey said, "learns to sense when someone's about to give him a beating he so rightfully deserves. Perhaps they're just here to file a complaint about one of your elixirs."

"This is no time for levity. I swear —"

"All right, all right," Corey sighed. "I'll have a word with them."

Whiteoak watched Corey walk away from the wagon toward the two men who'd been the cause of his concern. Looking at them from a calmer standpoint, they could have been a couple of cowboys out for a walk. Sure, they appeared cross but perhaps one of them was angry about a cheating lover or maybe both had lost their pay at a Faro table. Even as those optimistic alternatives drifted through his mind, Whiteoak knew they were too good to be believed.

Cheaters and swindlers did have a sense of when some of their past deeds were about to get them punched in the face. That's what separated the living practitioners of Whiteoak's craft from the dead.

Corey stood in front of the two men, talking quietly while keeping his hands near his gun belt. The two strangers listened to what he had to say, nodded, and then shifted their gaze toward Whiteoak.

When the professor snapped his eyes away from them, they practically rattled within their sockets.

First, the bigger of the two fellows laughed in a grunting manner. Then his partner started laughing as well. Before long, Corey joined in and gave the professor a subtle wave while heading back to Whiteoak's wagon.

"What did they say?" Whiteoak asked as Corey approached him.

Corey waved again, this time in the strangers' direction. "They're just here for the show."

"I don't think so."

"You're fussing for no good reason. I talked to them and they said it was nothing."

Whiteoak responded to that by charging at his friend with open arms. It was a short distance between them and when Whiteoak closed it, he wrapped his arms around Corey's midsection while driving both of them to the ground. At the same time Corey's back hit the dirt, a gunshot ripped through the air. Hot lead whipped over Whiteoak's back, followed by another bullet fired from a stranger's gun.

"They said they were fine," Corey gasped.

"What did you expect them to say? We're here to kill your friend the good professor?"

"Get off'a me!"

Whiteoak obliged by rolling to one side while drawing the .38 from under his coat. By the time he was laying on his back, Whiteoak's finger was tightening around his trigger. The pistol barked twice, spitting smoke and sparks from its barrel. The strangers scattered in opposite directions, but didn't go far. One of them hid behind a sign in the street advertising the medical services provided within the building across from Whiteoak's wagon and the other dropped to one knee while raising his hand to sight along the top of his pistol.

The man on one knee fired a shot that knocked a chip from one corner of the professor's wagon. His second shot came a little closer to the wagon's owner, but wound up digging a hole in the ground behind the professor. The other gunman peeked out from behind his sign and sent a bullet tearing through the air a few inches over Corey's and Whiteoak's heads.

Having drawn his gun, Corey fired at them while getting to a better position. Seconds later, several more bullets were spat in his direction amid thunderous reports. "Come on, Professor," he said. "Stand up!"

Whiteoak propped himself up on one elbow, firing again and again while shifting his aim from the sign to the kneeling man and back again. Eventually, he noticed the hand that was being offered to him and allowed Corey to pull him to his feet. Numbers rushed through his mind: the odds of him managing to hit one of the gunmen while firing so hastily, the chances of him or Corey being hit, the distance to a safe spot behind the wagon, and the dwindling number of bullets in his cylinder. By the time the last of those numbers reached zero, Whiteoak and Corey had reached the wagon.

"What the hell did you do to those men?" Corey asked breathlessly.

"They're after the bounty, idiot," Whiteoak replied while emptying the casings from his .38 so he could refill the cylinder with fresh ammunition from his pocket. "You're the one that told me about them, remember?"

"I do, but they don't strike me as bounty

hunters."

A fresh wave of gunshots tore into the wagon, sending wood splinters flying while drilling into the painted walls to shatter glass inside or ricochet off of iron pans. "What about now?" Whiteoak shouted. "Do they seem enough like bounty hunters, yet?"

"Doesn't matter. They're getting closer."

Corey was closest to the corner of the wagon, peeking around for a look at the two gunmen. Rather than push the other man aside or stretch his neck out farther around that same corner, Whiteoak dropped to his belly and wriggled under the wagon like an impeccably dressed snake.

The gunmen were, indeed, moving closer. Emboldened by their position and the lack of return fire, one of them ventured out from behind his sign while the other stood up and slowly walked toward the wagon. Before they could get there, a shotgun was fired from another direction that caught them both off-guard.

"Get away from there, assholes!" someone shouted.

"This ain't none of your concern!" the larger gunman said.

"We don't want trouble around here," shouted the dentist from the front door of his office. In his hands was a shotgun held in a way that made it clear he would put it to good use. "Now start walking or you'll get all the trouble you can handle."

From where he was, Whiteoak could clearly see the dentist as well as the two gunmen. Other folks' voices could be heard, but he couldn't discern any faces. Grunting to himself, the professor rolled onto his back and reached up with both hands to free a Spencer rifle from the brackets attached to the underside of his wagon. Once the rifle was in hand, he crawled out and got to his feet.

"You heard the dentist!" Whiteoak said. "Start walking or start dying!"

The two strangers knew when it was time to leave and did exactly that after lowering their pistols.

After the gunmen rounded a corner, Whiteoak lowered his rifle and smiled at the dentist. "You saved my life, sir! And here I thought you didn't approve of me."

"I don't," the dentist replied. "But we can't allow gunfights in our streets."

Suddenly, Whiteoak was nearly knocked off his feet by a clapping blow to his back. When he turned to look behind him, the professor was greeted by one of the ugliest smiles he'd ever seen. "You helped me look better than ever!" Bill said while displaying a set of crooked, chipped teeth that were now stained by Whiteoak's paint. "One good turn deserves another."

"Yes," Whiteoak said through a shallow grin. "It certainly does."

CHAPTER FIVE

"Why did you want to come back here?" Corey groaned.

"Because the Minstrelerro is the Mecca of Montana. It's the pride of the Rocky Mountains. Also," Whiteoak added, "it's the only place serving decent food at this time of night."

The hour wasn't late, but the only other restaurant in town that was still serving any hot food was a small shack a few streets away where the rats outnumbered the staff and customers by at least five to one. Even so, Corey didn't hesitate to reply, "I'd rather take my chances somewhere else."

"I get hungry after eventful demonstrations and tonight I'm craving pork chops. Can you get pork chops anywhere but here?"

"We could try."

"What do you have against the Minstrelerro?" Whiteoak asked as he used his knife to cut into the thick piece of pork on the plate in front of him. "It has character."

"What the hell is a Minstrelerro anyway?"

"It's a musician," said a tall fellow who approached Whiteoak's table, "known for wandering the deserts of West Texas, plying his trade and entertaining the masses."

When Corey looked up to him, the tall man extended a hand and said, "Harrold Carmine, at your service."

"You a friend of the professor's?" Corey asked.

"I'd like to think so."

"You certainly talk like him."

Straightening up so he towered over the two men seated at the table, Harrold gripped the lapels of his rumpled gray vest with both hands and nodded. "Considering Professor Whiteoak's credentials," he said through the long scraggly beard covering most of his face, "I take that as the deepest of compliments."

Corey didn't bother looking up at him. "What I meant is that you're both full of shit. I've been through every part of Texas and there's nothing called a Minstrelerro to be found."

"You're quite right," Whiteoak said. "I'd wager the minstrel part of the name reflects the singers who perform here at all times of the day and the last portion of the name was tacked on to add a bit of flair. After all, that does have a rather Texan feel to the word doesn't it?"

"It does," Corey admitted. "Also sounds like a few other things that ain't so flattering to you or this place."

"I'm part owner of this place," Harrold said in a sterner tone. "So you might want to watch your mouth. If you don't like it so much, you're free to leave."

"Nobody's leaving," Whiteoak said. "Not until I finish my meal, anyway. Besides, I invited Harrold to join us."

"When'd you do that?" Corey grunted.

"When I ordered my food. Why does that matter?"

"Because I wanted to know how much of my time you've wasted."

"Come now," Whiteoak said. "You wanted to have a word with me after my demonstration. Here I am."

"And here he is too," Corey said while motioning toward Harrold. "You've refused to talk about business until you were through with your damn food and now I'm guessing you want to hear whatever this man has to say."

Watching the two men with growing annoyance, Harrold said, "It's not polite to talk about someone like they aren't right in front of you."

"All right, then," Corey snapped while pushing away from the table. "You can return the favor by talking about me when I leave which is right now."

"At least listen to what Harrold came to say," Whiteoak pleaded.

Caught between sitting and standing, Corey waited a few seconds before dropping all of his weight back onto his chair. "Fine."

Harrold was on the verge of leaving, also. After a bit of coaxing from Whiteoak, he placed his hands on the edge of the table, leaned down and said, "Those two men who started shooting up your medicine show are bounty hunters."

Holding his hands palms up, Whiteoak gestured like a magician who'd just produced a dove from a folded handkerchief.

"So what?" Corey grunted. "You were right."

"Their names are Torence and Shay," Harrold continued. "At least one of them is from Wyoming. Could be both of them."

"Which is a lot more knowledge than we had before," Whiteoak pointed out.

"Great," Corey snapped. "We know the bastards' names. That should put us well ahead of any bullet they might fire at us."

Moving away from the table, Harrold said, "I have plenty to do around here, so I'll leave you two to continue your discussion in private."

"Thanks for the delightful meal," White-oak said cheerily. "And I apologize for my friend's rudeness."

"Not at all. It's been a long day."

After Harrold walked away and was immediately corralled into a spirited conversation with another batch of customers, Whiteoak turned to Corey and asked, "What was the meaning of that?"

"What?"

"That man had some valuable information and you treated him like a leper."

Corey shrugged. "Didn't seem like a lot of information to me. I never heard them names before, so that doesn't do us a bit of good."

"There was undoubtedly more to be learned from Harrold, except we won't know because you drove him away!"

"Aw, he'll be back. If he's got information worth knowing, I'm sure he'll come skulking about to look for some money so he can tell it to you."

"Exactly. And now we have to wait."

"You worried about the law asking questions regarding that shootout?"

"Of course not," Whiteoak scoffed. "The law won't know what happened for several more days."

That was one of the reasons Whiteoak enjoyed Hannigan's Folly. Not only was the town brimming with good liquor and plenty of customers for his wares, but it was at the northernmost tip of the Square Mountain Trail; the route connecting four small towns consisting of Hannigan's Folly, Jordan, Split Knee, and Westchester. None of those towns were much bigger than a mining camp. Most of their income came from providing supplies to prospectors, shelter for travelers, and pleasures for anyone with a taste for gambling, whiskey, or women.

Marshal Eliot Giddings was the sole lawman of the area who patrolled the Square Mountain Trail to check in with each town a few days at a time. He kept an office in each town that was supposed to be manned by a couple of deputies who worked for a meager salary to ride with him on the occasional posse, back him up in dangerous situations, and provide help for locals when a lawful presence was needed. The truth of the matter was that they were barely much more than thugs who kept the peace in one of the area's many brothels.

When he'd first arrived in Hannigan's Folly, Whiteoak was content to set up shop and milk the locals before moving on. Marshal Giddings paid him a visit, giving him all the customary warnings and vague threats to be expected from any law dog who tried to discourage a conman from plying his trade. But a funny thing happened after a few days. The marshal disappeared.

The locals he'd asked about Giddings all told him the same thing. The marshal was on his rounds. A bit more poking around told him that the marshal's rounds consisted of riding to all four towns along the Square Mountain Trail. Giddings spent anywhere from a few days to a week in each one depending on what was happening there that warranted his attention. If a trial was needed, he stayed longer. All most folks needed to know was whether or not the marshal was in his office or about how long he'd be gone. In the meantime, the locals policed themselves. Their methods weren't nearly as brutal as some of the towns Whiteoak had visited, but they kept each town from tearing itself apart.

Whiteoak made it his business to know every moving part of the lawman's system. He rode the trail himself, talking to locals, questioning deputies and even having a word with the marshal himself. In a short amount of time, Whiteoak was able to put together a fairly reliable system of his own that would tell him with a fair amount of accuracy when and where he could operate outside of Marshal Giddings' influence.

The locals were independent and the deputies were too lazy and corrupt to cause Whiteoak any concern. That only left the marshal who could only be a hindrance if he was around, which meant the law was an almost non-existent threat.

"So the marshal isn't in his office?" Corey asked.

"Not hardly," Whiteoak told him. "By my calculations, he should either be in Split Knee or possibly Westchester right about now."

"What about the deputy?"

"What about him?" the professor scoffed.

"Good point." Corey let out a short breath and looked around him. "Smelling that food is making me hungry. Where's one of them girls who bring the drinks around here?"

"Seems like you were the one who was more concerned about the law, my friend."

"What if I was? Not everyone makes it their mission to figure out the marshal's whereabouts down to the last step."

"So, what is it you wanted to tell me that

was important enough to come to one of my shows?" Whiteoak asked. "You haven't shown yourself since we parted ways shortly after arriving in Montana. What's the matter? You don't like being associated with the likes of me?"

"Since when has that mattered?" Corey asked.

"Since it seems you're about to ask me a favor and you've barely been civil to me since I've arrived."

Instead of trying to deny the accusation, Corey leaned on his elbows and said, "We go back a ways, don't we?"

"We do. And the last time we were in the same town, you were ten times the scallywag I ever was."

"Things have changed since them days. I'm trying not to draw attention to the man I was."

"Playing by the rules was never much of a concern for you," Whiteoak mused. "What happened? You find a woman whose pure and gentle heart set you on the right path?"

"There have been a few women, but let's just say I enjoy being a man who doesn't attract the kind of attention you seem to enjoy. I've got a few bounties with my name on 'em too, you know. I heard about the reward that was placed on your head because I try to keep track of things like that."

"That's good to hear," Whiteoak said.

Scowling, Corey asked, "What's so damn good about it?"

"A man who can be turned so drastically by something as fleeting as love isn't very trustworthy. Wanting to lay low is something I can understand a bit more."

"Then perhaps you'll lay low for a while?" Corey asked hopefully.

"Why would I want to do that? My business puts me squarely in the spotlight!"

"You've got a price on your head and so do I. What the hell else do I need to say?"

"Just get to whatever is on your mind."

Corey sighed, knowing all too well that trying to sway the professor's view based on good sense was like trying to bust down a brick wall using clever arguments. No matter how much thought went into that argument, the bricks would still split a man's skull. "There's a fella in these parts who might be able to help both of us with our bounty hunter problems."

"I'm sick of bounty hunters," Whiteoak said as he pushed his mostly empty plate away. "They seem to be coming out of the woodwork."

"Which is what happens when men like you and me don't take some time every now and then to lay low. Weren't you the one who taught me that?"

"That was a long time ago, but I do see the value of those sage words. Who's this man you're talking about?"

"His name's Jacob Parsons."

"I've been in town for a while, and so have you," Whiteoak pointed out. "We've both heard of Jacob Parsons. What's he to you?"

"Damn it, Henry, when'd you get so suspicious of your friends?"

"I'm suspicious of everyone. Things tend to work out better for me that way."

"After what happened in Kansas, Louisiana and every other place over the last couple years, you consider this to be *better*?"

"You should see it when things are worse."

"Jacob Parsons made a name for himself in the Dakotas," Corey said. "He's set up shop around here over the last several months. Spends most of his time in Split Knee."

"He's a gambler as far as I know."

"He also keeps his ear to the ground well enough to know a lot about the comings and goings of dangerous men."

Whiteoak smirked. "Sounds like someone worth meeting."

CHAPTER SIX

The ride to Jordan was fairly short; less than a day when taken under the right circumstances. By anyone's estimation, however, riding the mountain paths and narrow trails in a multicolored wagon wasn't exactly a right circumstance. As a show of disapproval with the professor's choice of travel methods, Corey rode ahead to leave Whiteoak in his dust. Instead of making the professor sorry for driving his wagon rather than riding one of his horses, Corey only wound up traveling alone.

A few miles outside of Jordan, as the sun was setting, Corey spotted the wagon ambling along at a pace that was only slightly faster than normal. The professor whistled a happy tune and he waved to Corey once he spotted the impatient man.

"Where the hell you been?" Corey demanded as Whiteoak drove along.

"I took a detour to Paris," Whiteoak

replied. "What does it look like?"

"Couldn't you ride any faster?"

"Penelope was getting a might anxious and I didn't want to rattle her. Isn't that right, girl?"

Whether the light brown mare pulling the wagon was responding to her name or was as anxious as her owner described, Penelope shook her head and let out a huffing breath. The spotted gray horse beside her snorted as well, but only a little.

"I don't care how your horses are feeling," Corey said. "You shouldn't have brought that wagon along for this ride."

"So you've stated. Repeatedly."

"And you still don't wanna listen."

"I also don't want my wagon to be molested while I leave it unguarded," Whiteoak said.

"Molested?"

"Robbed. Burgled. Set on fire. Whatever kind of dastardly acts someone might have in mind to take a swing at me while I'm away."

"So you plan on driving that thing all the way to Split Knee? It's twice as far from Jordan to there than it is from Hannigan's Folly to here!"

"I'm aware of the distances," Whiteoak said. "I can read a map and have probably ridden the Square Mountain Trail more than you."

"So you should already know that we're taking the long way around."

"Only by a few miles."

Corey looked up into the cold gray sky. Winter was still a few months away, but that didn't make it any warmer so high above sea level. The wind already had claws that would soon become icy daggers. Although the air was fragrant with traces of evergreen and running water, it still gnawed and scratched at those who didn't give it the proper respect. Turning up his collar, Corey said, "A few miles can make a world of difference out here."

"Indeed, it can. But there is a good reason for this detour, no matter how slight. There's a place in Jordan where I can leave my wagon and know it's safe."

"Most folks pay for a livery stall, Henry. Ever hear of one of those?"

"Most folks only have a horse to worry about, or a wagon half-full of common items. This," Whiteoak said while hooking a thumb at the wagon behind him, "is a box of miracles and highly valuable items. Are you aware of how much glass was broken with those shots that were fired at me the other day?"

"Them shots were fired at me too, you know."

"And if we were both hit, it wouldn't be as tragic of a loss than if some of my rarest items were obliterated by a stray bullet. Rarely do I leave my wagon unattended for long and when I do, I'd rather it was in the hands of someone I can trust."

"That someone's in Jordan, right?"

"He is. And his name —"

"I don't give a shit," Corey cut in. "Just know we're not driving that damn wagon all the way to Split Knee. There are still killers after us and that damn wagon of yours is slowing us down."

"It seems I should be more worried than you," Whiteoak said. "After all, you weren't there for that business in Kansas. It got pretty rough."

"I heard you tried to rob a bank."

"Succeeded is more like it."

Corey laughed. "Made a damn mess of it is what I heard."

"Who would tell you such a thing?"

"Plenty of folks heard about what happened. Also, you've bragged to me on more than one drunken night."

Whiteoak dismissed that with a backhanded wave. "All that matters is I came out of there a lot richer than when I arrived."

"You made a whole mess of enemies by robbing a bank being watched by a bushel of important men," Corey chided. "And to top it off, you didn't even try to hide who you were. Even the dumbest bank robbers usually remember to put a damn bandanna over their faces before they start waving their guns around!"

"If you want my help in this matter, I'd recommend a different sort of sweet talk."

"I don't want your help. You and I are just in the same pickle and I figured you'd want a friend at your side to pull you out of it."

"Remind me again why I bother keeping your company," Whiteoak said.

"Because I'm one of the few who know who you really are and what you really do and will still have the occasional drink with you."

"That cuts deep, sir."

Corey started to laugh, but realized Whiteoak wasn't merely spouting off. The professor's eyes were fixed upon the trail ahead of him and his posture had lost some of its proud straightness.

"You're right," Corey finally said. "I do need your help."

"I knew it."

"There's a chance some of the men who are putting up the reward for your head might also be after mine."

"What could you have done to anger those people?" Whiteoak asked. "We haven't worked together on a real job for some time."

"Maybe not the same job, but we've both been in similar lines of work."

Shifting his curious eyes toward Corey, Whiteoak studied him for a few seconds before saying, "You've started selling tonics?"

"No, you ignorant bastard! Robbing banks! See what happens when you step out of your wheelhouse? You start to lose your damn mind. You've always been the smartest fella I've ever known."

"Oh, well, thank you."

"Before you get yourself all built up, let me finish," Corey warned.

It took some doing, but Whiteoak managed to hold his tongue.

"When you and I rode together, we were both crooks," Corey said. "Then it became clear that I was more of a crook that wore a mask and you were a crook that stood up like a peacock and strutted in front of a garish wagon. I use a gun and you use your mouth. We may not have run in the same circles, but we were both doing what we were good at."

"Agreed," Whiteoak said crisply.

"Then you started getting too full of yourself with that mess in Kansas. You stepped into unfamiliar territory and you poked a whole lot of sleeping bears."

"It'd be difficult for me to disagree with you there."

"Afterward, when you came to me for help, I tried to warn you to lay low," Corey said. "Ever since you arrived in Montana, I've been trying to convince you to stay out of sight for a spell and stop doing those damn shows of yours."

Whiteoak shook his head without speaking.

"When I came to see you now, it was to warn you that you might get shot at sooner than you thought," Corey explained. "But I knew you wouldn't listen. Even when them two bounty hunters came at you in front of God and everybody, you still didn't seem overly concerned."

"And I suppose you're going to tell me you're just worried about me," Whiteoak scoffed. "Is that it?"

"What if it is? What if you've gotten so full of yourself that you need someone to tell you things like this or to watch your damn back to make certain nobody puts a bullet in it?"

"If you're so determined to protect me, do it from a distance so you don't have to be distracted by all the arrogant noise I've been making." With that, Whiteoak snapped his reins and the wagon moved a bit faster.

CHAPTER SEVEN

Jordan was barley large enough to be considered a camp. It was mostly a collection of tents with paths winding between them littered with broken planks of wood, dead animals, and the occasional cart that had fallen short on its journey through the mountains. Several tents were clustered together ahead of them, pinching the road into a bottleneck that was too narrow for the wagon to pass. Just as Corey was becoming uneasy, Whiteoak steered his team to the left where he cut between another pair of tents that were about the size of small cabins. Dim light and raucous noise emanated from both of those tents, branding them as either saloons or cathouses. Whiteoak snapped his reins, urging the horses to pick up enough speed to carry the wagon over the remains of an outhouse that had been tipped over to become partially submerged in the mud.

"You have any idea where you're going?" Corey asked. "Because I'm completely turned around."

"You've never been to Jordan before?" Whiteoak grunted.

"Course I have. And every damn time I come here, the roads are different than before. Was that Miss Stacey's back there?"

"Yes."

"So that would be the Ten Cent Saloon right across from it."

"Right again," Whiteoak said. "I suppose you're properly oriented now?"

After craning his neck to get a look around, Corey answered, "Just tell me where we're headed."

Whiteoak pointed straight ahead. "Right there."

The barn was on the side of the sorry excuse of a road they were using. It was so run down and full of holes that it blended with all the trash gathered around it. Without a single light inside of it, the shabby structure was nearly enveloped by shadows. As they approached, however, a solitary glow passed behind one of the broken windows.

"I don't like the looks of that place," Corey said.

"I thought you said you've been here be-fore."

"I have, but . . ."

"But only to visit Miss Stacey's and the Ten Cent?"

"Well . . . yes."

Whiteoak sighed. "And you always wonder why I've never wanted you along with me on the more elaborate jobs I've been put-ting together over the last few years. You don't pay attention to detail and you don't see anything unless it comes up to bite you on your nose."

"Well if your big, recent jobs all wind up like that bank robbery in Kansas, I'm glad you forgot to invite me along."

"For Christ's sake, stop throwing Kansas back at me!" Whiteoak snapped. "It's over and done. Let it lie."

The single glow within the barn now shone through a crack between the wide main doors of the building. The more Whiteoak and Corey bickered, the faster that glow moved. Before long, the doors were opened. The light emanated from a lantern held by a fellow in his late thirties wearing a pair of coveralls that were just as filthy as the camp surrounding him. Thin-ning hair sprouted at varying lengths from his scalp to form a poorly tended mop. As he lifted the lantern closer to his face, the man revealed sunken cheeks, a small nose and a pair of long, buck teeth.

"What the hell is all the noise out here?" the man asked. "Henry Whiteoak? Is that you?"

"It is, Jon," the professor replied. "Glad you recognized me."

"Spotted that wagon from a mile away. Who's that with you?"

"Jon Vorland, this is Corey Maynard. Corey's an associate of mine."

"You mean another huckster?"

Laughing, Corey brought his horse to a stop and said, "Not quite. Pleased to meet you." Although Corey leaned down from his saddle to extend a friendly hand, he was only left waiting for a few seconds before retracting it.

"What do you want?" Jon asked, shifting all of his attention to Whiteoak.

"Merely to partake in your services," the professor replied.

"Putting up your wagon or do you mean —"

"The livery services," Whiteoak said before Jon could finish his sentence. "Should only be for a few days, but could stretch a little longer. Do you have enough space available to accommodate me?"

"Should have it," Jon said while scratching his chin. "But it'll cost you a bit extra."

"Why?"

"Because that's a mighty big wagon along with two horses."

"There'll just be one horse," Whiteoak corrected. "The other will be accompanying me and my friend here."

Jon stepped closer. "Accompanying you to where?"

"That remains to be seen. All you need to know is what you'll be storing and for how long. Now, can you accommodate me or not?"

"Soon as we settle on a price, I got enough space to set you up. What else is there, Whiteoak?"

"Whatever do you mean?"

Grabbing the bridle of the professor's spotted gray horse, Jon said, "What else is there that you ain't telling me?"

Corey had been content to watch in relative silence for this long and saw no reason to speak up now.

"There's a lot I haven't told you," Whiteoak said in a tired, annoyed voice. "If you'd like to catch up on all of my exploits, you can buy me some drinks some other day and I'll tell them all to you. If you're worried about matters that directly concern you, don't be. The only reason I sought you out was for a place to store my wagon. If part of your fee now includes raking me over hot coals, then I shall politely decline and move along."

"Ain't no reason to move along," Jon said. Looking to Corey, he asked, "Is he always this fidgety?"

"You have no idea."

CHAPTER EIGHT

Once Whiteoak and Jon were finished haggling, the wagon was driven into the dark confines of the drafty barn. Just inside that shoddy building was the makings of another structure altogether. Several walls had been built in the corners to create smaller compartments that were concealed well enough to be nearly undetectable from the outside. That way, the barn could be secure while also looking as though it had nothing to offer. It was a simple feat of misdirection, but one that was very successful.

Whiteoak drove the wagon between two of the sturdy interior walls so his beloved vehicle was nestled between them. Both horses emerged from behind the walls and were soon unhooked from their harnesses to be led to the other side of the barn where four ordinary stalls were situated in a row. One of those stalls was already occupied by a black stallion with a white spot on its nose that watched patiently while Whiteoak's team was shown into their own stalls.

Corey had been helping with the tasks of putting up the wagon and stowing the horses' gear. Once the job was completed, he let out a breath and looked around at the mazelike collection of partitions and walls inside what had once been a drafty old barn. "So what the hell is all this?" he asked.

"Something I came up with."

"I figured as much," Corey said. "Looks like a rambling mess that's a lot more complicated than it should be." He looked over to Whiteoak with a grin on his face, but the professor wasn't enjoying the joke nearly as much. Taking some of the smarminess from his tone, Corey asked, "What's the reason for all the walls?"

"To keep what's inside hidden from the outside."

"Really? Does it work?"

Whiteoak stopped what he was doing long enough to shoot a glare at the other man. "When you were outside, did you know these walls were in here?"

"No."

"Then it stands to reason that anything behind the walls would remain out of sight, wouldn't you say?"

"I guess."

Returning to the task of putting the spotted gray horse in his stall for the night, Whiteoak snapped, "Then it stands to reason that thieves or any other brigands wouldn't feel the need to violate this place. Since Jon has yet to be robbed, my system works quite nicely."

"So this friend of yours hides things?"

"Don't we all?"

"Why do you need to hide your wagon?" Corey asked.

"I'm putting it somewhere it's safe," Whiteoak told him. "This wagon is my livelihood. It's filled with the creations that I use to earn my living. What's so hard to understand about me wanting to keep it safe?"

"If you just wanted to keep that wagon safe, you could have paid any number of folks back in Hannigan's Folly to watch it."

"Do you know anyone so trustworthy back in Hannigan's Folly?"

"I can think of more folks who fit that bill than what you'd find in this rat's nest of a camp."

Now that the first horse was safe in his stall, Whiteoak started putting the other mare down for the night. "Whatever you're leading up to, just get there already. I'm tired and have had more than enough of what you consider to be banter for one day."

"And I want to work together like we used to. All of our cards on the table, good ones and bad. It's the only way we can be any help to one another, especially since both of our lives are on the line."

Whiteoak's face was the same stony mask it always was whenever he wanted to distance himself from a nuisance. The annoyance that had been building in his eyes was just about to boil over when he let out a disgusted breath and turned away. In that moment, his gaze fell upon one of the fresher bullet holes that had been blown into his wagon. "I suppose you do make a valid point."

"I'm also certain you've rigged up some pretty nasty measures in that wagon of yours to keep it and all of your junk plenty safe without extra help, but I've rarely seen you move as fast as you did when we were leaving town. Those other times when you got the lead out of your ass, was when there was someone chasing you. I mean actual folks with torches or shotguns in their hands nipping at your heels and screaming for your hide."

Whiteoak's finger traced a circle around one of the bullet holes in his wagon. "It could be that those bounty hunters aren't the only ones with a grudge against me."

"Go on."

"There are a few others in town with an axe to grind."

Corey let out a tired sigh. "I don't have enough wind in my sails to drag it out of you. I think I'll find a comfortable bed for the night and consider you less of a partner and more of a load to bear."

Even though he knew some of Corey's tough talk was just that and not genuine promises of bad times to come, Whiteoak grudgingly told him, "Some of my customers were asking for refunds."

Despite not being a salesman himself, Corey had been around Whiteoak long enough to know that handing out a refund was almost as bad as opening a vein and filling an empty bottle with his life essence. "How many?" he asked.

"A dozen . . . give or take."

"Give or take how many?"

"Another dozen. Or two."

"Christ! What the hell did you do?" Corey gasped. "Paint some other part of them other than their teeth?"

Whiteoak didn't answer right away. From a man with the professor's propensity toward self-expression, that spoke more than his words.

At first, Corey's face became serious. Within the space of a few heartbeats, however, a sly grin began to take over. "What did you do, Henry?"

"It was the Fresh and White," Whiteoak told him. "Perhaps it wasn't quite ready for sale to the general public yet."

"Did you poison someone?"

"No! Nothing like that."

"Then what?" Corey prodded.

"It turned some folks' tongues gray."

"Their tongues?"

"Yes," Whiteoak said with a sudden sharpness in his tone. "And some of them might have experienced a bit of discomfort but that's only because they didn't follow the extensive instructions included on the label. It's not *my* fault if they don't choose to read the precautions before putting something in their mouths. What are they? Children?"

Crossing his arms and standing between Whiteoak and wherever he needed to be, Corey asked, "What else was there? A few gray tongues and some discomfort isn't much worse than the usual backlash you have to deal with when you set up shop in one place for longer than a week."

"And what makes you such an expert on the matter?"

"We've worked plenty together."

Having removed the harnesses from both horses, Whiteoak took them to the wagon and stored them in one of its many partially hidden exterior compartments. "Until you so recently decided to abandon our joint ventures."

"We parted ways for a while. It happens sometimes."

Whiteoak locked the compartment containing the harnesses and began stomping around the rest of the wagon, checking to make sure that every other compartment was shut and locked. "You know what else happens sometimes? Betrayal. Back stabbing. Traitorous machinations between friends."

"Those are all basically the same thing . . . I think . . . and they're also a bit dramatic. Did you forget about what happened in Virginia?"

"No. That job didn't go as planned, but —"

"It was a disaster. You wanted to convince a mortician that you could bring people back from the dead. What the hell were you thinking?"

"I was thinking he'd want to pay us to destroy the formula so he wouldn't be out of business."

"And you never once thought that he might just try to kill us and destroy the formula himself rather than take you up on the offer you made to sell it to him?" Corey asked.

"That's why you were there," Whiteoak snapped. "To guard against that eventuality."

"The occasional man trying to kill us . . . or rather, you . . . wasn't much of a surprise. It was to be expected. What kept tripping us up was you!"

"And how do you figure that?"

Sighing, Corey said, "You're a smart man, Henry. Maybe too smart. You think too hard and too long about everything from what you're gonna do to what you're gonna say and how you're gonna say it. After so much of that convoluted nonsense going around between your ears, you lose sight of the simple matters."

"Maybe you're right. I could use a simpler perspective now and then." With a smirk, Whiteoak added, "That's why it's good to have a simple man like you around."

"Thanks. I think."

Whiteoak patted Corey on the shoulder. "Don't think too hard. You might sprain something."

"So what else was there apart from the

gray tongues that caused you to pull up stakes and abandon Hannigan's Folly?"

"Not abandon," Whiteoak corrected while raising a finger to waggle for emphasis. "But there may have been a few other things stained as well."

"Apart from your reputation?" Corey chided. "Such as it is."

"Let's just say some of the ladies in town whose business involves being visually striking were some of the first ones to use my Fresh and White mixture."

"You mean the whores."

"What an impressive guess!"

"Not really. I noticed a bunch of the working girls flashing smiles that were a bit cleaner than normal."

"I see," Whiteoak said. "Let's just say that when they applied some of their more lucrative talents, they also applied a coat of paint to some very . . . peculiar places."

It took Corey a few seconds to mull that over, but when he was finished, he smiled broadly. "Are you telling me that when one of those ladies sucked on some fella's . . ."

"Lower extremity," Whiteoak cut in. "Yes."

"When she used her mouth on him, she turned his pecker white?"

"Yes," Whiteoak sighed. "And despite the fact that I assured him it would wear off with just a bit of vigorous washing . . ."

"Which I imagine some of those same ladies would be more than willing to do," Corey added.

"Exactly! A service for which, I offered to pay."

"Not a bad deal," Corey said.

"That's what I thought. But my offer of reparation was too little too late, since some of the gentlemen who were affected had already been discovered and severely punished for their actions."

Wrinkling his brow in concentration, Corey started shaking his head. "Just use common words, for Christ's sake, Henry."

"When the fella got his pecker sucked, the whore turned it white. And when that fella got home, his wife noticed the white pecker and started asking questions. My Fresh and White has also demonstrated certain . . . acidic properties when used in large quantities. On some of those men in question, the white coloration wasn't their only concern. There was also the loss of hair and some considerable amount of skin. Is that language common enough for you?"

"Jesus almighty," Corey laughed. "So you're running from angry wives and a bunch of fellows nursing burnt cocks?"

"Yes, and angry wives are not to be taken

lightly. Also, there's the matter of the whores themselves. A few of them were even better customers of mine."

"Sounds like this is leading somewhere interesting."

"They purchased some of my more exotic scented soaps."

"What kind of chemicals did you mix into those?" Corey asked like a child who couldn't wait to hear the next line of a fairy tale.

"Nothing, really. Just a few herbs to enhance the scent. What I hadn't foreseen, however, was how those herbs would interact with the chemicals I used in my Fresh and White." Seeing the expression on the other man's face, Whiteoak added, "Well, how was I supposed to know the two didn't mix? Science is an ever-changing art! We learn through experimentation."

"And what did you learn this time?"

Whiteoak sighed. "I learned that my Fresh and White compound, when mixed with certain soaps, may cause itchiness, burning and some other mild discomforts."

"Doesn't sound so bad."

"You try having those symptoms in certain private areas."

"Ahh. Yeah. I see where that could be bad. But bad enough to leave town?"

"Bad enough to make those ladies and a good amount of their customers mistake those temporary side-effects for a more serious disease that would then make those same ladies quite unappealing when it came to certain carnal duties."

Now Corey began to nod with true comprehension. "Them ladies were taken out of service for a spell."

"And their employers, certain large fellows with shotguns, don't take kindly to their cathouses losing that income. Even if the situation is temporary. So that, combined with the aforementioned angry husbands and wives . . ."

"Wives who can spread bad news like wildfire," Corey added.

"Yes. All those factors combined did make it rather prudent for me to leave town for a short while. By the time I return, all of those situations will have either remedied themselves or cooled down to a more manageable state."

"They'll remedy themselves, huh?"

Finished with putting his wagon and one of his horses up for the night, Whiteoak reached out to scratch the ear of the light brown mare, which was accepted with a gentle nuzzle. "It's nothing but a mild rash," he said. "I'm sure those girls have had worse. Tempers simply need to settle, is all."

"Tell me something. When did all of this happen? I thought you just gave your first demonstration of that tooth stuff right before we left town."

"I allowed some of my best customers to sample it ahead of time. Also," Whiteoak explained, "it seems the cathouses of Hannigan's Folly are quite well attended. Everything went from bad to worse in very short order," he said earnestly. "Taking my wagon along and keeping it out of sight seemed like a wise decision."

Corey slapped the professor on the back. "I guess thinking far ahead isn't such a bad thing all the time."

Although fatigued by the day's ride and the events that had preceded it, Whiteoak couldn't help but chuckle. "You should have seen the nether regions of some of those ladies. They were grayer than the top of a granny's head."

"Took it upon yourself to conduct the examination yourself, did ya?"

"I am a consummate professional," Whiteoak said. "And when I convinced one of those ladies to allow me to perform an even more extensive examination, her employer was most displeased. He claimed I was ruining even more of his livelihood and chased me out. When he caught me in her bed a second time, the discussion became much more heated."

Looking at the professor with a mixture of disbelief and admiration, Corey said, "You shove more into a few days than most do in a month! Don't you ever sleep?"

"Sleep in small doses is all that is required," Whiteoak replied with a wave of his hand. "Any more than that is merely laziness. That last altercation happened moments before we left town."

Corey thought about what he'd heard and put it all together in his head. Finally, he said, "That lady must've really been something. Was it Suzanna?"

"No. It was Lilly."

Corey whistled softly. "She's something else, but she's no Suzanna. Speaking of her, I owe you a thank-you."

"Why?"

"Because ever since she got hold of your formula, she's been working some real magic on me. Whatever is in that Fresh and White stuff adds a nice little something to when she's on her knees turning my pecker gray."

Whiteoak was shocked to hear that, but only for a moment. In the next moment, he was laughing heartily.

Corey laughed as well, but caught his breath long enough to say, "You should see her below the waist. After I got through with her, she resembles a skunk down there."

"A skunk? I highly doubt that!"

"Oh, she smells all fresh and dandy. I'm just talking about looks, white stripe and all."

The two men laughed together while leaving the livery. As they walked to one of the few places in town where they could each find a room for the night, they sang a merry round of "Oh, Susanna."

CHAPTER NINE

Instead of renting a room, Whiteoak opted to rent a tent for the night. It was barely large enough to cover his head, but certainly beat paying for a flea-ridden mattress inside a three-room shack that passed as one of Jordan's hotels. By the time he woke up and crawled out of the tent again, the sun was high in the sky and a crack of thunder rolled in the distance to the north. There were clouds in that direction, pouring rain onto the ground several miles away. Since the skies directly above him were mostly clear, he hitched up his pants and pulled his suspenders over both shoulders.

There was another tent a few paces away from his. As Whiteoak set his sights on a chuck wagon alongside the road, he kicked the bulky lump protruding from the side of that other tent. "Rise and shine!" he announced.

"Go to hell!" the lump replied.

"That's no way to greet such a fine day."

"It's a fine way to greet you, Henry," Corey said from within the tent. "Now leave me alone!"

"Someone's cooking grits," Whiteoak said. "Can't you smell them?"

After a slight pause, Corey poked his head out of the tent. "And bacon," he said while sniffing the air like a hungry dog. "Do you smell bacon?"

Whiteoak pulled in a deep breath through his nose. Puffing his chest out and hooking his thumbs around his suspenders, he said, "I was captivated by the scent of strong coffee but yes, I do believe there's bacon as well. Are you going to join me for a bite or would you rather hope there'll be some left when it's cold?"

Corey's head disappeared inside the tent. After a few seconds, it reappeared along with the rest of him. He still wore the same clothes from the previous day, only with considerably more wrinkles and stains than before. Standing up and scratching here and there, Corey glanced over to Whiteoak and asked, "What's the occasion?"

"To what are you referring, my good man?"

"You're dressed for church. And why are you so goddamn sunny? I thought you didn't like mornings."

"My likes and dislikes are unknown to anyone but me. I am an enigma and the world guesses about where I may turn next."

"Do you plan the foolish bullshit you say ahead of time or does it just come natural?" Corey grunted.

"It is part of the delightful tapestry that is me."

"You're full of yourself today. Just like every other day, I suppose. Aren't we riding on to Split Knee after we eat?"

"That was the plan," Whiteoak said as he tipped his hat to a mildly befuddled stranger.

"So you just got all gussied up for the sake of trying to impress the dregs in this place?"

"That is no way to refer to the good people of Jordan," Whiteoak said to the people in his vicinity. "And I'd much rather wash my clothes more often than walk about in yesterday's stench."

"Yesterday's stench is the same as today's stench, so what's the difference?"

"Today's stench is much more powerful," Whiteoak said with a withering glare. "To that, I can personally attest."

The chuck wagon was parked at a downward angle that lifted its back end several inches higher than the front. There was no slope in the road, but there was a great deal of mud which had engulfed the front two wheels and sunk that end, rooting the wagon to its spot. There were several people gathered near the wagon, most of which were either shoveling hot food into their mouths or clamoring for their orders to be heard by one man who somehow navigated the chaos surrounding him.

Whiteoak removed his hat and held it out to both point at the eye of the chuck wagon's hurricane while also nudging aside a few of the anxious customers. "What a fine day for some delicious food!" he declared. "My friend and I would like to partake in —"

"Get in line like everybody else," the cook snapped in a thick, Bulgarian accent. He wore a grease-stained shirt with sleeves that were rolled up to expose a pair of hairy forearms. His face was covered in soot from the cooking fire as well as stubble that had taken on the coarseness of a wire brush. A section of his wagon unfolded to allow him to reach inside for plates and some of the hot food. It wasn't until the man reached in and was handed a bowl of grits that Whiteoak realized there was another person inside the wagon helping the Bulgarian man serve his customers.

"We're here for breakfast, my good man," Whiteoak announced. "And I hear this is the best place in Jordan to be served."

"You'll be served when it's your turn," the Bulgarian said. "Get in line."

Whiteoak started to argue, but could see that he'd already been dismissed by the Bulgarian fellow. The others in line weren't any more accommodating, so Whiteoak placed his hat back upon his head and made his way to the back.

"Just act like you're important and that's what folks will think," Corey said. "Ain't that what you told me one time?"

"Yes. Now, shut up and wait in line."

"The great Professor wait in a line? What has this world come to?"

Whiteoak gnashed his teeth and did his best to ignore Corey's teasing. When the playful mocking didn't subside, Whiteoak turned on his heels to confront Corey. "Now listen here," was all he managed to say before someone knocked into him from behind.

"I am waiting at the back of the line!" Whiteoak fumed.

Two men shoved Whiteoak one more time. One of them, a man of average height and build, took an extra moment to grab Whiteoak's shirt front and push him back when he said, "Step aside if you know what's good for ya."

"I know what's good for me and you as well," Whiteoak said as he shifted his waist-coat to display the holster strapped around his shoulder. "Perhaps it's time for you to reconsider as well."

The man who'd grabbed the front of Whiteoak's shirt had a face that looked like it had been scratched apart by wildcats. Scars were laid on top of scars to form a grotesque patchwork of fragmented skin. Twisting his battered visage into something of a grin, he said, "Is that a fact?"

It was then that Whiteoak got a good look at the second man who'd bumped into him. Easily a head taller than anyone else in the vicinity, the man had a thick, rounded chest and arms like a couple of beef slabs dangling from a butcher's hook. His rounded features were partly covered by a thick beard and his eyes had the wide, wild qualities of a stunned bull.

"Of course," Whiteoak hastily added, "I'm only speaking from a professional stand-point. I know many things that are good for whatever ails you."

"Henry," Corey whispered. "Be quiet."

But Whiteoak either didn't hear his friend or was too far along in his own prattle to pay him any mind. Squinting at the first man's scars, the professor asked, "Are those burns? Must be painful. I have something that might be able to help you in that regard."

"You wanna know about pain?" the scarred man asked. Nodding toward the monster beside him, he said, "Strahan, teach these boys about pain."

Strahan grinned through the bush growing from his chin and wrapped one meaty fist within another so he could crack his knuckles. Stepping forward, he let out a slow breath that sounded like a slow leak from a steam engine.

As everyone near the chuck wagon backed away, the professor said, "Perhaps you're right, Corey. Sometimes maybe I do talk too much."

CHAPTER TEN

Strahan may have been large, but he wasn't fast. Like most big men, he made the mistake of thinking his size was enough to frighten an opponent into submission. If that didn't work, he could overpower someone once he got his hands on them. The trick was not to let them get their hands on anything but air. Professor Whiteoak had been on the receiving end of more punches than he cared to admit, which made this one even easier to dodge. After ducking beneath Strahan's swing, Whiteoak drove his elbow into the bigger man's ribs.

"What have you got here?" the scarred man said as he raised his fists. "Some kind of bodyguard?"

"I don't need anyone to guard me," Whiteoak said. "I do just fine on my own." Before the scarred man could reply to that, he was reeling from a punch that caught him in the mouth.

Corey grunted and scrambled to put some distance between himself and Strahan. Whiteoak couldn't tell much more than that without taking his eyes off of Strahan's scarred partner and he wasn't about to do that when he was close to landing another punch.

"Your friend's name is Strahan," Whiteoak said as he drove his fist into the scarred man's gut. "Tell me yours. I'd like to know who it is I'm pummeling."

Until now, the scarred man had barely gotten a chance to meet the professor's gaze. When he did, he unleashed a flurry of punches that peppered Whiteoak's torso like hail on a tin roof. The first several punches hurt. Once they started landing upon spots that were already aching from being hit, the blows started adding up.

Whiteoak covered up as best he could using both arms as a shield. In an attempt to protect one set of ribs, he turned that side away from the man in front of him. His scarred opponent's next punch cracked against Whiteoak's holstered .38, causing the man to recoil and take a step back.

Recognizing the opportunity, Whiteoak shoved the scarred man back further before sending a kick toward a prime target. Whiteoak's polished boot slammed between the scarred man's legs, doubling him over and dropping him to one knee. A gasp erupted from the men in the crowd who could sympathize with the scarred fellow's agony. Those who couldn't had never been in a fight.

Whiteoak turned to see if Corey was faring any better. For a moment, he couldn't find his friend at all. Then he spotted Corey sprawled on the ground, laying in a bloody mess eclipsed by Strahan's shadow. The big man was hunched over, drawing one massive fist back to drive it into Corey's face like a fencepost through dry dirt. One pull of a trigger stopped that fist a moment before it could do its damage.

"Enough!" Whiteoak said. The smoking .38 was still pointed at the sky, but the metallic click of its hammer being thumbed back was enough to draw all eyes in his direction. "Whoever you two men are, you're not welcome here. I suggest you leave."

With Strahan's fist over him, Corey wasn't going to let one second pass before scrambling out of its way. He jumped to his feet and placed one hand on the gun at his side, stopping just short of clearing leather. Since Strahan seemed torn as to what to do next, Corey said, "This ends right now or it turns into a shootout. Your choice. What'll it be?"

By now, the scarred man had circled around closer to Strahan. "This was just to deliver a message," he said. "Looks like we did that well enough. Let's go."

Slowly, Strahan relaxed his fist and took a less offensive posture. As his muscles lost their tension beneath his skin, everyone in the immediate area followed suit. The scent of blood was no longer in the air. The fight was over. It was time for regular life to move along.

"Are you all right?" Corey asked as the folks around him reformed the line leading to the chuck wagon.

Whiteoak winced while touching a sore spot on his side. "I'll be a hell of a lot worse once I get to jostling in the saddle, but I'll survive. What about you? It seems you caught the brunt of that unfortunate exchange."

"You got that right," Corey said with an uneasy chuckle. "Did wonders for my appetite, though. Let's get something to eat before we're kicked out of this camp." Corey snapped his fingers. "You owe me some money! You're buying breakfast."

Whiteoak and Corey both stepped into the line that reformed almost exactly as it had been before the fight started. Like most of the small settlements that survived without much law to speak of, the residents were accustomed to the occasional scuffle and weren't troubled by the sight of a little blood. More importantly, they didn't let those disturbances interfere with the important happenings of daily life. Of those happenings, receiving one's next meal was near the top of the list.

Once the line was reestablished and the cook resumed taking orders, Whiteoak dusted off his pants and straightened the line of his waistcoat. Eventually, he asked, "Was there anything else?"

"Like what?" Corey grunted.

"Like anything else you wanted to tell me?"

"Nope."

"Are you certain of that?"

"Yep."

The line moved forward and everyone in it took a few shuffling steps closer to the chuck wagon.

Whiteoak looked around at the others nearby. While he did receive a few wary or annoyed glances from those who held him partly responsible for delaying their next meal, none of them seemed outwardly aggressive. Whiteoak leaned closer to Corey and said, "It's something in regard to those two fellows."

"Which ones?" Corey asked while looking around.

"Don't play me for a fool," the professor snapped in a harsh whisper. "Those two who added a few lumps and bruises to what was shaping up to be an otherwise pleasant breakfast. That's who!"

"Oh, yeah."

"Were you hoping I'd already forgotten? Or were you just not going to tell me they were looking for you instead of me?"

CHAPTER ELEVEN

Having made his point well enough to snap Corey out of his temporary stupor, White-oak waited until they'd gotten their food and were sitting somewhere they couldn't be so easily overheard before resuming the conversation. Once they were settled on a long bench made from a few halved barrels and some weathered wooden planks, all he had to do was glare at his partner to spark a conversation.

"I already told you there was a price on my head too," Corey said.

"But you've implied I'm the main reason for all of the troubles in this neck of the woods."

"Not all," Corey admitted with a shrug. "But most of 'em."

"Who were they?"

"One of them was called Strahan," Corey said.

"I heard as much myself. Now tell me the

104

rest or I hitch my horses to the wagon and we part ways. That is, after I eat my breakfast, of course."

Corey sighed and picked at his generous portion of grits. "The other one, the fella with the scars all over his face, is named Giles."

"And they're bounty hunters?"

"Not exactly."

Whiteoak daintily picked up a hunk of bread which he used to sop up some of the gravy that had been poured onto his potatoes. The less fancy his surroundings, it seemed, the more the professor wanted to rise above them. His most recent attempt included savoring every bite of the same meal a pack of cowboys was devouring nearby and then dabbing at his mouth with a rumpled strip of fabric posing as a napkin. Once his face was sufficiently cleaned, he said, "I didn't think so. They weren't as persistent as any bounty hunter I've ever seen. So why were they so hell bent on picking you out of this crowd?"

"There's still a chance they were after you, you know."

"Hardly."

"How can you be so sure?"

"Because," Whiteoak explained while ticking off his points on his fingers, "while they may have approached both of us, they were content to walk past me to get to you. When they mentioned delivering some kind of message, they weren't looking at me. Finally, throughout my entire fight with Mister Giles, he seemed more interested in getting past me than actually putting me down."

A good deal of that was a hunch on Whiteoak's part. For some men, hunches were strange little ideas that panned out every now and then. To men like Whiteoak, they were sacred. Judging by the expression on Corey's face, this hunch would pan out.

"All right, so I'm fairly certain they were after me." After shooting a glance at Whiteoak, Corey stuffed some more food into his mouth and added, "Make that very certain," amid a spray of wet crumbs.

"What were they after?"

"Just like they said. To deliver a message."

Stabbing at his plate with a fork, Whiteoak said, "I may be in the business of selling dental products, but I do not enjoy pulling teeth. Don't make me yank out every word from you. We've known each other long enough to be past that."

"We've known each other a long time, sure. Then why didn't you invite me to lend a hand on that bank job in Kansas? I could've helped and gotten some money in

106

my pockets that I need a hell of a lot."

"You were in jail."

Shifting his accusatory glare elsewhere, Corey said, "You knew about that?"

"In the spirit of being tactful, I avoided bringing it up. We've all been nabbed in embarrassing situations and I just thought you'd rather not dredge up the fact that you were tossed into a cage for a short stretch of time because you couldn't keep your trousers on when it was time to —"

"All right, all right," Corey hissed. "What the hell happened to tactfulness?"

Smirking, Whiteoak took a calmer bite of his breakfast before asking, "Why were those two after you?"

"You remember the man I told you about before? The one who's got a beef with me and is willing to pay to have men resolve it with a gun?"

"Yes. I believe his name was Jacob Parsons?"

"That's the one," Corey said heavily. "He's a gambler and has been making a pretty decent living at it."

Whiteoak scowled while taking another bite. Eventually, he admitted, "I do enough gambling to have heard the name before."

"He's not trying to make a fortune on the gambler's circuit. Instead, he's been hustling card games in these parts where there's plenty of gold and silver money being tossed about by men who think they can get rich by risking everything they have."

"Sounds like someone we know."

"Yeah," Corey said. "Sounds like two people we both know and they're sitting here eating breakfast on this bench."

"If any man wants to get rich playing cards, he eventually rides the gambler's circuit," Whiteoak said, referring to the long list of well-known saloons and gambling dens where all the biggest and most infamous games were played.

"Jacob Parsons . . ." Corey stopped himself immediately after mentioning that name. He looked around, anxious to see any hint that he might have been heard. Even though Strahan and Giles were gone and nobody else was interested in him, Corey dropped his voice to a whisper and said, "Jacob Parsons may not be a big man on the circuit, but he soon will be. He's pulled together enough cash to stake some big games. Well . . . big for these parts, anyway."

"Let me guess," Whiteoak said. "He's been winning those games as well."

"Mostly."

The professor let out a mildly disappointed sigh. "Why is it that people are so willing to be fleeced? Even when they know they're contending with wolves."

"Yeah, well I don't know about all of that, but the gamblers around here have been lining up to play in Parsons's games. He wins enough to build up a good haul for himself, but not enough to scare folks away from his table. In fact, he's made a few men pretty damn rich when they won at his games."

"All part of his strategy, I'm sure."

"How do you know?"

"Because," Whiteoak replied, "it's just the sort of thing I would do if I were to attempt to make my fortune at the card tables."

"You'd wind up getting shot for cheating," Corey said.

"And you think Jacob Parsons isn't cheating?"

"If he was, there wouldn't be so many men out there wanting to play him. They'd more likely be lining up to put a bullet through his skull."

"If you spend any time at all on the circuit, you'll learn one lesson. Learning it fast means success and some degree of wealth. Taking too long to pick it up is a very short path to poverty. That lesson being this: everybody cheats. Some are just better at it than others."

"Well he's real damn good at it because

I've played him several times and have brought him to his knees on more than one occasion."

Raising an eyebrow, Whiteoak asked, "Were you cheating?"

"No!" Unable to stand up against the professor's continued scrutiny, Corey added, "Not every time."

"And that's the trick to successfully cutting corners in any endeavor. One must be skilled enough to excel on his own and sly enough to cheat when he has to without being caught."

"Why is it you always seem to be teaching instead of just talking like a normal man?"

"Because that's what good professors do."

Seeing that Whiteoak was more interested in praising himself than saying anything that might be immediately useful, Corey said, "Maybe you're right and maybe all gamblers cheat some way or another. I wouldn't know for certain because I ain't gambled enough to be an expert. What I can tell you is that I was holding my own and learning some damn fine tricks when I got pulled into a bunch of games with Jacob Parsons."

"Which, I take it, is where things went bad."

"In a big way. I got wrangled into putting everything I had on the line so it could be taken from me in what I know to be a crooked move."

"So he *was* cheating?"

"That's just it," Corey said. "I can't prove he was cheating, but I can't say for certain that he wasn't in that particular game. It's all so damn messy and it only gets messier the more I think about it."

"Good cons are like that," Whiteoak said wistfully.

"If I just took a wrong step and lost a big game, I could bear it. Might be sore for some time, but I can take a whipping as good as any man. But if I'm right, then that means Parsons is setting up a hell of a lucrative enterprise using the money that I worked damn hard to pull together and that don't set well with me."

"So, you'd like me to visit some measure of retribution against Mister Parsons?"

"I'd like to get my money back, that's for certain."

"And what about these men that are coming after you?" Whiteoak asked.

Reluctantly, Corey admitted, "I may have taken a run at him on my own, which was one of the things I was doing when we parted ways after first coming to Hannigan's Folly."

"What did you do?"

"Roughed up some of his men. Took a swing at him."

"And?" Whiteoak prodded.

"And . . . I might have burnt one of his smaller businesses to the ground. It was just some pig sty of a general store that would've fallen over on its own anyways. Wasn't much more than a tent that couldn't stand up to a stiff wind. There wasn't even any merchandise in there, but I did find some cash tucked away. Made a small profit, but I mostly wanted to piss him off."

"I'd imagine you succeeded. Why didn't you tell me as much when we first met up after arriving in Hannigan's Folly?"

"Because Parsons was away at the time," Corey explained. "I thought he'd skipped town with the money he took from me and everyone else he'd swindled so he could start whatever venture he's funding."

"What venture might that be?"

"I don't know and I don't much care," Corey said with a grunt. "Now that I know Parsons is in Split Knee, all I want is to get at least some of my money back. If I can't have that, I wanna take a chunk out of his hide for making me look like a fool in front of anyone who saw or who's heard about that game."

"Since gamblers don't have much to do

between hands other than drink and talk, I'd say a great number of them have heard about that game," Whiteoak pointed out. "Also, it seems he may be justified in being cross at you."

"I know, I know. But this whole mess started with him cheating me! I'm the one that was wronged!"

"What truly interests me is this venture you mentioned. For a man with that many funds at his disposal and the ambition that Parsons seems to possess, such a thing could be very profitable indeed."

"Which is why I didn't want to just tell you about it straight away," Corey said in a frustrated tone. "Once you get the scent of money in yer nose, you can't shake loose of it. It's shit like that that turns simple jobs into complicated ones."

"It's also what turns poor men into rich ones."

"See? Right there," Corey said while jabbing a finger at the professor. "I want to propose a job and you've already got your sights set on what's after the job. Maybe even a long ways after it. See why I just wanted to let you think it was a simple matter of bounty hunters?"

"I'm offended that you thought you couldn't confide in me. After everything we've been through, certainly not all of it was good, but it should have been enough for you to know me better than that."

"Oh, I know you just fine. I know that if you heard about a couple of bounty hunters putting you and me in their sights, you'd be fine with helping me take them down. You may not be the best with a gun, but you're a hell of a planner and sly as a fox which always is good in a pinch."

"Why, thank you," Whiteoak said with mock humility.

"But," Corey continued, "if you knew I was involved with a gambler who was pulling together a pile of cash for some scheme, you'd get those damn wheels turning again and we'd be right back where I don't wanna be."

"What wheels? Where don't you want to be? I'm the one who followed you here, remember?"

"I'm talking about the wheels in here," Corey said while tapping a stern finger against the professor's forehead. "And where I don't wanna be is smack in the middle of another one of your plans where you barely know what the hell you're doin' until you've almost gotten yourself killed."

Whiteoak slowly shook his head, swatting away Corey's hand like he would a persistent moth. "If you think I'm the sort of man who'd leave a friend in a lurch just to chase a profit, then you don't know me at all."

"Christ, here we go."

"Those men who came after me during my show back in Hannigan's Folly. Are you telling me they're working for this Parsons fellow, as well?"

"No," Corey replied. "They're real bounty hunters."

"And Mister Parsons truly doesn't know a thing about finding who sent them or how I might put them off my scent?"

"If there's anyone in these parts who'd know such a thing, it'd be Jacob Parsons. He's used hired guns and bounty hunters to do some of his dirty work a few times. I figured if he didn't know about the men after you, he'd at least be able to point us toward someone who did."

"And this cash he's acquired," Whiteoak said craftily. "Were you planning on splitting it with your partner should we be able to help take it out of Parsons's hands?"

"If it's a fair cut, naturally."

There was a glimmer in Whiteoak's eyes, which lasted for a few seconds before he covered it with his hands. Pressing his fingers against his brow, the professor rubbed and fretted before saying, "I don't know. I thought we were friends, Corey. This mistrust you've shown truly hurts."

"Every friendship has some mistrust," Corey replied. "If it didn't, it'd be a marriage."

"Did you come up with that bit of nonsense on your own?"

"No. You did. It was one of those little sayings you like to spew out when you're trying to sound educated."

"I don't know," Whiteoak said. "I think I'd come up with something better than that."

"You were drunk."

"Ah."

"Are you still in on this job with me or not?"

"What's the split?"

After a brief consideration, Corey replied, "Seventy-thirty. It is my money after all."

"Fifty-fifty," Whiteoak replied. "Your money, my neck on the line."

"My money as well as my neck being right there with yours. Sixty-forty."

"Always good to do business with a friend," Whiteoak said through a beaming smile.

Chapter Twelve

"Where is he?" Strahan snarled.

The man on the receiving end of that question was the same one who'd cooked most of the food that was sold at one of the most popular chuck wagons in Jordan. He wasn't the Bulgarian who took the orders, but the little fellow who worked the cooking fires, tended to the supplies and stashed money inside the wagon itself. "Who?" he sputtered. "Where is who? I don't know what you're talking about!"

"The asshole that I was beating to a pulp before I was interrupted by the other asshole. The one in the fancy clothes."

"Oh, they left."

"When?" Strahan asked.

"After they got their food."

"Where'd they go?"

The little man shook his head vigorously. "I don't know. All I do is some of the cooking and whatever other needs to be done while Stan takes the orders."

"Who's Stan?"

"The owner. He was outside taking orders."

"Where is he?"

A few minutes later, Strahan was in a different section of the camp with a different man dangling from the end of his fist. Stan put up a fight at first, but didn't last long once he'd been thumped in the gut by one of the larger man's fists. After a short line of questioning similar to the one given to the smaller cook, Strahan got some more definitive answers.

"They're headed south," Stan said.

"When'd they leave?" Strahan grunted.

"Less than an hour ago."

"Where are they headed?"

"Westchester, and the fellow with the fancy clothes said he needed to get there by tomorrow morning."

"Tomorrow morning, huh?" Giles said while scratching his chin. "You sure that's what he said?"

Strahan stood in front of him, wiping blood from his knuckles onto his filthy shirt. Looking down at his fist, remembering how he'd ended his questioning with both Stan and the smaller cook, he nodded and replied, "I'm sure."

"Folks tend to lie when they want you to stop beating on them. You sure that ain't what happened this time?"

"I only beat on them a little," Strahan said.

"I want you to be sure."

"I am."

"Good," Giles said. "Because if they want to see Westchester by tomorrow morning, that means they'll need to ride in an awfully big hurry."

"But they already left," Strahan told him. "Think we can catch up to them?"

Giles grinned while laughing once under his breath. "They're two strangers who might've rode the Square Trail once or twice before. We know these parts better than most anyone. We can catch up, but we'll have to be quick about it. Saddle up the horses and I'll let Sarah know where we're headed. Meet me at the south end."

Strahan nodded and lumbered away. Giles rushed over to a tall, square tent that was roughly the size of a sitting room. Pulling open the front flap, he looked inside and found a man sitting in a rusty barber's chair getting his hair trimmed by a short woman with reddish blond hair and pale skin.

"Sarah," Giles said. "Come here for a second."

The man in the chair had his feet out-stretched, eyes closed, and hands clasped over his midsection. Opening his eyes, he scowled at Giles and said, "Wait your turn, asshole."

Before Giles could silence him with a colorful threat, the man was pacified by the woman's hands as she patted his cheek while walking around the chair. "I won't be long. You just sit tight and I'll be right back." As she spoke, she slipped her fingers through the customer's hair as though she was scratching a dog near her feet. The man responded in kind, relaxing immediately and putting an end to his barking.

As she stepped outside, Sarah said, "What is it? I'm running a business here."

"Me and Strahan are gonna find Corey Maynard and bring him to Parsons."

"He's not alone, you know," she told him.

"Yeah, I know. He's with some dandy in a silk suit. After the beating we put on them earlier and the one they'll get, Parsons shouldn't have any trouble convincing Maynard to go along with the plan."

"Why didn't you have him agree to it when you had the chance yesterday?" she asked critically.

"Because things were about to get out of hand and having Maynard scared and reckless is better than having him dead." Putting an edge to his tone, Giles added, "I know how to do my job. Just do yours!"

She acknowledged that with a sneer as she turned away from Giles and marched into the tent.

"What took you so long, darling?" her customer grunted. "I ain't got all day to sit in this chair."

"Yes, you do," Sarah replied as she reached out to run her fingers through his hair again. And like any lapdog, the customer settled down and obeyed his master.

A short time later, Giles and Strahan were on their horses riding out of Jordan. There wasn't a distinctive end to the camp, but rather a thinning out of smaller tents that eventually gave way to open country like water slowly trickling from a spigot before petering out. There were a few others on the trail as well, either heading into Jordan or out to one of the nearby spots where prospectors plied their trade. The two gunmen thundered straight past them, changing course just before stampeding over them.

For just under a mile, there was only one useable trail leading southwest away from Jordan. After that, there was plenty of room for more adventurous souls to be creative in the route they chose to traverse the rocky terrain. Some trails were only known to a few while others were simply too treacherous to be used by anyone but the most experienced scouts and riders. Giles and Strahan were already thinking ahead, figuring which would serve as the fastest shortcut to meet back up with the main trail. Even if Corey and Whiteoak chose an alternate path, Giles was confident in his knowledge of the Square Mountain Trail that he could catch up to damn near anyone other than an Indian that was raised in the wilds of those mountains.

As the horses picked up speed, the trail flowed past them like rushing water. Giles raised an arm, finger extended, pointing in the direction he wanted Strahan to go. There was a crack that sounded through the air, accompanied by a sharp burning that raked along the bottom of his outstretched arm and dug into his side just below the armpit. Along with the burning came an impact that twisted Giles in his saddle and threw him off his horse's back.

Strahan pulled back on his reins, bringing his horse to a stop several paces further down the trail. By the time he turned back around to get a look at his fallen partner,

Strahan's pistol was in his hand. Merely having the gun in his possession, however, wasn't enough to prepare him for the next shot. Preceded by another crack, the shot ripped through the air within inches of Strahan's face, causing the big man to recoil and nearly slip from his saddle. Rather than fall in a way similar to his partner's unceremonious dismount, Strahan climbed down and stumbled away from his horse.

"Someone's shooting at us!" the big man hollered.

"That," Corey said as he rode around a bend where he'd been concealed by a cluster of trees, "would be my partner who is a ways off with a rifle pointed at you both right now. If he doesn't get you, I promise I will."

Giles fumbled to remove the pistol from his holster using his bloody arm. When the weapon was free, he tossed it to the ground. Grudgingly, Strahan followed suit.

Chapter Thirteen

Whiteoak wasn't far away. Laying stretched out on his belly atop a boulder fifty yards from the trail, he'd gained the advantage of distance and high ground which meant everything to a man with a rifle. The Spencer rifle was a reliable weapon but in Whiteoak's hands under those circumstances it was deadly as lightning thrown down by the gods themselves. By the time he arrived at the bend where Corey was holding Giles and Strahan at gunpoint, the professor had his weapon reloaded and the line of his clothing back to rigid perfection.

"This ain't a wise move, Maynard," Giles said.

Corey looked at his partner and then at the gun in his hand. "Funny, but I was thinking it turned out pretty good."

"Mister Parsons doesn't like it when men steal from him. You knew that and you stole from him, anyway. You must be stupid, especially knowing what happened to the Hendricks brothers."

"Then maybe I should put the two of you down right here and now," Corey said. "Save me some grief in the future."

"You won't."

"And why's that?"

"Because if you wanted us dead," Giles replied, "you would've killed us already."

"That was him showing kindness," Corey said while pointing at Whiteoak. "But this right here," he said as he raised the pistol in his hand so he was sighting along the top of its barrel, "only answers to me."

Before Corey could draw another breath, Whiteoak stepped forward. "The man on his knees is correct. At least, about one thing. I don't want you dead. That was my choice and, dare I say, impeccable aim to stop you temporarily rather than permanently. Of course, that decision can be overturned at any time if need be."

Corey looked over to the professor with a question in his eyes. To that, Whiteoak merely nodded confidently and straightened his posture to a more commanding stance. While he was clearly uneasy with every moment spent talking to the gunmen instead of putting them down, Corey respected Whiteoak's silent request and allowed the professor to take the lead.

"First thing's first," Whiteoak said. "You two need to be wrapped up and put somewhere safe. Or," he added while picking out a tree a short ways off the path, "somewhere relatively safe."

The professor kept the gunmen in his sights while Corey used a length of rope taken from his saddle to tie them to the tree. Neither of the prisoners was content to be bound that way, but a few clubbing blows from Corey not only settled them down but also allowed Corey to vent some steam.

"There," Whiteoak said while Corey was tying the last knot in the rope binding Giles to the tree. "Now we can talk like civilized men."

"I'll show you civilized," Strahan growled as he struggled against his ropes.

Whiteoak scoffed at that. "I doubt that. Let's start out with an easy question, shall we? Where will we find Jacob Parsons?"

"The Mountaintop," Giles spat. "Everyone knows that."

When Whiteoak looked at him, Corey nodded. "It's a saloon."

"I know it's a saloon! Does that sound like a place where Parsons may be found?"

"One of them, yeah."

"Good. Now what's this venture Mister

126

Parsons has been working on?" Whiteoak asked.

"Venture?" Giles replied.

"You know what I hate more than just about anything?" Whiteoak said as he sighted along the top of his Spencer. "Repeating myself for no good reason. It wastes time and proves that someone wasn't paying any mind to what I've been telling him."

"That's true," Corey added. "He really does hate it when folks don't listen to him jabber."

"He's been riding up into the mountains a lot, if that's what you mean," Giles said.

"Anytime someone leaves town or their camp, they're riding into the mountains," Whiteoak pointed out. "Be more specific."

"I don't mean the Square Mountain Trail," Giles continued. "I'm talking about into the mountains where hardly anyone goes."

Finding himself more interested in what was being said, Corey asked, "You mean like a mine?"

"Not any mine I ever heard about. Least it's not on any of the maps."

"Shut yer damn mouth!" Strahan roared.

"Oh, pipe down," Giles said. Looking Whiteoak straight in the eyes, he said, "You really are dumb as a sack of rocks, ain't you?

If that's all you want to ask after going through all that trouble."

"You still haven't told me what this venture is," Whiteoak pointed out. "Is it a mine? And if so, is it gold? Silver? Or is it something else? These mountains are full of promise for all kinds of businessmen."

"That's where you're gonna have to ask Mister Parsons if you want to know so bad," Giles said. "And, if you ask nice enough, he may even let you buy in. Now how about untying these ropes so I can put a good word in for you?"

Corey stepped up. "What was the message Parsons had for me?"

Giles looked to him and replied, "Oh, yeah. I nearly forgot about that."

"I haven't."

"He says you still owe him money and if you don't give it to me and Strahan, we're supposed to beat you to an even bloodier pulp than before."

"Doesn't look like you're in much of a position to do that," Whiteoak said.

"We'll just see about that. We was also supposed to send a message to anyone else out there who might think about getting on Parsons's bad side. Once word spreads how we whipped the two of you like stray dogs, that message will spread well enough."

"What else do you know about this venture?" Whiteoak asked. "Tell me!"

Blinking and eventually shifting his gaze toward the professor, Giles said, "Oh, are you still here?"

"You'll know I'm here once I start working on you," Whiteoak promised. "All I need are some tools from my wagon. The sharp, pointy tools that even the most unscrupulous dentist would refuse to use on his patients."

"Do your worst."

"Oh, I certainly shall!"

Whiteoak was still spouting rage at the two men bound to the tree when Corey grabbed hold of his arm and dragged him away. After losing sight of the prisoners, Whiteoak snapped his eyes toward Corey and asked, "What do you think you're doing?"

"Saving you from embarrassing yourself," Corey replied in a low voice. "Or perhaps embarrassing yourself further."

"What?"

"What you're saying, the mean looks, the threats you were about to make . . ."

"I wasn't . . ." Reminding himself how well his friend could spot a lie, especially one made under duress, Whiteoak said, "There may have been threats forthcoming, but I wasn't embarrassing myself."

"They weren't buying a word of it."

"Oh, I think they were. At least, some of it, anyhow."

Corey shook his head.

As if to illustrate his point, Giles and Strahan could be heard speaking to each other in calm, easy voices.

"Fine, then," Whiteoak conceded. "Our main goal was to capture them and prevent them from returning to Split Knee to inform their employer and we've done that. Why not try to get more out of them?"

"What do you mean more? We ain't got nothing out of them so far."

"I beg to differ. We know where to find Mister Parsons which saves us some time. We know he's been heading off into the mountains."

"Off to God knows where," Corey said. "That's a real big help."

"If his own men don't know where he's going, then it must be someplace really interesting. I don't know about you," Whiteoak said with thinly veiled excitement, "but I couldn't be more anxious to meet this old acquaintance of yours."

CHAPTER FOURTEEN

Giles and Strahan were left bound to a tree with bandannas shoved in their mouths. They were just off a trail that saw some degree of traffic, so Whiteoak figured someone would happen upon them eventually. To keep his conscience relatively clear, the professor purposely overlooked the knife strapped to Strahan's boot. It would take them some time to get to the blade, but they'd be free eventually. There were so many better ways for a man to sully his conscience than leaving the likes of those two to die.

With that bit of business concluded for the moment, Whiteoak was content to follow Corey's lead through the mountains. Having acted as a scout and trapper for several years, Corey knew dozens of trails that would suit their purpose. They rode from one trail to another, charging single file through narrow gorges and skirting narrow ledges that could break the bones of anyone unfortunate enough to fall onto a decayed pile of the others who had no business tempting their fate so high above sea level.

The reason why Whiteoak had told the cook back at the chuck wagon that he was going to Westchester was to put a sense of urgency into Giles and Strahan when they came racing after them. Despite the success of that plan, Corey wasn't very appreciative. He still wasn't appreciative when Whiteoak reminded him of it after making camp that night.

"Why can't you admit it?" Whiteoak asked as he sat down onto a half-buried stump and stretched his legs out.

"Admit what?" Corey said.

"That I was a help in that fight."

"What fight?"

Whiteoak snorted once, which was something close to a laugh. He started to make the noise again, but stopped. "Are you serious? The fight where we bested those two gunmen who were after you."

"Wasn't much of a fight. More like an ambush followed by a surrender."

"And I was instrumental."

"Sure, whatever you say as long as it'll make you shut up for a while. What the hell difference does it make?"

The sun was long gone and the last hints of its light were fading from the sky, leaving the air cool and growing colder by the minute. Animals rustled through the trees and bushes, feeling out the prey that would be out that evening. Taking no notice of that whatsoever, Whiteoak said, "You never gave me credit for being anything other than a salesman."

"Ain't that what you are?"

"I served in the Army, you know! Shouldn't that command some modicum of respect?"

"Were you an officer?"

"No."

"Then I won't salute you." After a few more moments spent poking the campfire with a stick, Corey said, "You did pretty good back there. Although, you did miss one of them."

"My bullet went exactly where it was meant to go. Neither of those men would have done us much good if he was dead."

"And neither of them are doing much good tied to that tree," Corey added.

Slowly, the remaining rays of sunlight were choked out by the oncoming night. The winds grew from cool to cold as the mountain sank its snowy teeth into every bit of exposed skin on the two men. The horses shifted their weight and lowered their heads to the chill, settling in for a quiet night. Unwilling to give in to the silence just yet, Whiteoak asked, "What's this venture I've been hearing about?"

"Which?"

"If you think you'll wear me out on the subject, you're sorely mistaken. We're in the middle of nowhere with nary a saloon in sight. I've got time and nothing else to fill it."

"Jesus Christ."

"We can talk about religion later, if you like. Right now, I want to hear about the venture Jacob Parsons is undergoing."

"You're a real persistent cuss, you know that?"

"Yes, sir, I do," Whiteoak said through a grin.

"Tends to strain a man's nerves sometimes."

"I know that as well."

Despite himself, Corey couldn't help but laugh at the professor. Shaking his head, feeling the day's fatigue settle in, he said, "I don't know much about it. Honest. It's got something to do with a still up in the mountains."

"A still? Those aren't exactly rare and

they're not hardly worth fighting for."

"There's more to it than that. I just don't know what. I was hoping to get close enough to Parsons to see for myself. Maybe even buy or win a few shares in the endeavor if it seemed worth the trouble."

Suddenly, Whiteoak's face brightened. "Ah ha! You thought it was some kind of new liquor or possibly a fuel source for locomotive engines!"

"The former might've occurred to me, but I don't know what you mean in regard to the latter."

"You wanted to acquire some of it and sell it to me," Whiteoak continued, overpowered by his enthusiasm. "That's why you've kept it so close to the vest and that's why you held out for so long. You were trying to procure a deal ripe enough for me to want to invest in as well!"

Corey shrugged. "You do tend to get all riled up about anything that can be mixed, brewed or otherwise concocted."

"Yes, I do," Whiteoak said while rubbing his hands together vigorously. "Tell me everything you know on the subject."

"I already did. The only way I got Parsons to part with any more was to convince him to wager the information in a card game. When I finally got close, the stakes were so damn high, I had to go into one hell of a deep hole to match the bet. I lost and now I owe Parsons that money." Whiteoak scoffed under his breath.

"What's so funny?" Corey asked.

"Nothing. I just thought you were a better gambler than that. At the very least, you should have been able to stay afloat without losing your shirt."

"I know how to play the game," Corey said with a growing amount of venom in his tone. "But he wouldn't have parted with what I wanted on anything but the largest wager."

"Then you pick a better spot to make your stand."

Corey started to defend himself with vigor, which broke down into an angry sputter. When words finally came to him again, they were, "Real easy to judge after the fact."

"I'm just saying that the strength of your hand doesn't mean much to a true artist at the card table."

"Artist, huh? Don't you mean cheat?"

"When it comes to playing games of chance?" Whiteoak said. "Of course that's what I mean!"

"Men get killed for cheating at cards."

"Only men who don't know how to do it

properly."

The posture that Corey took when he heard that was similar to a pose Whiteoak might have stricken if someone had accused him of being a bartender instead of a dubiously licensed physician. "Are you accusing me of being a bad card player or a cheat?"

"Which do you think is worse?"

"A cheat, of course."

"And that's why you're poor," Whiteoak said. "Cheating is just a bad name put onto a craft that's as intricate as it is old. We've had this discussion plenty of times already."

"I know and it always ends the same. Cheating ain't right and them that get shot for it deserve every ounce of pain they get."

Whiteoak shook his head and gazed at the polished surface of his boot. "Your grammar becomes increasingly atrocious when you know you're wrong about the subject at hand."

"And you sound more like a goddamn politician when you're stringing bullshit onto a line."

"And what is that supposed to mean?"

Drawing a breath that didn't do much to calm him, Corey said, "I wasn't about to cheat to get what I needed. I had a damn good hand and if anything, that son of a bitch Parsons was the one who was cheating."

"I'd imagine so. And who wound up with the short end of that stick?"

Despite knowing the answer, Corey wasn't about to say it out loud. Instead, he gnawed on it like a piece of gristle that was too tough to swallow with the rest of his meal.

Whiteoak never required someone on the other end of a conversation for him to keep it rolling. Without skipping a beat, he lifted a finger victoriously and said, "Mister Parsons knew what he had was too valuable to part with, so he kept hold of it by any means necessary. You just weren't prepared to do the same to take it from him."

"I wasn't prepared to get shot is more like it."

Shrugging, Whiteoak said, "If you don't have the stones to push your bets as far as they need to go, you'll never win. Didn't you even suspect that Parsons might cheat?"

"Maybe."

"Then, you either do the same and better or you lose. That's all there is to it."

"I'd rather find another way to get one over on Parsons than slither in the grass alongside of him."

The professor grinned. "Then it's good you brought me along."

CHAPTER FIFTEEN

Of all the stops along the Square Mountain Trail, Split Knee was the one that most deserved to be called a town. Its buildings and tents were situated on a steep slope that led into a rocky terrace overlooking a deep ravine half a mile away. Due to the height of the rocks upon which the town was built and the depth of the ravine, Split Knee seemed perched on the edge of a catastrophe. Newcomers often complained of feeling as though they were about to plummet to their deaths, the pits of their stomachs writhing inside of them as if the descent into hell had already begun. Once they got their bearings and came to grips with the fact that the ravine wasn't nearly as close as it appeared, the feeling usually passed. If it didn't, those newcomers moved along.

Shifting in his saddle, Whiteoak winced and took a steadying breath.

"Been a while since you've been to Split

Knee?" Corey chided.

"I'm fine," the professor replied unconvincingly. "Penelope might be a little uneasy, however," he added while patting the mare's neck.

Corey wobbled in his saddle, mimicking the sway of a drunk that was about to fall onto his ass in the gutter. He kept it up, even though the professor wasn't looking directly at him. All he needed to do was sway just a bit more in a rocking pattern to catch the other man's attention.

"All right!" Whiteoak said. "Enough!"

"You're too accustomed to rolling around in that traveling museum you call a wagon. It softens you up for when you're out riding the trail like a real man."

"I am a real man, thank you very much. I'm just a man who doesn't like the thought of skidding down the side of a mountain."

"I've only got one more thing to say in regard to that swirling sensation in the bottom of your gullet."

Looking over to Corey, Whiteoak said, "What's that?"

"Welcome to Split Knee."

The two men continued their ride into town with Whiteoak keeping his eyes pointed forward and his mouth shut most of the way. That was almost as uncharacteristic for him as the satisfied smirk on Corey's face. The professor's condition lessened somewhat as they approached town. Not only was there more to catch his eye, but the slope of the mountain upon which Split Knee had been built appeared to ease up thanks to the houses, shops and other buildings scattered nearby.

Apart from a twisted series of alleys and narrow footpaths slicing through town like a web of old scars, there were only a few streets of note within Split Knee with three smaller ones that were more recent additions. At the top of the town was Summit Street, running east to west at Split Knee's highest elevation. Taylor Street ran parallel to Summit, bisecting the town like a belt around a fat man's waist. Those two were connected by three others that ran north to south named First, Second and Third Avenues. On Third Avenue, just below Taylor Street was Cross Way, which was a short street that didn't extend far enough to meet up with Second Avenue. At either end of Cross were two smaller roads running south to the lowest border of town. Not surprisingly, they were named Left Avenue and Right Avenue. While Split Knee had many things to offer, creativity wasn't one of them.

"I must say," Whiteoak declared as his

eyes wandered from one building to another along the southernmost stretch of First Avenue, "this excursion has definitely taken a turn for the better."

Corey nodded and took in the same sights as the professor. Some of those sights were blonde, others had darker hair, but they all wore loose clothing that was unbuttoned to display full, feminine curves. "Leave it to you to come into town through the whore's district."

"Am I to believe you don't appreciate the company of pretty women?"

"I didn't say anything of the sort. All I meant was that you were the one who picked this route into town and were real insistent about it."

Catching the eye of a woman with long brown hair and olive skin, Whiteoak tipped his hat and asked, "Can you blame me?"

"Nope. Not a bit. I was hoping we might be able to conduct some business before you sow your wild oats and such."

"My friend, a true man of the world sows his oats at every opportunity. He also learns that every moment of every day contains such an opportunity."

Corey sighed. "We doing business or not?"

"Where exactly is this business you're proposing?"

"That way," Corey replied while pointing north. "Summit and Third."

"The Mountaintop Saloon?"

"That's the place. You been there?"

"I have, on many occasions," Whiteoak told him. "Only this visit to Split Knee already seems to be affording me a new perspective."

"Because you're not riding in on that wagon?"

"Precisely. While there are many advantages to traveling with my equipment and advertisements, there are certain benefits to being somewhat more discreet."

"A one-legged dog howling with its ass on fire would be more discreet than you in that damned wagon," Corey chuckled.

"Be that as it may, I think there are many opportunities besides the ones involving Mister Parsons in this town."

"You say that in every town, no matter how many times you been to them."

"Such is the way for a true adventurer and entrepreneur."

"If that last word means asshole, then I agree."

"Why don't you tell me more about Parsons," Whiteoak said. "I've heard of the man, but not enough to consider myself prepared for this venture."

"What have you heard?"

"That he's not to be trifled with at the card tables. There were also some rumors connecting him to the deaths of at least half a dozen men. I can't say for certain how much of that is true, but there was enough for me to steer clear of him."

"You were right to do that," Corey said as he nodded to a pair of busty working girls leaning over the porch railing of a two-story cathouse. "He's not much of a businessman, but he does own pieces of most of the gambling halls along the Square Mountain Trail. Takes a cut from games in other saloons as well. Faro, roulette, you name it."

"A man with varied interests. I like it. How did he acquire a hand in all these games?"

"Buying them or beating the right men to a pulp until he got what he wanted," Corey replied.

"I see. Nothing I haven't dealt with before."

"When you're dealing with this fella, just do me a favor, Henry."

"Of course!"

"Try not to piss him off."

Whiteoak smirked. "You know I can't make a promise like that."

144

CHAPTER SIXTEEN

The Mountaintop Saloon may not have been the tallest building in town, but it looked down on the rest of Split Knee like a lord presiding over his kingdom. Three floors, dwindling in size from bottom to top, mirrored the shape of the town itself. Whether or not the design was purposeful was unknown since the original owner and designer of the saloon had been gunned down long ago on Taylor Street. All most folks knew about the saloon anymore was that it served the best beer in the county and was the place to play for the highest stakes.

Whiteoak and Corey were tying their reins to a hitching post outside when the sound of loud music drifted through the air. The piano and banjo players competed to be heard over the voice of a singer who fought to overcome the boisterous yelling and laughter of the customers filling the saloon to its rafters.

"Now this is more my element," Whiteoak declared. "Every time I come to this town, I fall in love with this establishment a little more."

"Weren't you tossed out on your ear the last time?"

"Where did you hear such a vicious rumor?"

"I read it," Corey said as he started walking toward the saloon's front door. "In a newspaper."

"Oh, well, I suppose that's a mildly credible source."

Any embarrassment or aggravation that had been on the professor's face was chased away once he stepped inside the Mountaintop Saloon. The bar was at the back of the room and stretched along that entire wall. To order a drink, customers had to wind their way through the shifting maze of card tables, chairs, roulette wheels and Faro spreads as well as the people drifting between them. Those people came in all shapes and colors, ranging from men in expensive suits all the way down to vagrants without enough cash to afford a bath in the last several months.

Whiteoak beamed while tugging at his lapels to straighten the front of his coat.

"Shall we test the waters or dive right in?"

"It probably wouldn't do to just stroll up to Parsons and let him know why we're here. That is," Corey added while looking around, "if I knew where he was. Do you see him?"

"No," Whiteoak replied without making an effort to search the faces surrounding him. "How about we scout this place properly?"

"Might as well."

The professor set his sights straight ahead and started walking. As he maneuvered between the tables, he listened to the voices of gamblers and thieves, catching glimpses of the cards they held while guessing about the lies they told. He could feel anger, anxiousness, exultation and fear crackling through the air like the charge that came before a bolt of lightning struck the earth. Each of those men had fortunes to make or lose. They wore guns on their hips and only a sharp observer of character could tell whether or not they had the sand to pull their triggers. Henry Whiteoak smiled. If he ever had a true home, it would feel a lot like this place.

Before he'd walked halfway across the room, Whiteoak was spotted by one of the young women who wound their way from one customer to another like bees sampling a field of ripe blossoms. She was slightly shorter than the other girls, but had a bright enough fire inside of her to outshine her competitors. It showed through in the confidence in which she carried herself, the directness of her gaze and the easy familiarity in her beaming smile. Of course, a young, naturally curvy body and tightly cinched corset didn't hurt her cause.

She strutted toward Whiteoak with her hands on her hips and enough sway in her movements to cause her long brown hair to rustle as if in a breeze. The closer she got to him, the more her eyes narrowed into a playful scowl. "Is that Professor Henry Whiteoak I see?"

Opening his arms to accept a hug, he replied, "None other, my dear!"

She did hug him, but followed it up with a slap across the face. Of course, Whiteoak reacted to it as though his head had been knocked off his shoulders.

Corey chuckled. "I see you've made friends everywhere."

"Friends don't pack up and leave town without a moment's notice," she said without taking her eyes off of Whiteoak.

Rubbing the part of his cheek that had barely been hit with enough force to make a red spot, the professor said, "There were some hostilities with those rowdy miners. Don't you recall?"

"Oh, I recall," she said. "I also recall that you sold them a collection of rocks instead of the agreed-upon merchandise."

"Let me guess," Corey said, truly savoring the moment and all of Whiteoak's discomfort. "He was supposed to be giving them gold? Silver?"

"It was supposed to be Attracting Stones," she explained with a hint of a grin beneath her scowl. "Isn't that what you called them?"

"They were magnets," Whiteoak told her. "Made to attract precious metals instead of the common ones that only attract iron scrapings."

"But they didn't work past his demonstration?" Corey ventured.

The young woman nodded. "That's right. And those miners were none too happy about it."

Whiteoak raised his eyebrows and held his hands up to shoulder level as though he was being robbed. "I told them the effects of those stones wouldn't last very long. It's not my fault they didn't act quickly enough to take advantage of my product's copious benefits."

"That's what I love about this one," she said while patting his cheek with a bit more care. "He just keeps talking until he's either covered his ass or set a torch to it."

"Or," Corey added, "until he's done both."

The woman turned her rich brown eyes toward Corey and looked him up and down, sizing him up. "Have we met?"

"No, but I've seen you around. You're one of the whores who works this place."

While the scowl on her face had been playful before, it was all business now. "What did you call me?"

Whiteoak stepped between them and explained, "Giavanna here is not a whore. She's a saloon girl."

"What's the difference?" Corey asked.

"The difference," she said sternly, "is that one shares a bed with trash like you and the other wouldn't do such a thing if the world was coming to its end."

Keeping his neutral tone, Whiteoak said, "Saloon girls drum up business for the place by charming customers into buying drinks, steering gamblers toward the proper games and generally keeping warm blooded men from leaving. She does it quite well, too. Gia, this is my friend Corey Maynard."

Corey extended a hand. "Pleased to meet

you, Gia."

She shook his hand with the bare minimum of affection. "I've seen you in here before as well. I believe you've been slapped in the face by every girl in here apart from me."

Whiteoak raised an eyebrow while looking over to his friend. "Did you proposition one of Gia's coworkers for something distasteful?"

"Yes, so let's move on."

"Why don't you move on?" Gia said. "I'd like to have a word with Henry. Alone."

There was no room in her icy tone for negotiation so Corey didn't bother trying. Instead, he sighed and walked away while muttering, "I'm gonna have a drink."

"A drink," Gia grumbled while motioning to the bartender, "that will be double the regular price."

Some of the smaller tables weren't meant for hosting card games. They were nothing more than rounded boards nailed to the posts supporting the ceiling intended only to be a place to rest a few drinks. Whiteoak leaned against one, resting an elbow on the wooden surface while plucking the watch from his pocket so he could dangle it by its chain. "It's good to see you again, Gia."

"What is it, Henry?"

"What's what?"

"Don't play that game with me," she said while propping both elbows on the small round table and leaning closer to him. "What's the reason you're here? It must be something good to bring you back down the Square Mountain Trail so soon."

"Can you blame a man for traveling through so much rugged terrain for a glimpse of that pretty face?"

"That line of bull only worked on me once and even then . . . just barely."

Dispensing with his flowery speech, Whiteoak told her, "I'm here because some men are out to kill me and my friend there."

"Anyone I know?"

"In my case, it has to do with a job that went awry in Kansas."

"You mean that bank job you were bragging about?" she asked.

"Bragging? Hardly. A man in my position stays alive by protecting his secrets."

"Except when he's drunk," she whispered. "Or when he's trying to convince a woman that he's something other than a fancy pants blowhard driving a garish wagon."

Whiteoak started to deny the charge and defend himself, but something sprang to mind that stopped his efforts before they could begin. "Was that the night of the dance at that place on Taylor Street?"

She nodded. "You were so eager to get your hands on me that you wouldn't stop talking about one exploit after another. I figured most of them were lies, but I heard a few things since then that convinced me the story about your Kansas bank job might have some truth behind it."

"If you thought they were lies, then why did you allow those words to separate you from your dress that night?"

"Because you spoke them with such . . ."

"Style?" Whiteoak offered. "Grace?"

"You were loud," she said. "I had to take you somewhere quiet just to shut you up."

"And after that? What's your excuse for that?"

"Maybe I wanted to see how well you handled that gun of yours," Gia said as her fingers drifted to the silver handle of the .38 poking out from under his waistcoat.

It took some effort, but Whiteoak was able to snap himself out of the spell that was drawing them closer together. "Do you know Jacob Parsons?"

"Is he the one that means to kill you?"

"He's the one that means to kill Corey."

"Who?"

"My friend. Come now. He may not be the showman that I am, but surely you haven't forgotten already."

Scowling as though she'd taken a bite of a rotten apple, Gia said, "I haven't forgotten. Maybe you and I should pick up where we left off and let your friend take his chances with Jake Parsons."

"Does it annoy you so much that he mistook you for . . ." Seeing the anger creep in around her edges as he drew close to comparing Gia to another kind of working girl, Whiteoak shifted his words to, ". . . for something you're not?"

"He's not the first and won't be the last to call me a whore," she said off-handedly. "Seeing men look at me that way makes my skin crawl."

"It's also something you've used to your advantage, I'm sure."

"Yes, but I don't have to like it."

Placing a hand on her arm, Whiteoak said, "Then let's get our business squared away so we can find some privacy where I can rub you the right way."

Gia smiled at him, which turned into a laugh. "I'm sorry," she said once she caught her breath. "Is this where I'm supposed to bat my eyelashes and hurry to do whatever you want?"

"Yes."

"You truly are a brazen, arrogant peacock, Henry."

"I try. I'm also a peacock who still has a good portion of money tucked under his feathers. If you do right by me, I'll see that you get your share of it."

"What's so important that you finally decide to take notice of Jacob Parsons?" she asked. "Last time you were in town, you were content to steer clear of him."

"Last time, he was just another fellow surrounded by gunmen who wasn't interested in my wares."

"And too dangerous to be approached for one of your schemes?" she added.

"Yes," Whiteoak told her. "That too. In any game, there are players, those who get played, and those who are best left out altogether. Surely you know what I mean."

"Of course I do. Now tell me what's got you interested enough to risk coming back to Split Knee so soon after you were kicked out."

"It was quite a while since I left town."

"But when you return, it's real quiet and without your wagon," Gia pointed out.

"That doesn't mean anything."

"All right, then. Since nothing means anything and you're just wandering into this place on personal business, I'll leave you alone to get to it."

When she started to walk away, Whiteoak grabbed her arm to reel her back in. "Parsons can help my friend and I both get out of hot water by talking with the people necessary to call off the killers that have been sent after both of us."

"There's a price on your head."

"That's right and a man with Parsons's influence can be a big help in redirecting any killers sent all the way from Kansas. He may even be more influential than that. In any case, he's making things rough for my friend which, by extension, makes things rough for me. Lessening the heat from any source would be splendid."

"Especially," she said, "for someone who attracts as much heat as you."

"Precisely. Do you know anything that might be of any help in that regard?"

Gia nodded. "Lots of men come through this saloon full of big talk meant to impress the ladies. It doesn't take much to point all that talk in the right direction."

"Which is why I came to you," Whiteoak said. "Why all the back and forth talk on the subject if you already knew where I was headed?"

"Because I wanted to see if you'd be up front about it."

"I should have been."

"Actually," Gia confided while tapping the end of Whiteoak's nose, "if you didn't lie a little or beat around the bush, I'd suspect something was terribly wrong with you. As it is, it seems you're pretty much your normal self. Also, I like to watch you squirm."

"Well, you got what you wanted, I'd say. How about giving me what I want?"

"Later," Gia told him while tracing her fingertips along the professor's chest. "For now, how about I introduce you to Jacob Parsons?"

Chapter Seventeen

The table where Parsons played poker wasn't in the main room of the Mountaintop Saloon. It was tucked away in the back of the second floor with walls so thick that the music from the main room below could hardly be heard. The air smelled of expensive cigars and the perfumed skin of beautiful women. Those cigars were clenched between the teeth of the men playing the game while the perfume adorned the skin of women sitting upon those men's laps.

When Whiteoak tried to approach the table, he was stopped by a delicate hand. Holding him back, Gia whispered, "He doesn't like to be disturbed."

"This is an important matter," Whiteoak said in a voice that was just loud enough to carry through the room. "I'm sure he can spare a few moments."

If Parsons took any notice of Whiteoak's announcement or the authority he instilled in his tone, he gave no indication. He was somewhere in his late fifties with thin silver hair parted down the middle. His face wasn't exactly beefy, but it hung on him like a mask that was one size too big. While his cheeks may have drooped somewhat, his eyes were those of a hungry owl looking for the next mouse to be torn to shreds. His attention was instead focused on the man directly to his right.

"You called me?" Parsons said sharply. "With a pair of fucking jacks?"

The man sitting next to Parsons may have been dressed in similarly expensive material as his host, but he didn't have the same fiber beneath all the silk and clean cotton. "It's called gambling, Jacob," he said nervously. "I gambled and won."

"What you did isn't gambling. It's an idiotic play that brands one of us a fool. Are you admitting to being an idiot?"

"No. I won the hand, didn't I?"

Parsons shifted in his chair so he could more directly face the other man. "What did you just say?"

There were two others at the table. One of them, who also happened to be farthest away from Parsons, said, "Let's just get on with the game. I'm sure you'll have plenty of time to win your money back."

"That's not the goddamn point!"

When Parsons raised his voice, nobody wanted to answer back. Some of the ladies decorating the men's laps tried to quietly move away from the table.

"Where are you going, honey?" Parsons said to the girl closest to him. The one on his lap didn't try to get away, but looked like she was hoping for any chance to do so. The woman Parsons had just addressed smiled and eased back down onto her benefactor's lap. Looking back to his main target, Parsons said, "When I want to play with idiots, I do it in the main room. This is supposed to be a game for professionals, not cowboys looking to throw away their money on a whim."

The gambler with the jacks said, "It's all a part of the game. I bluffed and you bought it. Don't be a sore loser, Jake."

Parsons's smile looked more like a slightly curved line that had been scratched into a slab of rock by a dull chisel. "Sore loser? Me? Is that what you think, Andy? After all this time we've known each other."

"We have known each other a while," Andy said. "And I know how you get when you've had a few too many beers."

"I'm a student of the game," Parsons replied with dignity that somehow felt greasy. "The reason I hold my games up here is so I won't have to deal with idiots who play with nothing more than blind luck."

"It ain't luck. You want me to explain why I chose to bluff the way I did or would you rather continue playing? The cards will fall your way eventually, just like they do for everyone else."

"Don't talk to me like I'm a fucking child."

Andy held his hands palms up just a few inches above the table. "You're right, Jake. I'm sorry. I made a stupid play and got away with it. Sometimes it's all a man has left."

"Were you cheating me?"

"Don't go down that road," Andy replied gravely. Picking up the deck of cards that had been gathered in preparation for a shuffle, he said, "If you want to inspect these, be my guest. If you want to switch them out, that's your right. Just don't call me a cheater."

"Actually, I think I would like you to tell me why you made such a fucking stupid bet. I mean, someone who's smarter than an average milking cow would know better than to pull that kind of thing in here."

One of the other gamblers chuckled nervously and said, "Let's all just take a breath and have another drink. I'm buying."

"You hear that?" Andy said in a relieved tone. "I think he's got a point."

"I've got a point too," Parsons said. In the space of a heartbeat, he brought up a hand that had been beneath the table near his knee and slammed it down. The impact of the hammering blow was enough to rattle every chip on the felt-covered surface, crushing Andy's hand between Parsons's fist and the deck of cards he'd been holding. It wasn't until Andy tried to pull his arm back that he realized it was pinned in place by a slender knife in Parsons's grip.

"Jesus!" yelped the gambler who'd so recently tried to barter a peace between the two men.

Parsons shifted the muscles in his face to mock a grin. "Go get the drinks you promised. Andy here was going to enlighten me on the finer aspects of playing this game I love so very much. Isn't that right, Andy?"

Although Parsons seemed to be enjoying himself, Andy wasn't anywhere close to that. He squirmed at first, only to find that moving his pinned hand in the slightest only caused more of his tender flesh to scrape against sharpened steel. Shifting his efforts to his other hand, he grabbed hold of Parsons's hand in an attempt to pull the knife up and away from where it had been

Chapter Eighteen

When Whiteoak came back down to the main area of the saloon, the first thing he saw was Corey leaning against the bar with a drink in his hand and a smile on his face. Whiteoak crossed the bustling room, stood directly beside Corey, placed both hands flat upon the surface of the bar and stared straight ahead.

"Shut up," the professor said before a single word could pass Corey's lips.

Paying no heed to the stern command, Corey asked, "What the hell was going on up there?"

"I told you to shut up."

"How come you're not upstairs slinging cards with Parsons? Did you lose your money already?"

Ignoring the man next to him, Whiteoak lifted a finger to politely catch the barkeep's attention. Once he had it, he ordered a shot of fire water and watched eagerly for it to be poured into a glass in front of him.

"Did Parsons frighten you?" Corey asked in a mocking, infantile voice. "Did he chase you out of there?"

"No," Whiteoak curtly replied.

Grinning wider, Corey looked over to the woman who'd taken her sweet time in winding through the crowd to stand at the bar with them. "Did you see what happened?" Corey asked Gia. "Please tell me you saw everything."

"I saw it," she said.

"And was it bad? Please tell me it was bad."

Before Gia could tell Corey anything, Whiteoak said, "I went up there to see the lay of the land and I saw it, all right? Let's not say anything more about it than that."

"Parsons is known to get rough during his games," Corey said as if sifting through the thoughts that were racing in his mind. "I imagine something like that happened."

"It was something like that," Gia told him.

Corey slapped the bar triumphantly and let out a barking whoop. "Damn! I wish I could've seen you scurry out of there like a whipped dog!"

"You want to see someone get rough?" Whiteoak said while tapping the rim of his glass to signal for a refill. "You're about to see that and a whole lot more if you don't lower your voice with absolute haste."

"Sorry, Henry," Corey said as he slapped the professor's back. "But I should've warned you that Parsons wasn't some easy mark."

"You did warn me. Several times, in fact, during the ride from Hannigan's Folly."

"Oh. Well, then, you should've listened. I'm gonna see if I can find this redhead I've been eyeing while you were upstairs making a fool of yourself. She's got the plumpest backside I ever seen."

"That would be Misty," Gia told him. "And she's right over there."

Corey looked in the direction she was pointing and immediately spotted what he was after. Misty had a slender build with small, perky curves up top and wider, luscious hips that were accentuated by the skirt she wore. Her pale skin and beaming smile gave her face a luminous quality and the dark red waves of hair spilling down to her shoulders were more than enough to capture the attention of several men around her.

"Looks like you've got competition," Whiteoak said.

Straightening his shirt and pressing down some of the wilder sprouts of hair he could find with anxious hands, Corey said, "Not for long. Don't wait up for me." With that, he marched across the room like a soldier on his way to plunder a small village.

"She's gonna eat him alive, isn't she?" Whiteoak mused.

"Oh, yes," Gia replied.

"Why haven't I seen her around here before?"

"She's new. Just came into town from somewhere back east about a month ago."

"East . . . where?" Whiteoak asked.

"Virginia, I think. Why are you so interested?"

Admiring the view as Misty shifted her weight and tossed her hair while laughing at something one of her admirers said, the professor replied, "Because a place with exports like that is most definitely worth a visit."

Gia brought his eyes back to her by placing her fingers on Whiteoak's chin and turning his head. "Weren't you here on some kind of business? Something to do with Jacob Parsons, I believe."

"Yes, indeed. And as you've seen, some groundwork has already been laid to that end."

"Groundwork?" she scoffed. Although some of the smirk remained in her eyes, Gia did an admirable job of clearing most of it from the rest of her face. "No offense, Henry, but there wasn't much accomplished up there apart from you stammering a bit before running away."

"Exactly. And that's what Parsons saw as well."

"Oh," she said skeptically. "Well done, then."

Whiteoak took hold of her arm and drew Gia in close. "What I want you to do, when Parsons asks about me, is tell him exactly what you just told me. Or, something to that effect anyway."

The longer she studied his face, the more Gia found lurking behind the professor's eyes. "What are you cooking up?"

"I still have business with Parsons and it involves getting in on one of his card games. One of the good games upstairs. Not one of the many that I'm certain he plays down here among the riff raff."

"If your business is still about a price on your heads, perhaps you should talk to those men over there," she said while nodding toward a section of tables within spitting distance of where Corey was getting better acquainted with his nicely proportioned redhead. "Because they intend on collecting it."

Both men sat hunched over their table

with shoulders pulled down low and heads hanging so the brims of their hats covered everything but their chins. Now that they were getting up and looking over toward Corey, Whiteoak could make out a whole lot more.

"Those two work for Parsons?" he asked in a hurried whisper.

Gia shrugged. "Men like them work for anyone who pays well enough and Parsons can pay better than most."

"Do they know we're here?"

"They've been watching ever since you came strutting in this place like a peacock with your tail feathers on full display. That's the problem with a man like you," she added while playfully tapping Whiteoak's chest. "You're too smart for your own good. Sometimes you overlook the simple things."

"I was thinking we'd run into them again, but figured we'd be in the open where making a move would be difficult. If they can catch Corey off his guard somewhere quieter, that could be difficult."

"You'd best hurry, then," she said as Misty led Corey by the hand toward a short set of steps that led to a row of doors at the far end of the room. "Because he's about to find himself about as far off his guard as a man can get."

CHAPTER NINETEEN

A row of doors led from the main room of the saloon directly into private rooms that were just large enough to hold a bed, a chair and a small chest of drawers with a water basin on top of it. The rooms were provided for customers who couldn't wait to get their hands on one of the many whores working at the Mountaintop and were rarely used for more than a few minutes at a time.

"All right, darling," Corey said as he pulled open the door and followed Misty inside. "Time for us to get down to it!"

"Room's extra," she informed him while tugging at the lacing that kept the front of her dress closed. "You want the half hour or hour rate?"

"Better put me down for an hour," he replied. "I got some big plans for you."

She smiled as though she hadn't heard that from every other man accompanying her into one of the private chambers. If

Corey had asked for a fifteen-minute rate, she would have at least respected his honesty. As it was, she was more than happy to tack on the additional fee to her list of services that were about to be provided.

"Why don't you make yourself comfortable?" Misty said while easing the front of her dress down. "And I'll do the same."

Since she was standing next to the chest of drawers, Corey moved over to the chair positioned in the back corner of the room. He eagerly stripped off his shirt and boots and set them on or near the chair so they wouldn't be in his way. His gun belt came off next, which he draped over the back of the chair before starting on his pants.

"You ready for this, honey?" Misty asked.

Corey's eyes widened. "Hell, yes, I am!"

Misty smiled and slowly turned her back to him. She bent at the waist, placed one foot up on the frame of the bed and hiked her skirts up to reveal the smooth, pale curves of her perfectly rounded backside. "Go on, then. Don't keep me waiting."

Whatever words Corey meant to say were lost amid the anxious, anticipatory laugh that bubbled up from the back of his throat. The sounds he made shifted into a series of deep breaths as he positioned himself behind her and placed one hand on the small of her back. Moments before he could fully indulge himself, the door rattled behind him.

"Someone's in here," he said while easing into her. "Find another room!"

The door rattled some more as it was opened. The floor beneath them trembled beneath solid impacts of boots thumping against the boards like rocks being dropped from the saloon's roof. Corey turned to look over his shoulder while the rest of his body was still attempting to relieve the tension that had been building inside of him for the last several minutes. "What the hell?" he grunted when he got a look at the face of the man who'd barged in on him.

Strahan's bearded face filled most of Corey's field of vision. Beneath the tangled whiskers was the wicked smile of someone enjoying what he was about to do. In stark contrast to what most occupants of that room wanted, Strahan balled up his fist and pounded it against Corey's cheek in a short, clubbing blow.

Corey staggered to the side where he immediately bounced off one of the small room's walls. "Who the hell?" he grunted.

"You don't remember me?" Strahan asked. "How about this to remind ya?" He pulled back the same fist he'd used to end

Corey's party with Misty and drove it straight into the other man's chest.

Corey's next breath came in a wheezing gasp as he reflexively clutched the spot where he'd just been hit. Before he could absorb any more punishment, he flopped onto all fours and scurried the short distance to the chair where he'd left his gun belt. He got there only to encounter one problem: there was no pistol in his holster.

"Where is it?" Corey groaned as he turned to look at the bed.

Misty was huddled on the bed, pressing herself against the wall as flat as she could. She knew all too well that it was best to move aside when two rams were about to lock horns.

When Corey snapped his head around to get a look at Strahan again, all he could see was the large man's fist. With no regard for grace or accuracy, Corey rolled away from the incoming swing and tripped himself up on the chair. He cleared a path for Strahan's fist, however, which was his only intention for the hasty maneuver. Corey scrambled to get himself upright again while Strahan turned and cocked his arm back for another punch.

"I remember you now!" Corey said while pulling his pants back up. "You're one of those assholes who we left tied to a tree after you ambushed me a few towns ago."

"You got that right," Strahan replied. "And all I needed to do was wait for you to come to Split Knee, walk straight into Mister Parsons's own place and take yer britches off."

Corey stood up and shrugged. "It seems silly when you say it like that."

Strahan unleashed the punch he'd been preparing with a savage growl. If it had connected, it could very well have separated Corey's head from his shoulders. But the man for which the blow had been intended ducked beneath it and drove an uppercut into Strahan's midsection. Corey's knuckles thumped against tensed muscle as he chopped away with one hammering fist after another. He planted his feet, kept his head low and continued to hit Strahan's ribs, stomach and midsection with everything he had.

When the barrage eventually stopped, the only sound that could be heard was the chaotic mess of voices from the main room and Corey's labored breathing. After a few seconds, Strahan's voice drifted through the air when he asked, "You done?"

"Ummm . . . yes," Corey replied. "I believe I am."

Since there was no shirt collar for him to grab, Strahan clamped one hand around Corey's neck and held him in place so he could pound his knuckles into his jaw. Corey's head snapped to one side and blood sprayed from his lip. Grabbing onto Strahan's wrist, Corey attempted to loosen the big man's grip. He started kicking Strahan's shins, which didn't do much since he was in bare feet and lacked any hard leather to add to his attack. Corey was lifted off his feet and tossed against another wall. Strahan kept hold of his neck, pinning Corey in place.

"Where's that professor friend of yers?" Strahan asked.

Corey's face reddened as all the blood swirled within him like a flow of angry bees trying to escape his skull. As the pressure increased and Strahan's grip around his throat tightened, Corey saw something that brought a partial smile to his face. He couldn't be certain that he wasn't hallucinating the sight of an arm extending from the wall near the chair in the corner, but the elegant, well-tailored sleeve wrapped around that wrist brought some measure of hope along with it.

"He may be . . . closer than you think," Corey croaked.

As Strahan turned to see what had caught Corey's eye, the hand attached to the arm in the wall angled upward to point a pistol at the room's occupants. Before the trigger could be pulled, the wall buckled under a solid thump. Dust exploded from between the boards, followed by another spray mixed with splinters of wood as the entire back wall cracked apart and two men tumbled into the already crowded room.

Giles was one of the men and Whiteoak was the other.

"Sorry to intrude," the professor said. "But it appeared as though you needed some help."

Whiteoak attempted to add a roguish wink to his dramatic entrance, but was cut short by Giles's fist slamming into his chin.

CHAPTER TWENTY

Having landed mostly on his side when breaking through the wall, Whiteoak rolled onto his back and took a swing at the man attacking him. The scars on Giles's leathery skin showed that he'd weathered worse storms than fighting with a medicine man, but he reeled from Whiteoak's punch and staggered back through the jagged remains of the rear wall. Whiteoak's fist did have some muscle behind it, but it was the chunk of wood within it that nearly put Giles down for the count.

Whiteoak looked at his fist in disbelief after sending the other man reeling. When he saw the scrap wood that he'd inadvertently grabbed, he didn't hesitate to press his advantage further. He scrambled to his feet, cracking the plank against Giles's head with enough force to turn the flimsy wood into sawdust. Still gripping his pistol in his other hand, Whiteoak thumbed back the hammer and pointed it at Strahan.

"Still think you can collect on that bounty?" the professor quipped.

Strahan answered by swatting away the professor's gun hand and driving a meaty fist into Whiteoak's chest. The impact drove all the air from Whiteoak's lungs and dropped him onto the cot. When he forced his eyes open again, Whiteoak found himself staring directly into Misty's face. "Why, hello there," he said in something close to a drunken stupor.

Strahan loomed over the professor like impending death, balling his hands into tighter fists. His mouth curved into a wicked sneer as he began to lunge forward and deliver a punch that would put Whiteoak through the floor like a cheap nail. Just as his arm was about to surge forward, it was stopped by a hand that gripped Strahan's elbow.

Using his hold on Strahan's arm to turn the big man around, Corey punched him in the face with three chopping blows. Strahan shrugged off the first punch and part of the second, but the third dimmed his lights a bit. Blood pouring from his mouth and from several cuts on his face, Strahan renewed his attack on Corey by punishing the other man's ribs with a solid uppercut.

Having pulled himself together somewhat, Giles stood up and stepped through the broken wall. His other foot hadn't cleared the jagged chunk of cracked wood near the floor when he heard a smooth, mildly slurring voice from the vicinity of the bed.

"Ah, ah," Whiteoak warned. "Best let them work this out between themselves."

While Giles wasn't inclined to obey the professor's wishes, he was swayed by the pistol in Whiteoak's hand that was pointed at him. Giles sized up his opponent, noting the way Whiteoak propped himself up on the cot while looking at him with hooded eyes. Although the professor's hand wasn't quite steady, it would have been next to impossible for him to miss a shot from that distance. Giles relaxed his posture and stayed put.

Corey ducked under one of Strahan's swings and hit the big man's gut before leaning out of the way of another incoming punch. He didn't seem to be doing enough damage to put the big fellow down, however, and even a glancing blow from Strahan hurt worse than a solid punch from any other man. Knowing that Strahan wouldn't stop swinging until he was put down for good, Corey did his best to avoid taking any more damage. Such a task was far from easy in such tight quarters.

Seeing that he'd gained the familiar advantage of sheer power over an opponent, Strahan put both fists to work. His swings were slow, but landed with impressive force. Since Corey kept busy twisting and turning and repositioning himself, those punches slammed mostly against walls and furniture while only occasionally making contact with a fleshy target. Corey knew he couldn't withstand much more even if he did only take partial hits. The effort of dodging was wearing him out, but he knew he wouldn't need to worry about it for much longer. One way or another, the fight would be over very soon.

As soon as he felt the edge of the cot's frame beneath him, Corey snapped a punch to Strahan's nose. That portion of the big man's face, like the rest of it, was already a gnarled mess. Even so, no man could take a punch to the nose without feeling a jabbing pain explode through his skull and set his eyes to watering. The punch wasn't intended to be a finishing blow, however. It was meant only to make the big man angry enough to put all he had into his next attack. In that respect, it was a rousing success. Strahan bared his teeth in a savage display, swinging his right hand like the hammer of a raging god.

At the last moment, Corey twisted aside to let the fist sail past him and into the frame of the cot. Although a few of Strahan's knuckles scraped against his side, Corey managed to clear enough of a path for the rest of the blow to be absorbed by wood and nails. Strahan let out a pained grunt before staggering forward as his momentum carried him toward the floor. After that, Corey was on him like a tick latched onto its next meal.

Wrapping both arms around Strahan's neck, Corey tightened his grip and cinched it in with everything he had.

"Would you like some help?" Whiteoak offered from where he stood watching the scuffle as though he had money riding on its outcome.

"No," Corey grunted. "Stay where you are."

"Is that sarcastic or do you truly want me to stand fast?"

"Damn it, Henry. Just shut yer mouth and sit still for a change!"

Having drawn some measure of strength from those words, Corey leaned back and choked Strahan hard enough to drop the big man to his knees. Strahan wheezed and swung his arms over his shoulders in futile attempts to swat Corey off of him. Where his moves had been slow before, they were now more sluggish and Corey dodged them with ease.

Seeing his partner in real trouble put a sense of urgency into Giles who tried one more time to re-enter the room.

"Ah, ah," Whiteoak chirped while pointing the pistol at him. "No need for more of a mess in here."

Giles tensed his muscles, but refrained from doing much more. He lost more steam when he saw Strahan wilt beneath Corey's continued assault. Now that he had the big man down, Corey moved around from behind Strahan and dropped straight down. Since he still had a firm grip on Strahan's thick neck, he took the big man down with him to land with his rump on the floor next to the broken cot. Strahan's chin cracked against the cot's frame with an impact that was considerably harder than any punch he'd taken thus far.

For a moment, it seemed Strahan might recover from the blow. He reached out with one hand to grip a portion of the cot's frame and used the other hand to brace himself against the floor. It became apparent that he didn't have the strength to prop himself up and Strahan flopped onto the floor.

"What the hell?" Corey said as he turned his attention to Whiteoak. "Where did you come from?"

"Questions later," Whiteoak urged. "Right now, we need to take these two somewhere out of the way. Fortunately, I know the place. First of all, get them out of their hats and jackets."

CHAPTER TWENTY-ONE

The Parlour was one of the smaller cat-houses on First Avenue, but also one of the finest. From the moment customers walked through its front door, their senses were caressed by smooth textures, sweet smells and the velvety coos of the women who stepped forward to greet them. Naturally, Henry Whiteoak approached The Parlour as he did most things. He circled past the easy and most obvious entrance to find one that escaped the sight of common folk. The side door wasn't marked and didn't have a handle. Only after Whiteoak started knocking on it, did the rectangular outline of a doorway become visible among the dusty grit of the wall facing the alley. It was how the regulars got inside so they weren't spotted by wives, relatives, or members of the clergy who were on their way to meet their own sinful needs.

Within the span of a minute, the door was

opened by a bulky man dressed in dark clothes brandishing a shotgun. Whiteoak flashed him a smile and asked, "Is Sissy available?"

The gunman's eyes narrowed and he grunted, "You got that money you owe me?"

"What money?"

"For that tonic that was supposed to clear up the rash I had."

"Had?" Whiteoak asked. "As in a past ailment?"

"You heard me."

"So that means it's gone!" Gesturing as though he'd just created a sunset, Whiteoak declared, "The tonic worked."

"It cleared up on its own after nearly driving me out of my damn mind from all the itching."

"I promised results, not a definite time in which to expect them. Now, is Sissy here or isn't she?"

The gunman glared down at Whiteoak, deciding whether or not to squash him like so much rotten meat. Reluctantly, he said, "She's in her room."

"Thank you, friend. I remember the way."

Just past the doorway was a coat room and beyond that, a narrow hallway. Whiteoak strutted happily toward the more populated part of the house and pulled in a long breath. All those pleasant scents filled his nose and it wasn't long before his eyes were also given a treat. A woman with long brown hair and a thin face entered the hall from the other end. She smiled when she saw a man in front of her, but smiled wider once she recognized that man's face.

"Professor Henry!" she said. "I didn't think I'd see you in town for a while. Wasn't someone out to kill you or put you in jail or something like that?"

"Perhaps," Whiteoak said with a shrug, "but you can't keep a good rogue down. Is Sissy available?"

The woman approached him until she was close enough to step into Whiteoak's boots. Placing her hands on his shoulders and kissing his cheek, she whispered, "Sissy? Wouldn't you prefer someone with a bit more experience?"

"For what I want at this particular moment," he replied with a wink, "she's got all the experience I could want."

Well beyond the point of being taken aback so easily, the woman shrugged her shoulders and gave Whiteoak a fleeting, intimate touch while moving past him to continue down the hall. At the end of the hall was a large room that was The Parlour's namesake. Taking up at least a third of the entire first floor, the room was elaborately furnished and decorated from top to bottom. Its floor was covered in expensive carpeting and the walls were painted a luxuriously deep, dark red. Although the women milling about the room were clothed, their dresses were loose enough to show plenty of smooth, fragrant skin.

Whiteoak leaned over to get a sniff of silky, perfumed hair while fighting back the urge to forget everything that had brought him to The Parlour. A few of the women turned to look at him as he skirted the edge of the room on his way to a staircase that led to the second floor. Most of those recognized the professor, but were unable to give him more than a nod in greeting due to the several men who were sharing the room with them. Those men glanced in Whiteoak's direction, but were much too preoccupied to do much more than that before turning their attention back to the lady closest to them.

After climbing the stairs in a rush, Whiteoak found himself in another hallway which he hastily navigated until he came to a room marked by an elaborate C. He knocked, waited for about a second and a half and then knocked again.

"All right," snapped the young woman

who pulled open the door. "Give me a second to . . . Henry? Is that really you?"

Raising his eyebrows and opening his arms, Whiteoak said, "Most irrefutably!"

Her name was Cecily, but everyone who'd shared her company for more than an hour called her Sissy. She wasn't the tallest girl in The Parlour and her figure wasn't the curviest, but there was something else about her that more than made up for it. She had a spark inside that lit up her eyes like a summer's day and wispy golden hair to match. When she moved, there was an exuberance about her that allowed even the oldest soul to recapture some measure of youth and a playfulness that played even better in the bedroom. Dressed in a short robe that she'd been holding shut with her hands, she wrapped her arms around Whiteoak to hug him while curling one foot up off the floor.

"I didn't think I'd see you for a while!" she said. "Are those men still after you?"

"Which ones, darlin'?" Whiteoak chided.

"The ones who thought you stole their horses after robbing them when they were drunk."

The professor's smirk dimmed a bit. "Oh. I forgot about them. Are they still in town?"

"That doesn't matter. Come in," she said while taking hold of Whiteoak's hand and dragging him into her room. The space was decorated sparsely, but still managed to reflect the exuberant soul of its owner. The linens were soft and bright. The flowers on the table were fresh and fragrant. The window was open to show a sky that was wide and full of possibilities. When she spun on her heels to face him again, Sissy's robe opened to reveal a trim, tight little body covered only by a few loosely fitted undergarments of white cotton. "I missed you," she purred.

"And I you," Whiteoak said. "But there's something important I need to discuss."

"Can't it wait?"

"Not really."

Ignoring that response, she locked her hands behind Whiteoak's neck and lifted her mouth to his so she could kiss him eagerly and excitedly. When his hands found their way to her hips, her slender frame began to tremble.

"I . . . really need to have a word with you," he said when he bought himself a moment to take another breath.

"Do you honestly want to talk? Now?"

"Yes. It's quite urgent."

Sissy pulled back from him enough to get a full look at his face. She unclasped her hands from around his neck and tugged at the edges of her robe. It fell away from her like beads of sweat dripping down the curve of her spine. The material rustled slightly as it passed her hips and pooled in a pile around her feet. "What about now?" she asked.

Whiteoak's eyes drifted up and down along her body, taking in every detail from the angles of her shoulders and the lines of her pert little breasts all the way down to the trim muscles of her thighs and the glorious promise between them. "Perhaps I could take a moment, but after that I will most definitely need to speak with you."

Sissy grinned wantonly. "Most definitely."

CHAPTER TWENTY-TWO

When Whiteoak returned to the Mountain-top Saloon, it was also through a lesser used entrance. He was much more careful to remain hidden this time, which wasn't too difficult considering the amount of noise and general revelry that was going on at that time of night. Keeping his head low, the professor motioned to the men following behind him so they could form a moving barricade keeping him out of sight from most of the rest of the room. The other two were bulky enough for the job and young enough to occasionally be distracted by the fresh female faces around them.

Stepping into the side room where he'd found Misty earlier, Whiteoak made certain nobody had followed the three of them before closing the door.

"What the hell took you so damn long?" Corey asked from where he sat on the cot. He held a pistol in each hand, keeping one pointed at Giles and the other at Strahan. Both of those two men were slumped over, bloody and unconscious, which did nothing to ease Corey's nerves.

"I was procuring us some help just like I said I would," Whiteoak explained. Motioning to the men he'd brought that were now crowding the room with their muscled bulk, he added, "See? As promised."

When both of the younger men looked at him, Corey nodded toward the broken back wall and said, "Grab them and take them through there back to . . ."

"To The Parlour," Whiteoak finished. Unable to help himself, he added, "Said the spider to the fly. Heh."

Although mildly amused by the damage done to the room, the men Whiteoak had brought stepped over the wooden rubble to pick up the men that Corey had been holding at gunpoint. When the prisoners stirred, the young men thumped their fists into each gunman's face to put them back to sleep again. Carrying Giles and Strahan like so much dirty laundry, the men started walking toward the door.

"No," Whiteoak said. "Wrap them up in blankets or something so they're not seen. At least, not their faces. And when you leave, go through there," he said, while pointing into the shadowy space behind the busted wall. "There's a door that leads to the kitchen. Should be empty at this time of night."

"What the hell are you talking about?" Corey asked.

"It's late," Whiteoak replied. "The kitchen's closed. Should be a straight shot with no witnesses."

Grabbing Whiteoak's jacket, Corey pulled him to the other side of the room. If he was hoping for privacy, neither of the two young men seemed interested in much else apart from their appointed tasks.

"You'd best explain yourself," Corey snapped. "It's been a hell of a night and I'm fresh out of patience."

"Those two are doing exactly what we discussed before I left. They're taking Parsons's hired muscle to somewhere they won't be a bother to us."

"And where did you find them?"

"They work at The Parlour," Whiteoak said, causing both of the younger men to look in his direction like dogs who'd happened to overhear their own names. Waving for the two to continue what they'd been doing, Whiteoak continued, "It's a cathouse down on —"

"I know what it is," Corey snapped. "Since

when do you have so much pull at that place? What are you? Part owner or something?"

"No," Whiteoak chuckled. "There is one particularly sweet girl who works there that has taken a shine to me." Leaning over to Corey and nudging him with his elbow, the professor added, "She'll bend over backwards for me, both literally and figuratively."

Visibly disgusted by the image that put into his mind, Corey said, "So you just asked her to send a couple of men to help you drag some warm bodies away?"

"Not in so many words. I told her these two were trying to kill us and needed to be dispatched so I could clear the matter up."

"For once, you actually got by with the truth? That's mighty strange."

"I don't think I appreciate that insinuation, sir."

"You weren't supposed to," Corey replied. "You sure they'll stay put once they get to the cathouse? I mean, those two aren't gonna keep knocking Giles and Strahan about the head whenever they start to wake up, are they?"

"No. Maybe. I didn't ask for details, just that they be restrained and kept out of sight. The cathouses on First Avenue have always been competitors with the saloons up here on Summit Street since both basically provide similar services. With men like Parsons in charge of these establishments, that competition tends to be very fierce. They've come to blows more than once and asking someone to do a favor that would blacken the eye of their opposition, so to speak, didn't take much convincing."

Corey still had some questions regarding specifics of the matter, but he set them aside. Competition between First Avenue and Summit Street was widely known throughout Split Knee and the professor's powers of persuasion were just as well known to anyone who'd ridden with the man for more than a day. "All right," Corey said. "But what about *that*?" he asked while pointing at the broken wall at the back of the room. "Were you going to explain that or did you intend on blaming it on rats eating away the wood?"

Whiteoak looked over to admire his handiwork. "It's a pickpocket room. You didn't know about those?"

"Why don't you tell me?"

"You really didn't know about them?" Adopting a tone that even a child would find condescending, Whiteoak said, "You see, these girls who work here don't really love you and the men they work for love you even less. While those girls are letting you paw at them for money, their employers figure out ways to snatch the rest of your valuables. One of those ways are these rooms connected to other rooms where others can sneak up and pick your pockets while you're preoccupied."

"Through those panels that opened where you reached into the room?"

"Didn't you ever wonder why the chair upon which most every man will put his clothes and gun belt is always located against the wall in such an opportune spot?"

"I suppose I never thought it was such a good spot," Corey said. "Just one place instead of another."

"And that is what separates men like you from men like me."

"You mean separates the cheaters from them that are cheated."

"Well," Whiteoak said reluctantly, "yes."

"And you knew this was one of them pickpocket rooms before I went in?"

"I had a good idea. I mean, little rooms all in a row like that are a hint. Besides, even if I did know for certain, you didn't give me much of a chance to tell you anything before you traipsed off with that redhead."

"But you must've known I was in trouble,"

Corey pointed out. "Otherwise you wouldn't have busted in at all."

"I was out here watching for Parsons to send his hired guns to stir up some trouble. I'd assumed they would come after me since I was out here for all to see, but that was erroneous."

"Or just plain egotistical. You do think the world revolves around you, so why not think everyone sees you as the worst threat there is?"

"Be that as it may, I spotted the big fellow having words with several of the girls working in here who then pointed toward the room where you were taken. The smaller man went in another direction so I decided to take him out of the picture first. He went through a door that led to the corridor running behind those rooms where unsuspecting men like you are taken."

"And you couldn't have gotten to him before my gun was lost?" Corey fumed.

"The doors were locked and it took a bit of time to open them. Also, Giles wasn't exactly forthcoming when it came to stepping aside so I could lend a hand with Strahan."

All Corey needed to do to verify that statement was take another look at the man in front of him. Whiteoak's face was battered and his clothes were a rumpled mess. For him, that was the equivalent of sailing through a hurricane. Also, since they were still breathing while Giles and Strahan were under wraps, Corey figured he couldn't complain too much more than he already had.

"So, what now?" Corey asked as he rubbed a spot on his face that had taken a particularly severe amount of punishment. "Giles and Strahan are out of the way, but that can't last forever. They'll either break loose or be killed by the boys who've got them now. Either way is trouble for us."

Whiteoak smiled, showing a set of pearly, if somewhat blood-smeared, teeth. "Now," he replied, "is when we press our advantage."

"*Advantage?* Just what the hell do you consider an advantage?"

The professor looked over to the section of the cot that was more or less intact. The slanted set of boards supported some blankets and part of a thin mattress which was also sturdy enough to bear the weight of the redhead who'd remained silent while trying to make herself as small as possible. Misty sat huddled on that section of the cot with her knees drawn up tight against her chest and arms wrapped tightly around them.

Now that she'd been noticed, she started to shake her head and press herself even harder against the wall.

"No," she said urgently. "Don't kill me. Please. I didn't want a part of any of this."

"Any of what?" Whiteoak asked in a cool, neutral tone.

"I was just supposed to distract him, that's all."

"You mean him?" Whiteoak said while pointing to Corey.

She nodded.

"Of course you were," Whiteoak declared off-handedly. "Anyone could have surmised that much. You've got one more job to do."

Misty crawled from the spot where she'd been huddled and started tugging at the bits of clothing she'd pulled on. "Anything. I'll do anything."

"Nothing like that," Whiteoak said as he pulled the front of her blouse shut. "I want you to get dressed, leave this room as though everything is under control and then leave this saloon."

"But," she protested. Misty stopped herself short when the professor snapped a finger up and held it directly between them as though he was suddenly, and very urgently, counting to one.

"You'll leave this saloon and head to The

Parlour on First Avenue. Do you know where that is?"

"Yes."

"Who would try to talk to you after you're through with an appointment like this?"

"Morgan," she replied. "She'll want her cut of the money and tell me what I'm supposed to do next."

"You'll hand over the money you owe." Whiteoak then reached into a pocket to retrieve a small bundle of bills. Peeling off a few, he said, "This is what you'll hand over. Whatever money you got from Corey is yours. All of it." Handing her the rest of the money in his grasp, Whiteoak added, "This too."

Misty had been afraid and shaky before, but she brightened up considerably. "What should I do when I get to The Parlour?"

"Whatever strikes your fancy. If anyone asks what happened in this room, you tell them whatever you need to in order to make it seem things here went smoothly enough. If they mention any peculiar noises that may have occurred, you'll say things got a little rough but only in the carnal sense. If they mention other men asking about Corey, tell them they must have gone into a different room. You hear?"

She nodded while tucking the money into

a little pocket sewn into her blouse against her chest.

"Whatever you say to any curious parties," Whiteoak continued, "just make certain . . ."

"That everything is business like always," she cut in sharply. "Got it. You know, this isn't the first time I've had to cover for someone after they left my bed."

"These are slightly more dangerous circumstances than you're accustomed to," Whiteoak said.

"You might be surprised what I'm accustomed to."

He nodded and leaned in. "You were paid well," the professor said in a lower, rougher tone. "I expect my requests to be followed to the letter. If they're not, I'll do things to you which you are most certainly not accustomed to. Do you know who I am?"

"P . . . Professor Whiteoak. The medicine man."

"And do you know everything I have in my wagon or in the vials I keep on my person?"

"Not . . . exactly."

"That's right, so you have no idea what I can inflict upon someone who crosses me."

Even though she wasn't as frightened as Whiteoak was hoping, Misty looked at him with enough trepidation to make it clear his point had been adequately made. "I'll go to The Parlour for a while and if anyone asks, there wasn't any trouble in here," she said. "At least, nothing to worry about."

"Very good. Run along now."

No matter what she thought of the people in that room, Misty was clearly glad to be away from them.

"Just try to keep your head down," White-oak said. "Do your best to stay out of sight."

"And what are you gonna do?"

"What I do best, my good man," White-oak said while straightening the line of his suit. "What I do best."

CHAPTER TWENTY-THREE

When Whiteoak and Corey left Misty's room, they went through the narrow hallway exposed by the broken wall. They kept their heads down and moved swiftly through a side door into an alley and didn't stop until they were on Taylor Street, which was the halfway point between Summit and the southernmost border of town. They stayed there for an hour or two, passing the time with a few drinks at a little bar in the lobby of a hotel that obviously didn't see a lot of customers. The beer was passable and the barkeep was relentless in his attempts to sell them more, but the place served its purpose well enough.

The owner of the hotel was a short fellow with thinning hair slicked down against his scalp like a set of wavy lines scribbled onto the top of his head. He approached Corey and Whiteoak with open arms and an exaggerated smile on his lips. "Is there anything else I can get for you two gentlemen? Anything at all?"

Whiteoak looked at him carefully and then narrowed his eyes. "Weren't you losing your hair the last time I saw you?"

Patting the side of his head to press down one of the few strands growing there, the owner replied, "It's a troublesome condition, but I do what I can."

"No. You were practically bald when I was here last. You're looking quite well, sir."

"Um . . . thank you."

Corey was more than happy to stay out of the conversation until he felt Whiteoak's boot knock against the side of his foot. Knowing the signal, Corey played along by spouting, "Bald? That can't be. You look like a man in his prime."

The lie was confused and half-hearted, spoken by a man who was too tired to make it any more convincing than that. However, it landed fairly well since the person on the receiving end of the deception was desperate to hear those words from anyone. The hotel's owner stroked his pathetic collection of tresses as if it was a mane. "Why, thank you."

"I don't know if you remember me. I'm Professor Henry Whiteoak."

"Oh!" the owner said. "I do remember

seeing you when you came through town some time ago. Driving a colorful wagon, weren't you?"

"I was. This isn't a business trip, though, so the wagon was left behind. This is my friend Corey Maynard."

When the owner extended his hand in greeting, Corey reluctantly shook it. When he broke contact, he turned around to lean against the bar and face the man behind it. Taking a page from the barkeep's book, Corey kept his mouth shut and let the others gab.

"You look different than you did before, Professor," the owner said. "A little less fancy, I'd say."

Dusting off a few specks of dirt from the front of his trousers as if that would help the generally rumpled and sporadically torn appearance of his clothing, Whiteoak chuckled, "A bit disheveled, to be certain. We ran into some unsavory characters."

"Town's full of them, I'm afraid. What can I do for you?"

"A drink would be good for a start," Whiteoak replied. "One for me and my friend here."

"Naturally. The usual?"

"Nothing but. I trust you're still using my formula to improve the taste and quality of your liquor?"

"Naturally," the owner said with a wink. "Haven't had a complaint yet."

While the owner filled two glasses with whiskey, Whiteoak leaned against the short bar and said, "Also, I would consider it a personal favor if you could spread the word that I'm in town again."

"Ah, yes. Advertising."

"That's the idea. Be sure to let folks know when I got here so they'll know exactly when I started brewing my newest mixtures. That information will become very valuable once I give my demonstration."

"Interesting," the owner said as he set the whiskey glasses in front of Whiteoak and Corey respectively.

"And just to show my appreciation, I'll see to it that you receive a ten percent discount on your normal orders."

"Hmmm."

Leaning over to the owner, Whiteoak nudged him and added, "If you tell them I've been here most of the day and night working on my wares, I'll bump up your discount to thirty percent. Just for the duration of this visit, of course."

Now the owner truly perked up. "Thirty percent! I'll tell folks right away, starting with my neighbors."

"That's what I like to hear!" Whiteoak downed the whiskey in one gulp, slapped the glass onto the bar and headed for the door.

Although he was clearly lost in the conversation, Corey was more than willing to have a free drink. Once his glass was emptied, he set it down next to Whiteoak's and followed in the professor's trail. Once outside, he fell into step beside Whiteoak and growled, "What the hell was all that?"

"He's one of my best customers. Buys every drop of hair restoration tonic I can brew, not to mention the liquor flavoring I've recently perfected."

"What was the rest of that nonsense? We're supposed to be keeping our heads down, fer Christ's sake!"

"For everything, there is a reason, my good man."

Corey hopped a step in front of the professor to block his path. Stopping Whiteoak with a firm, open-handed jab to the dandy's shoulder, Corey said, "I'll hear that reason right now or you'll hear the sound of my fist cutting through the air on its way to your jaw."

"Calm yourself and lower your voice."

"I'll be calm once this bullshit is over."

"Says the man who got me involved to

begin with."

"True," Corey said, "but as always, you've taken a bad situation and shaken things up until they're a whole lot worse. Damn this all to hell. We should just get out of town while we have the chance."

"Why? So we can watch over our shoulders for the next time Parsons or one of his men decide to take a run at us?"

"Unless you've got a better idea."

Whiteoak showed him a beaming smile. "Of course I have a better idea."

"Shit. I just walked right into that."

Draping an arm over Corey's shoulder, Whiteoak steered him toward First Avenue. "The purpose of visiting our friend with the thinning hair was to make sure he's a good witness to the fact that you and I were here instead of at the Mountaintop at this particular moment. In a short matter of time, that fellow will spread that knowledge to several others who, when asked, will all attest to my whereabouts."

"What good will that do?"

"To put what happened back at the Mountaintop with Giles and Strahan in the proper light."

"But . . . if we can prove we weren't there . . ."

"Then it will seem as though Giles and

Strahan didn't do a very good job," White-oak said. "In fact, it will seem they were slacking on their duties altogether before leaving the Mountaintop to conduct some business of their own."

"So that's why you put them two from The Parlour in Giles's and Strahan's clothes?"

"Exactly. Men with reputations like theirs earn a certain amount of fearful respect, which means other folks try not to look them over too hard when they pass. In fact, normal folks are just happy to see dangerous men like that move away from them without incident. At worst, a few patrons of the Mountaintop will see two men who looked suspiciously like Giles and Strahan leaving with an even more suspicious load that Parsons will almost certainly assume is you and I wrapped in blankets."

"What if he doesn't think that?" Corey asked. "If we ain't leaving town soon, then he'll know for certain we're more than dead weight wrapped up in blankets."

"Which will only create more uncertainty. Look, we don't need to uphold much of a ruse for very long."

Corey swiped his hand across his sweating forehead. "Thank God. Your ruses give me a headache."

"All we do is get under Parsons's skin for a while. Stir up some confusion. Create some questions in his mind."

"That ain't hard under any circumstance."

"Exactly. And we also have to lay some foundations for some things I'll be telling Parsons the next time I see him."

"And when's that?"

"As soon as I go to The Parlour to freshen up and see to it that our helpers and their unconscious burdens have arrived safely."

The two of them walked a few more steps before Corey asked, "You sure this is a better idea than just riding away from here?"

"The Square Mountain Trail has been a healthy source of income for both of us. Are we to simply run away from it like dogs with our tails tucked between our legs?"

"We'd be living dogs."

"But dogs, nonetheless," Whiteoak pointed out. "I thought you wanted Parsons and his bounty killers off of our trail!"

"All this goddamn scheming of yours is making my head hurt. Right when I think I got you corralled, things get even more convoluted."

"Convoluted is another word for interesting, my friend. Besides, the short and easy paths never lead anywhere worth being."

"Head's still hurting," Corey groaned.

"That's just the whiskey. An unfortunate and largely uncommon side effect of my additive, I'm afraid."

CHAPTER TWENTY-FOUR

For a man who relied so much on his appearance, Henry Whiteoak didn't take very long to put himself together. His preparations were down to a science more precise than when he mixed the tonics he sold. Despite the short amount of time he took and the fact that his extra suit wasn't able to be cleaned and pressed after being pulled from his saddlebag, Whiteoak looked every bit the distinguished gentleman when he left The Parlour less than half an hour after he and Corey had arrived.

His stride was fast and purposeful when he walked back up to Summit Street.

His steps were sure and strong when he marched into the Mountaintop Saloon.

His voice was confident when he asked to have a game of cards with the highest stakes in the house.

His eyes didn't waver when an armed man stormed down the stairs to get a look at him and not so much as a single bead of sweat appeared on the professor's brow when he was asked about the reason for his presence there.

"Why, to play cards of course," was Whiteoak's reply.

The gunman went back upstairs, returned a few minutes later and escorted Whiteoak up to the second floor where Jacob Parsons still sat at the same place he'd been before.

"Where's your friend?" Parsons asked.

"Last time I checked, he was with a redhead who works here," Whiteoak told him. "If you want more than that, you'll have to find him and ask yourself. I'm not his wet nurse."

"What do you want here?"

"There's plenty I want. For the moment, I'll settle for a seat at that table. I believe there's an empty one right there."

Parsons looked across at the unoccupied chair and then back to Whiteoak. "Plenty of games going on downstairs."

"But the biggest stakes are up here. And if you're not about to put it all on the line," Whiteoak added as he approached the empty chair, "then why the hell bother?"

Parsons wore a mixture of expressions, all of them stirring beneath a nearly impenetrable layer of stone. There was suspicion and wariness, to be sure, but there was also curiosity. It was the former upon which Henry Whiteoak built his business.

"Well, then," Parsons said. "I suppose it never hurts to have another man at the table. That is, if you have enough to cover your bets."

When Whiteoak reached under his jacket, the gunman who'd escorted him upstairs as well as another armed man drew their pistols. The professor kept his hand still for a moment before slowly pulling it out so his money could be seen. "Just buying in," he explained cautiously.

"You got enough to last more than a few hands?" Parsons asked.

"Does it matter?"

Parsons shrugged and took a drink from the beer mug in front of him. "Not really. Soon as you're flat busted, I'll have you tossed down them stairs."

"All right, then," Whiteoak said. "Let's play."

Chapter Twenty-Five

The game was played like a war, moving fortunes back and forth as sides were taken and battles were waged. There were casualties along the way, including two of the men who'd been sitting at the table when Whiteoak first arrived. The professor didn't get a chance to learn much about them since they weren't of a mind to engage in conversation or offer any personal tidbits that might be used against them. More than likely, they were simply too wrapped up in their own game to bother making idle chit chat with the likes of a known conman. Once their luck took a turn for the worse, they became distracted which made them easy enough to be picked off.

Whiteoak took the first one down by bluffing with a busted flush. He chipped away at the second until Parsons eventually swooped in to make the kill and drag what was left of that one's chips in to join the rest that were piled in front of him. When those two were gone, only two others apart from Parsons and Whiteoak remained. One was a Chinese man with a wispy black beard sprouting from a pointed chin. He gave Whiteoak his name amid a flurry of exotic syllables and had no intention of repeating himself. Because of his frosty demeanor, Parsons had taken to calling him Chill and the name stuck. The Chinese fellow didn't seem to mind and responded to the moniker as if he'd had it since birth. The other man was named Denton. He had a round face which seldom bore anything more than a partially interested expression. Since he rarely did anything other than fold, he might as well have not been there at all.

The only other people to venture into the dimly lit room where the high stakes game was played were the girls who brought drinks or rubbed the shoulders of whoever tossed them some money. For a brief moment, a slender man scurried over to Parsons's side before rushing back down the stairs to the first floor. Whiteoak watched that one closely, noticing the interest that sparked in Parsons's eyes whenever the skinny fellow whispered into his ear. He couldn't make out what was being said, but the bit of news made him scowl at Whiteoak a bit harder. The professor knew it was time to make his move.

"I raise," Whiteoak announced.

"After checking and calling the last two rounds of betting?" Parsons asked.

"That's right."

They were playing seven-card stud and three of the four cards that lay face up in front of each player had already been dealt. Parsons glared down at the cards spread in front of Whiteoak, studying them as if he hadn't already committed them to memory. Whiteoak had the six of clubs, ace of spades and nine of diamonds which had been given to him in that order. "What's the raise?" Parsons asked.

"Two hundred."

Chill had a pair of threes showing along with the ten of clubs, which wasn't enough to keep him from tossing his hold cards onto the pile of discards.

"The last card dealt was the nine of diamonds," Parsons said. "What the hell difference could that have made to you?"

Whiteoak shrugged while picking something out of his teeth. "Why does that matter?"

"It matters because it upholds the integrity of the game, that's why! Without integrity, I might as well play with a bunch of children who just want to look at the pretty pictures painted on the cards!"

Whiteoak looked down at the cards in his hand, admiring them as though he'd just now fully appreciated how the ink was arranged upon their faces.

After letting out a frustrated breath, Parsons grinned. "Oh, you must have a couple of nines in reserve. Makes sense, since you were shaky at first and now you come out guns blazing."

"That could make sense, I suppose."

"You were here earlier when I had to teach someone else a lesson, right?" Parsons asked in a menacing tone. "You saw firsthand how highly I regard a game played in the proper fashion."

"Oh, it was difficult to miss that point," Whiteoak said. "But even you make the occasional bluff. That's part of the game as well."

"Yes, it is. Playing like an *idiot* won't be tolerated. Understand the difference?"

"Indeed I do," Whiteoak declared.

"Good. I raise."

"Call," Denton said hastily.

Keeping his eyes on Whiteoak, Parsons nodded toward Denton and said, "That one's drawing to a flush, but you've already got something."

Whiteoak shrugged and kept picking his teeth.

Shaking his head, Parsons chuckled to himself and grumbled loud enough to be heard by the others around him, "Dumb son of a bitch doesn't know how lucky he is." In a more conversational tone, he asked, "Where's your friend?"

"Don't know," Whiteoak replied. "Haven't seen him for a while."

The grin on Parsons's face grew a little. "It's up to you, smart man."

Whiteoak checked his cards and then checked them again. "Call."

The cards were dealt by the tall brunette woman who'd been tending bar earlier. She was one of a trio of ladies who rotated between serving drinks, pouring them and dealing. She flipped the fourth up card to the remaining players which was a jack of hearts for Whiteoak, a three of diamonds for Parsons and a three of spades for Denton.

"Looks like I got that last diamond you were fishing for," Parsons said smugly. Denton grunted something under his breath and pretended not to care. "Your move, Professor," Parsons said. "I doubt you got much help from that jack."

"How do you think you know what helps

me?" Whiteoak asked with irritation gnawing at the edge of his voice.

"Because I've played this game like a professional. Now make your play or get out of the way."

Since Parsons seemed so pleased with himself after making that speech, Whiteoak let him revel in his moment for a short while. When that faded and Parsons became agitated again, Whiteoak let him stew a bit more. Right before Parsons cut loose with another tirade, Whiteoak pushed in a healthy raise.

"I see I was right about them nines," Parsons said. "I call."

Denton sighed while studying his cards to make certain none of them had magically turned into the suit he was hoping for. Grudgingly, he called as well.

They were dealt one more down card before Whiteoak threw in a large bet.

Parsons shook his head and laid his cards down. "Still can't beat those nines," he said as though he'd just secured himself a major victory. "You ain't about to wring another penny out of me."

Denton put in a small raise, causing Whiteoak to smile brightly. "Call!" the professor said before showing the cards he held. Apart from an ace, there wasn't much to speak of. It was enough, however, to make Denton curse under his breath.

"Luck is all it is," Denton said while making a grab for the backside of the closest working girl. "Don't do a damn thing against real skill, though. You'll get yours."

Even though Denton was already distracted by what was under the skirts of the girl he'd grabbed, Parsons couldn't take his eyes off the cards splayed in front of Whiteoak. "A pair of aces?" he sneered.

"Yep," Whiteoak replied cheerily. "Isn't that a hoot?"

"Goddamn pair of aces isn't a hoot. In seven-card stud, it's barely a hand!"

Whiteoak gathered up his cards and looked them over. "But . . . aces are good."

"Are you serious?"

Looking over to Chill, Whiteoak asked, "Aren't aces good?"

Chill shrugged and shoved his cards toward the brunette dealer.

Parsons threw his cards at her angrily. "You thought aces were good against what everyone else had?"

"The rest of you didn't have much," Whiteoak pointed out.

"But you thought *aces* were good against three sevens or maybe a flush?"

Whiteoak blinked innocently in a way that

was obviously intended to rub Parsons the wrong way. And because the effort was so obvious, it worked in a spectacular fashion. "I won, didn't I? So that means my aces were good. The game is about more than just what cards you hold. You see —"

Parsons slammed his fist down onto the table with enough force to drive a nail through it. "Don't presume to tell me anything about how this game is played. You, sir, are feeble-minded at best and wildly overconfident at the worst."

"If that's the worst, then I'm doing pretty good," Whiteoak chuckled. "Am I right, fellows?"

Chill and Denton shrugged and nodded respectively.

Shifting his eyes back to Parsons, Whiteoak said, "If I'm making you so upset, then I could leave. Let me just collect all these chips and I'll be on my way."

"The hell you are. If you think you can win a pot that size and then skip away with your money, you're sadly mistaken."

"So I'm a prisoner?"

"No," Parsons snarled. "You're a prick and a coward."

Whiteoak's eyebrows shot up and he recoiled. "I beg your pardon?"

It was Chill who said, "If you get up and

leave without giving anyone a chance to win some of their money back, then you are a coward."

Denton nodded solemnly. "I'm inclined to agree. That may not be a rule of the game, but it's unspoken law at a poker table."

"And what if I did decide to leave, Mister Parsons?" Whiteoak asked in a steady voice that had none of the feigned emotion from a few moments ago. "What would happen? Would you call your men to beat me and take your money back?"

Settling back into his seat, Parsons allowed the merest fraction of a smile to show in one corner of his mouth. The move was as slimy as it was calculated. "That's most certainly an option. But I am no coward and I can win back ten times that amount of money whenever I choose. If my men did happen to cross your path and if there was an altercation afterward, it would be strictly for the pleasure of seeing a snake like you bleed."

Whiteoak cleared his throat and began stacking his chips into neat piles. "Well, then. Let's continue the game."

CHAPTER TWENTY-SIX

The game went on for a few more hands before getting interesting again. In that short amount of time, Whiteoak had managed to win the diamond cufflinks off of Chill's sleeves. Other than that, he kept his head down and his plays safe as he watched the one thing at the table that truly mattered. Jacob Parsons was smug as ever; even more so once he felt certain he'd cowed the man who'd beaten him through what appeared to be dumb luck and sheer mindlessness.

It was Whiteoak's turn to bet after the third up card, the nine of diamonds, had been dealt. He looked down at the other two, the ten of hearts and queen of diamonds, while shuffling his chips with his left hand. "Tell me something," he said. "Why seven-card stud? Most games downstairs are five-card stud or draw. Do you folks just prefer to buck the trend?"

"We prefer larger pots," Parsons replied. "Are you in this one or not?"

Beside Whiteoak, Chill had the king of diamonds, four of hearts and the ace of clubs. Parsons had the three of spades, eight of hearts and king of spades on display in front of him and seemed to be quite pleased with it since he'd been betting heavily from the start. Denton was out of the hand and couldn't care less about the game since he had a girl on his lap redirecting his priorities.

"I'm in," Whiteoak said as he met the raise with a sufficient amount of chips.

Parsons grinned. "Still drawing to that straight, huh? Not a wise play."

"Few would refer to me as a wise man," Whiteoak said.

"Now that's got to be the first thing that's come out of your mouth that I believe."

The next cards were dealt face up. Whiteoak received the ten of clubs and Chill got a four of that same suit. The six of spades landed in front of Parsons, which didn't elicit much of a response. Chill was first to bet and he led out with a modest amount of chips.

"Raise," Parsons said right away as he shoved in triple the number of chips that Chill had committed to the pot.

"Oh my," Whiteoak sighed. His fingers glanced over the edges of his chip stacks, counting them at a lightning pace.

"You've got enough to cover it," Parsons declared. "Only question is if you've got enough balls."

Whiteoak's eyebrows raised and he straightened in his chair. "Call."

Shaking his head, Chill dumped his hand faster than a drowning man shaking free of an anchor chain.

The last card was dealt face down to the surviving players. Parsons pushed in a sizeable bet without a word.

After counting his chips one more time and glancing down at the cards in his hand, Whiteoak locked eyes with Parsons and said, "I want a loan."

"How much?"

"To cover a raise of two thousand. I've got a couple hundred left here and I need the rest."

"You're that confident in your hand?"

"Yes," Whiteoak said without blinking an eye.

"You can have the loan, but you'll need more because I'm raising another two thousand."

"Why not make it six?" Whiteoak asked.

"So . . . another four makes your loan . . ."

"No. I call that raise and raise it another six."

None of the girls working that room were pretty enough to distract Chill and Denton from what was happening at the table. They watched the exchange between Whiteoak and Parsons with the fearful reverence of spectators at the edge of a battlefield. And, like those morbid sightseers, they were just as cautious not to do anything that might draw any fire in their direction.

"That'd be almost ten thousand that you'd owe me," Parsons growled. "You sure about that?"

After some more calculating inside his head, Whiteoak nodded.

"Then you'll have to make it an even fifteen if you want to cover the raise I'll make after that," Parsons declared.

"You make your flush?" Whiteoak asked.

"There's one way to find out."

Whiteoak drew a long breath and let it out. "How do you expect me to cover that kind of raise?"

"Frankly, I don't. But if you're so hell bent on making a show of it, there's always that wagon you ride around in."

"My wagon?" Whiteoak gulped.

"That's about all you got that's worth much of anything, ain't it? It sure as hell isn't worth that kind of money, but you might come close after tossing in everything that's wrapped up inside that rickety eyesore. And the horses, of course."

"Now that's just cruel. Those horses and I have been through a lot."

"Tell you what," Parsons said as he shifted in his seat to lean forward a bit. "You can keep one horse for yourself, just so you have something to ride out of town with."

"I believe what you meant to say is, 'something upon which I could ride out of town.' "

The look in Parsons's eyes was nothing short of lethal. "Just for that I'll take both horses, you uppity prick."

"All right. But if I win, I'll want something to cover your debt as well."

"You think I'm not good for it?" Parsons asked.

"You may be good for it . . ."

Parsons tensed as though he was about to jump across the table at the professor. Before that could happen, Whiteoak added, "You're most certainly good for it, but I doubt you've got that kind of cash on hand."

"I could get it for you in a few days."

"That won't be good enough. I mean, your two men have already attacked my friend on more than one occasion. What assurances do I have they won't do so again, if only to make an example of us?"

"I already heard about what happened downstairs," Parsons said. "Not only did one of the whore's rooms get smashed apart, but everyone seemed to walk out of there fine."

"Did they?" Whiteoak asked. After a few quiet seconds had passed, he shrugged his shoulders and said, "I guess it doesn't really matter if my friend and your men had a tussle or if your men simply took care of some business of their own and then carried the bodies out so nobody would notice," he added with a chuckle.

"Just make your goddamn play."

"We still need to settle the raise. I'm putting up my wagon and its contents, but you must put up something in return."

"What the hell do you want?"

"The bounty that's been placed on the heads of me and my friend Corey Maynard," Whiteoak replied. "I want it removed."

"If you win, I guess I could manage that."

"Don't take me for a fool. You could manage it quite easily since you were the one to offer the bounty."

Meeting the professor's gaze, Parsons said, "I said I'd do it."

"But that's not enough to cover such a large amount."

"You're wasting time!" Parsons barked. "And you're putting on a fucking show when all you have to do is play the goddamn game!"

"All I'm doing is making certain that I can walk out of here with my winnings if I do happen to take this pot. Past experience has already told me that it would be unwise to wait around for you to give me the money since it would most likely be delivered to me by the same men who've already tried to cause me bodily harm."

"From what I've heard, you don't have to worry about them two."

Whiteoak put on an expression of wounded innocence. "Didn't you hear that my friend barely managed to run out of that room with his knickers on after your two men stormed in? And surely you heard that those same two men came out carrying another pair of men wrapped up in sheets to carry them out of the saloon. If not, you haven't heard correctly, sir."

For a moment, it seemed Whiteoak's line of bullshit hadn't had an effect. But then a small inkling of doubt crept into Parsons's eyes that told the professor he'd heard a thing or two along those lines. At the very least, he'd been told enough to conflict with the story he'd been hoping was the truth. All of the false leads and dead ends Whiteoak had put into place served their purpose, creating a nervous uncertainty that gnawed under Parsons's skin. "You've got to win the hand first, asshole," he said. "Do that and then we'll discuss payment. Are you in or out?"

"I raise."

Parsons shook his head. "You just wanna keep raising until one of us dies from old age? You already got your loan and another on top of that. You don't have anything left to your name, you fucking idiot! Shit or get off the pot!"

"How eloquent. I'm not folding."

"So that means you're in," Parsons said with frustration dripping from every word. "Now go ahead and show me the straight you've been putting together to scare me with."

"I believe what you meant to say was, 'the straight with which I've — ' "

Parsons slammed his cards down with enough force to knock over most of the stacks Whiteoak had built in front of him. "There you go," he said while shoving the queen and ten of spades next to the other three spades that had been face up in front of him for most of that hand. "What've you got to say now?"

"Not a lot," Whiteoak sighed as he laid his cards down in a pile. "Other than I thought you were bluffing." There was a deuce of hearts on top of the pile and the deuce of diamonds beneath it.

"A pair of deuces?" Parsons sneered. "All of that for two goddamn pair?"

"It beat what you had showing and I thought it beat what you were trying to pass off."

Parsons blinked and looked at the cards one more time. "You're all balls and no brains, Whiteoak. I knew that the moment I saw you strut in here with them fancy clothes. All you needed was someone to weather the storm of all the fucking chatter long enough to put you down."

"You'd need that," Whiteoak said as he snapped a hand out to grab Parsons by the wrist when the other man tried to scoop in the pot. "But you'd also need more than a flush to beat a full boat." With that, Whiteoak spread his hold cards all the way to show the ten of diamonds at the bottom of the pile. "Now, about that discussion regarding your payment of this outstanding debt."

CHAPTER TWENTY-SEVEN

Parsons was fuming even more than usual when someone got the better of him. So much so that Chill and Denton quietly moved away from the table so they could observe the conflict from a safer distance. Once at the small bar, they took their drinks in one hand and their women in the other.

"You come in here, playing like a dim-witted child," Parsons said. "That's bad enough, but excusable since you still covered your bets."

"Speaking of covering bets," Whiteoak started, but clipped his sentence short when Parsons drew a snub-nosed .32 from somewhere under his vest and rested that hand on top of the table directly in front of him.

Continuing as though he'd drawn a short breath instead of a lethal weapon, Parsons said, "You make one of the single worst plays I've ever seen and then you have the gall to slow play the winning hand? You must be insane."

"Slow play?"

"Don't play dumb with me, asshole. That business when you made it look like you just had two pair knowing goddamn well that you had a full house."

"Oh, that. A simple bit of theatricality. Force of habit, I'm afraid. Sorry if it offended you."

Thumbing back the pistol's hammer, Parsons said, "You bet your ass it offended me. You crack wise again and you'll be a whole lot sorrier."

"Just a part of the game."

"It's an insult to me and nobody insults me in my own place at *my* game. Losing is one thing, but pissing right on my shoes and expecting me to just wipe it off is something else. If you didn't know that much, then you're more than just a terrible fucking poker player." Furrowing his brow, Parsons added, "Perhaps you're a cheat as well."

"Now I take offense to that, sir," Whiteoak sternly replied. "I may be a great many things, but I am most certainly not a cheat."

Of all the bluffs the professor had run that night, his most recent statement was the largest. It also had the most riding on it since Parsons already had more than enough reason to shoot him. Everyone else in the room watched intently. Perhaps they knew Whiteoak was lying about the honesty of his game or they might have figured it was only a matter of time before Parsons pulled his trigger anyway.

Whiteoak kept his gaze level and his hands steady.

Before long, Parsons grunted while relaxing his gun hand. "You're too bad of a card player to be much of a cheat," he grumbled.

"But I did win that hand," Whiteoak gently reminded him. "So, there's the matter of payment."

"I told you I can pull together the money in a day or two."

"And in that time, your men could put me down. Surely you can understand if I'm a bit leery where that sort of thing is concerned. I already witnessed those two extracting some bit of bloody business earlier this evening."

"Wasn't any business of mine," Parsons said.

"My associate mentioned something about a fight over a whore and some damage that was done to the room."

Parsons looked over to Morgan who was now pouring drinks for the men at the bar. She nodded and said, "There was some sort of fight in Misty's room. Big hole in one of the walls."

"Christ almighty," Parsons groaned. "I told Giles them panels were a bad idea. All they do is piss folks off once they see what's going on while they're fucking."

"Panels?" Whiteoak asked innocently.

Parsons waved the question off, seemingly growing more tired with every passing second. "You want the bounty off you and Corey Maynard's heads? Fine. It's off. What else?"

"I've heard from various sources that you're taking part in a certain business venture. I'd rather not disclose my sources . . ."

"You heard it from Corey Maynard. That prick made it his business to hear everything that's been going on around here every time he's in town. He's like a fly buzzing around a pile of shit, that one."

Since things seemed to be going his way for a change, Whiteoak passed up the opportunity to point out that Parsons had just referred to himself as a pile of shit. Folding his hands upon the table he spoke in a civil manner. "From what I've heard, this business of yours has the potential to be very profitable."

"What did you hear, exactly?"

"That there's a venture taking place in the mountains."

"Lots of ventures in the mountains, friend," Parsons said. "Fortunes are made and lost in them hills."

"You know damn well what I'm talking about. If you had more than one venture in the mountains at this moment that was lucrative enough to settle this debt you now owe me, then your fortune is much larger than most anyone else's within several nearby states."

"Maybe you'd be wise to take whatever I give you and be on your way. Remember those two men you mentioned earlier? Giles and Strahan? They're loyal to me and I pay 'em well enough to stay that way. One word from me and your silver tongue will be yanked from your skull with a pair of blacksmith's tongs."

"If you're expecting me to quake at the sound of that," Whiteoak said calmly, "then think again. That's not the first time I've been threatened. You want to set your dogs loose? Go right ahead. I'll sit here and wait for you to give the order."

"Don't test me."

"You can barely play cards. Why should I think you'd ever pass a test?"

Parsons slammed his fist down again.

"What the hell did you do? Kill Giles and Strahan? Bribe them?"

In the same tone of voice he'd used to feign ignorance on so many other recent matters, both large and small, Whiteoak asked, "Whatever do you mean?"

"Morgan!"

Upon hearing Parsons summon her, Morgan hurried from behind the bar to approach his side. "What would you like, Jacob?"

"Where are Giles and Strahan?"

"I don't know."

"Find them!"

She left the room and was gone for only a minute or two before climbing the stairs once again and crossing the dimly lit parlor on the second floor. In the time she was gone, Parsons sipped his drink while Whiteoak rolled one of his chips back and forth across the knuckles on his left hand.

"Some of the girls saw them leave," Morgan reported. "It was a while ago after the fight in Misty's room."

"What about Misty?"

"She's gone too."

"What do you mean?"

"She's not here. Sometimes the girls will go home or somewhere else to freshen up after entertaining a rowdy guest," she explained.

"How about this?" Whiteoak said as he pushed his chair back and stood up. "I'll give you some time to put your affairs in order, arrange my painful demise and whatnot, and then return for my payment. If anyone asks what happened while I was up here, I'll be sure to let them know about your troubles paying your debt and your difficulty in locating your two gun hands. I may even be able to find a way to work it into my presentation when I'm demonstrating my newest elixir designed to cure a man of his vile impulses to gamble and climb onto the bodies of sinful women." Glancing toward Morgan and the ladies at the bar, he added, "Present company excepted, of course."

"Sit down."

"Or what?" Whiteoak asked. "You'll shoot me? After the injury you gave to that poor fellow at your earlier game, I'd think you'd be hard-pressed to find anyone else to play with you after killing me. In fact, you'd be piling up a good deal of offenses for which you'll have to answer once Marshal Giddings visits this town again."

Removing his hand from the .32, Parsons stood up and left the gun on the table. "Better yet, why don't we both take a seat somewhere more private?"

"I'd rather not follow you into any locked rooms."

"If you want to hear about the business I'm conducting in the mountains, you'll join me to someplace we can talk without being overheard. Trust me. You'll be happy you did."

With a flourish of his hand, Whiteoak snatched the .32 from the table and dropped it into one of his pockets. Waving his now-empty hand toward the door, he said, "After you, kind sir."

CHAPTER TWENTY-EIGHT

"Pack your things," Whiteoak said as he rushed into one of the smaller rooms on the first floor of The Parlour. "We're leaving."

"Pack what?" Corey asked. "I never brought anything to unpack."

"Oh, sorry. I got swept up in the moment and reverted back to instinct. Be that as it may, we're leaving."

"What the hell happened? Do you realize I'm babysitting two prisoners here?"

"Yes, and it's a long story." Whiteoak stopped in his tracks, shook his head as if he was listening to loose change rattling inside and then added, "Reverse that."

"You're crazy," Corey sighed.

"Funny, that's what Jacob Parsons told me."

"I suspected it plenty of times, but thought you were eccentric because you were smart. That ain't the case, though. You're genuinely crazy. Also, smart, I'll give you that, but ec-

242

centric doesn't cut it. Crazy does because that's what you are."

"How are Giles and Strahan holding up?"

"Last time I checked, they were still unconscious."

"Where are they?"

"Upstairs," Corey said. "Are you gonna tell me what happened or not?"

"I'll give you the short version on the way," Whiteoak replied, which was exactly what he did as he and Corey hurried up a narrow set of stairs to the second floor. Using a string of choppy sentences but unable to help himself from sprinkling in a generous dose of colorful words, Whiteoak outlined the high points of his poker game with Parsons. The professor was reaching for the knob to the door of the room where the two gunmen were being kept when Corey slapped that hand away.

"You cheated in a game with *Jacob Parsons*?" Corey said. "That son of a bitch can barely tolerate when someone makes a lucky draw on him."

"I didn't cheat. I simply waited for my moment. Until that moment came, I had to keep him tightly wound and overly confident. One of those two things are natural for a man like him at any given time, but maintaining the proper balance of both was tricky."

"Don't try to make it sound like you planned this whole thing. If you didn't cheat at the right time, then you expect me to believe you waited for luck to turn your way?"

"No!" Whiteoak snapped. "It wasn't luck. It was patience and setup. I'd heard plenty about Parsons before seeing him up close and all of the stories I heard seemed mostly true when I saw how highly he regarded himself at the card table. Someone treating him as anything other than a god of poker was a personal affront to him, which was something I knew I could use. Stoking his confidence by bungling a few well-timed plays was the bulk of what I had to do until the tides of fortune shifted my way as they inevitably shift toward anyone's favor in the course of due time."

"What about those men in there?" Corey asked while nodding toward the door in front of him. "They're killers and unless you've got some sort of plan for them, we need to put them down like the rabid dogs they are."

"They're not rabid dogs. Dogs, maybe," Whiteoak amended, "but not rabid. They follow orders to earn their pay."

"I suppose you knew they'd be coming for us?"

"Didn't you?"

"Yeah," Corey replied. "Eventually."

"There you go. Deductive reasoning at its finest."

Gritting his teeth, Corey said, "Sometimes I don't know when you're bullshitting me."

"That last bit I said was one of those times. Anyway, we both knew they'd be coming. The only difference between you and me was that I wasn't preoccupied with a sweet smelling little redhead when they arrived. Once things were in motion, the trick was to keep them under control before turning them in our favor. First was to make sure those killers weren't an immediate threat to us," Whiteoak said while ticking off his points on his fingers. "Second was to put them out of the way where nobody knew exactly where they were. Well, nobody but us."

"I'd rather just kill them," Corey said.

"And I'd rather not have a murder charge hanging over me like the sword of Damocles. Stealing and verbal thievery are on one side of the fence and murder is a long ways on the other. That fence being the law."

"In case you forgot, the law don't take

kindly to stealing, either."

"But certain lawmen are more open to bribery or reason when they catch a thief. A killer is another kind of animal and is frequently dealt with in a much deadlier manner."

Hearing those words did a good job of calming Corey. He took a deep breath, let it out and nodded.

Whiteoak placed his hands on Corey's shoulders and leaned in to talk to him in a voice that wouldn't carry past the two of them. "This whole process started the moment I watched Parsons stick a knife through another man's hand just to prove a point. I turned my back and left as swiftly as I could, marking me as something of a coward in his eyes. That way, when I returned for a game, he already thought he had a leg up on me.

"The game itself was to set up the moment when I went for the throat! I had to make certain Parsons grew confident enough to stretch himself beyond his means once I ratcheted up the betting and keep him angry enough so that he wouldn't back down when every lick of common sense in his head told him to lay down his cards. That anger is also why it was essential to take care of Giles and Strahan."

"Is that why we had those two boys dress up in Giles and Strahan's clothes?" Corey asked.

"Parsons had to think his hired guns were still out there ready to jump when he told them to."

"Confidence," Corey pointed out.

"Exactly. But there also had to be some doubt concerning them since they hadn't shown their faces, turned up dead or answered the summons that Parsons inevitably sent out for them throughout the game. The best thing about building another man's confidence," Whiteoak said through a devilish grin, "is knowing the precise moment to start tearing it away. Parsons never took me seriously until it was too late and he was in too deep."

Corey's eyes widened. "How much did you get off of him?"

"Everything he had in front of him at the table, but the money isn't the best of it."

"What about the bounties on our heads? Were those taken away?"

"Yes," Whiteoak told him. "But that's not the best, either."

"We're free and clear with pockets full of a rich man's money? What the hell else is there?"

"Remember that business venture you

mentioned?"

"Yeah," Corey said hesitantly.

"Parsons and I sat down to have a nice talk about that. He provided some details that he most definitely wouldn't have parted with before."

"What kind of details?"

"For starters, a location that's a whole lot better than just 'somewhere in the mountains.' He also told me who he's dealt with out there and how to approach them. I think we should have a pretty easy time of introducing ourselves and becoming partners in a very lucrative endeavor."

"Do you even know what the endeavor is?" Corey asked. "Because I never made it that far when I was looking into it on my own."

"That's because you didn't have me at your side," Whiteoak said proudly. "They're brewing a chemical that will swiftly become a treasured commodity to nearly every company with deep pockets in this and other countries. The possibilities are limitless!"

"You say that about hair tonic."

"But this time I'm genuinely excited about our prospects. Can't you see it in my eyes?"

"You had that same excited look when you're talking about hair tonic."

"Forget the hair tonic," Whiteoak snipped. "This is something big. The chemical that's being brewed up in the mountains has uses that even Parsons doesn't know about. The details are too complicated to talk about now . . ."

"Why? Because I'm too stupid to understand?"

"No, because we're standing in front of a door about to walk in on a pair of killers."

After a brief silence, Corey said, "Yeah. I guess that's true as well."

Whiteoak smiled and tightened his grip on his friend's shoulders. "It's a chemical mixture that's highly flammable in one form and easily digestible in another. Depending on how it's mixed, it can be used as a fuel for steam engines or as a medicine that's strong enough to burn out nearly any type of disease."

"That's what Parsons told you?"

"It is."

"And don't you think that sounds a little . . . suspect?"

"Of course I thought that," Whiteoak said. "But if even a fraction of it is true, it can be worth a lot of money to someone with the knowledge and means to make either of the mixtures and produce even one end product. That certain someone could also find new methods of using the formula to even greater results."

"And that person's you," Corey said skeptically.

"I do have knowledge of chemicals. Otherwise, I would have poisoned someone by now."

"What about them people in Louisiana?"

"That was a fluke," Whiteoak said dismissively. "And they didn't die. You're missing the point here. Whatever business venture is out there, it's big enough for Parsons to hold on to it for this long. He was trying to keep it to himself and only let it go once he was backed into a corner with no alternative. Don't you see? This could be massive!"

Corey managed to nod convincingly enough for the professor to let go of his shoulders and turn back to the door. "Just do me a favor," he said while preparing to enter the room. "Leave these two to me."

CHAPTER TWENTY-NINE

Corey always carried a pistol, but wasn't partial to any particular make or model. The gun in his holster at any given time was whatever he could find and this time it was a bulky Army model Colt. He drew the firearm while pushing open the door, bringing up the pistol and cocking back the hammer in a smooth series of motions.

"Wipe that bad look off your face before I blow it onto the wall along with the rest of your fucking skull!" he roared.

Trailing in behind Corey, Whiteoak hadn't even had a chance to notice the expressions worn by either of the two men who sat tied to their chairs. Giles kept his head slumped forward, leaving Strahan to hold up his chin so he could fix a predatory glare upon anyone who walked in the room.

"If you were gonna shoot us, you'd have done it by now," Giles said without giving Corey more than a partial upward glance.

"That was before we got what we needed from your boss," Corey said. "Henry, did we get what we needed from Parsons?"

"Most certainly, yes," Whiteoak replied.

"And these two here," Corey said while pointing to the prisoners using the Colt's barrel, "got nothing better to do than kill us."

Whiteoak shrugged, allowing his partner to take the lead in the conversation for a change. "So it would seem."

"Then, can you think of a reason for us to keep them around?"

Whiteoak tapped his chin and crunched his face into a mask of exaggerated thought.

"You kill us and Parsons will hunt you down," Giles said.

"Who'll hunt us?" Corey replied. "You two are the best he's got, right? And look what happened to you. I think I'll take my chances with any other boys he may have in reserve."

"You better hope we don't never get free," Strahan warned. "When that happens, I'm gonna rip your fucking head off and piss into the stump."

"Very colorful," Whiteoak mused. "But there's nothing in it for you. The bounty's been removed from both me and my friend here. Also, lifting a finger against us will make your employer very upset."

Corey approached Strahan's chair and started to holster his Colt. Before the weapon was halfway encased in leather, he brought it up again and cracked the point of its grip against the bigger man's cheek. The impact wasn't hard enough to knock Strahan out, but it opened a deep gash in his flesh. "I warned you about looking at me like you're a bad man."

No matter how much rage was boiling inside of Strahan at that moment, he choked it down and tempered his glare.

"What about you?" Corey asked Giles. "Got any fire in your belly?"

"You'll find out soon enough," Giles replied.

"Probably, but not before you have to answer to Parsons about letting us ride on out of town and leaving you two behind. If I were you," Corey added, "I'd let it drop and just try to cover my own ass. Or you could come after us again," he said as he started dragging Strahan's chair backward toward the door. "It worked out so good for you this time around. Of course, it goes without saying that if me or my partner see you again, even from a ways off, we'll shoot you down and chalk it up to self defense."

"You wouldn't see it coming," Whiteoak

said after he'd gotten behind Giles's chair and started dragging it out of the room. "Just a crack in the distance, a whisper in the ear and everything becomes dark. I've seen it more than enough times to know that's how it goes."

Giles strained to look over his shoulder at Whiteoak. The cold certainty he found in the professor's eyes lent more than enough credence to his words. Before descending the staircase, the two young men who'd dragged them across town showed up to help carry the chairs to the first floor and out the back door Whiteoak had used earlier.

After making its way to an alley not too far from The Parlour, the strange procession set the chairs down amid several piles of old, broken crates. Grinning down at the two gunmen, Corey knocked out Giles with one punch to the face. Strahan proved to be a bit tougher, but slumped forward after a few chopping blows to his already bloodied skull.

"Them two might not be right again after so many knocks to the head," one of The Parlour's helpers pointed out.

Corey merely shrugged and said, "That's what they get for being such pricks."

After Corey walked away to get the horses,

Whiteoak approached the two men from The Parlour. "Here," he said while handing one of them a thick wad of cash. "This is for your trouble. Split it between the two of you."

Weighing the money in his hand, the young man tipped his hat. "Thank you, Professor."

"We're leaving Split Knee for the discernable future, so that leaves you and the others at The Parlour to deal with any repercussions regarding this incident."

"Reaper . . . cussin'?"

"Corey and I kicked up a good amount of dust," Whiteoak said. "Think you can handle things once it settles?"

"Oh, that! It's like I told you before. This isn't the first time there's been a feud between Summit Street and First Avenue and it won't be the last. Hell, this wasn't even the worst."

"Good to hear . . . sort of," Whiteoak replied. "Wouldn't want to leave the wrong people in a lurch. Thanks for the helping hand."

Having split the money between himself and his partner, the young man led the way back across the street. "I'll tell Sissy you said goodbye."

Whiteoak was about to leave the alley to

meet Corey and the horses, but stopped and turned back around. The grin on his face started small but spread into a wicked smile as he reached into a jacket pocket and removed something from where it had been stored. Chill's cufflinks were exquisitely made and definitely valuable. From the moment they'd been tossed into the middle of the table at Parsons's game, Whiteoak envisioned how well the diamond accessories would enhance several of his favorite shirts.

"As good as these would look on me," he said while reaching out to tuck one cufflink into each unconscious man's pocket, "they'll look even better on you. Think of it as an apology for all the rough treatment. Or," he added slyly, "there's always the chance that Parsons might find out what you've got and recognize where they must have come from. Now that would spark an interesting conversation, wouldn't it? I'd like to be a fly on the wall for that one."

The professor straightened the two men's clothing to cover the fact that he'd planted the cufflinks and took a moment to admire his handiwork. "On the other hand," he mused, "perhaps I should leave word that you two were accepting money from me the whole time. That way Parsons would find out for certain. It'd be a shame for both of us to miss out on that interesting conversation, after all."

CHAPTER THIRTY

Whiteoak and Corey left Split Knee as soon as they could. They left even before they could fully supply themselves for a ride lasting more than a day. Fortunately, both of them knew the area well enough to point their horses toward a small trading post just north of town. Even though they didn't attract much attention from the few people there, both men kept their hats pulled low to cover a good portion of their faces while purchasing supplies from a grizzled old mountain man selling wares from the back of his wagon. There were some appetizing smells drifting from a large tent nearby, but the men stuck to the jerked venison they'd purchased instead of treating themselves to a plate of hot stew. It was more important to put some more distance between themselves and anyone who might be trying to land on Jacob Parsons's good side.

"We may still be in a bit of a pickle around

here," Whiteoak whispered as he loaded his saddlebags with a portion of the supplies that had been purchased.

"Really?" Corey scoffed. "Do you think so?"

"Even though Parsons took the price off our heads, it may take a while before word spreads that it's gone."

"That's if he takes the price off."

"Parsons took a humiliating enough loss to me," Whiteoak said. "The last thing a man in his position wants to do is add to that by painting himself as a liar on top of everything else. For a businessman of any sort, that kind of damage is irreparable."

Corey shook his head. His saddlebags were stuffed full so he cinched them closed and buckled them in place. "There's business and there's personal. What you did to Parsons, making a fool out of him in his own place in front of men who will surely tell the tale to their friends as soon as possible, was as personal as it gets."

"I realize that. But that bounty is what concerns me right now."

"I don't think you need to worry about that one."

"You don't?" Whiteoak asked hopefully.

"Nah. You should be worried about the next group of killers that Parsons sends after us. Most likely, they won't be working for a bounty. They'll be plain old killers working for a wage and the favor of a powerful man like Jacob Parsons. Also, he's got friends who will have no qualms with putting a bullet through our heads for free."

Whiteoak climbed into his saddle and shrugged. "It doesn't do us any good to worry. Best to be on our own way."

"That's it, huh? You kick over the hornet's nest, poke that same nest with a stick and then go about your way?"

"A tired analogy, but yes. If you don't stir things up, then what are you doing?"

"Living without being shot at?" Corey offered.

"Perhaps, but there's always the chance that trouble will find you, anyway. If all you want to do is muddle through without risking anything then that's not living. It's surviving."

Corey climbed into his saddle. "You got something against survival?"

"I do when that's all there is. I'd rather think there's more to a man's life than making it through one day to see the next. Without risk, there's no reward other than whatever occasional little pleasantries are tossed your way like so many scraps. Here you go," Whiteoak sneered while extending an empty hand to Corey. "Good dog. Run along now. Be good and don't make any trouble. Maybe next time, you'll get a piece of old bread to go along with that."

"You think trying for something better is the same as going out and looking for the most trouble you could possibly find? There are a few notches in between them two, don't you think?"

Whiteoak thought it over and made a sour face. "I suppose there are. I'd rather aim for the higher end of the scale than settle for the middle. That's how I got to where I am today."

Both men snapped their reins and headed for the edge of camp. It didn't take long for their horses to put the little settlement behind them. "Where you are today?" Corey said with a chuckle. "A fast-talking medicine man who rides around in a garishly painted wagon selling sugar water to dumb locals?"

"Yes! And it's glorious!" Whiteoak exclaimed while opening his arms to embrace the world around him as though he'd been the one to wind it up and set it in motion. "Without my fast talk and slightly crooked ideas . . ."

Corey laughed and then half-heartedly tried to pass it off as a cough.

"Yes, I said *slightly* crooked," the professor said. "No matter what you or anyone else says, I've pioneered some dandy innovations right along with the ones that serve no purpose other than to fund my liberated existence. Do you know what I did for a living before I acquired my wagon?"

"You were in the Army," Corey sighed. "You told me about it plenty of times."

"After the Army."

After thinking for a moment, Corey said, "No. That's actually something you never talked about."

"I was a clerk and a chemist and a teacher."

"All at the same time?"

"No," Whiteoak said. "I drifted from one job to another, each one was considered respectable by the community I was in. I hated every second of it. There were tasks to do, ways to do them and that's all there was. Do something a particular way, do it the same way again and again, sleep, eat, do it all again."

"My ma was a teacher," Corey warned. "You saying there's something wrong with earning a living that way?"

"Not at all. There are people in every profession who love it or excel at it and they do their vocation proud. I didn't have any

262

passion for what I did. That's the difference between living and surviving. Passion!" When he spoke that last word, Whiteoak clenched a fist and held it up to the sky. "Without passion, you don't have anything to offer. You're just filling space. Even someone in the most upstanding job there is can become nothing but a lump unless they bring passion along with them. On the other hand, a passionate soul can bring a spark to anything they do, no matter how lowly the task."

"And you're passionate about swindling?"

"Sometimes." Leaning over in his saddle toward Corey, Whiteoak asked, "You're not exactly a clerk or teacher yourself. Don't you find a thrill in what you do? Otherwise, why do you do it?"

"Man's gotta eat."

Whiteoak kept looking at his partner until a smirk broke through Corey's stony features. "There it is!" Whiteoak gloated. "I knew it."

"Man's also gotta be smart when chasing his passions," Corey pointed out. "Children are the ones who run head-first into every damn thing without thinking first."

"True."

"Then why don't you think about what you're doing out here? Doesn't anything seem suspicious to you?"

"You still think riding into the mountains after this business venture is a foolish pursuit?" Whiteoak asked.

"Even if there is something to it, there's bound to be danger. And don't tell me the bullshit about nothing good ever coming easy."

Freezing with his mouth partway open and a finger raised, Whiteoak eased back and said, "I wasn't."

"Doesn't this whole story about this concoction or whatever seem a little familiar?"

"How so?"

"Familiar, as in resembling a sales pitch that a snake oil salesman might give about a tonic he cooked up in a wagon somewhere."

"Every so often," Whiteoak said whimsically, "those concoctions prove to be a whole lot more than what they started as. And if those cooks in the mountains don't know what they have, I could turn it into something stupendous."

"What if it's nothing?" Corey asked.

Whiteoak looked up and pulled in a breath of crisp mountain air. "Then we will have ridden through the mountains with money in our pockets and strong horses beneath us. I don't see that as being so very bad."

Corey sighed and shook his head. "It can turn out a whole lot worse than that and you know it."

"I do, but it's good to have someone to remind me every now and then."

CHAPTER THIRTY-ONE

The next time they saw civilization was late the following afternoon. Westchester was a small town to the northwest of Split Knee. There weren't many miles between the two towns, but it was an arduous ride to make the trip from one to the other. That portion of the Square Mountain Trail had been washed out so many times that, in several places, the path dwindled to a ribbon of dirt amid rocks and thick overgrowth. Not only did the gravel make it hard to see the trail, but also made the horses' job that much more difficult since chunks of the ground tended to loosen beneath their hooves.

When the trail could be seen, it wound between large boulders and cut through rushing streams flowing with snow that had melted to surge down in a strong current. At times, even the famed big skies of Montana were all but hidden by a thick canopy of branches and leaves. Just before catching a first glimpse of Westchester, Whiteoak thought for certain they'd taken a wrong turn and had looped back around to retrace their steps. Eventually, several thin trails of smoke hanging against the clouds brought their eyes down to the chimneys at their source and the town itself was revealed.

After a tough night filled with the ever-present threat of gunmen tracking them down to exact bloody vengeance, the sight of Westchester was enough to bring weary smiles to both men's faces.

"There it is," Whiteoak said. "Thank the Lord."

"There better be a steak in that town," Corey growled. "If there ain't, I'm gonna raise some hell."

No hell was raised in Westchester that night. Corey got his steak, Whiteoak lost himself in a beer and both of them slept in warm beds.

The next morning, Whiteoak found Corey sitting at a table in the little dining room of the hotel where they'd spent the night. Only two of the four small tables were occupied, the second of which had a pair of trappers sitting at it chomping loudly on a tall stack of pancakes.

"Thought you'd be asleep for a while longer," Corey grunted as Whiteoak sat down across from him.

"Sorry to disappoint you."

"Feels like all I've been lookin' at lately is your damn face."

"I could mention a similar complaint in regard to you, but I have better manners than that," Whiteoak pointed out.

"Well my manners ain't too good first thing in the morning, so keep the conversation down to bare essentials. In fact, keep it down to nothin' unless it's really important."

Whiteoak opened his mouth and drew a breath but before he could utter his first word, Corey added, "And if you think it's important, think about it some more to be sure."

The professor did that and closed his mouth again. He then stood up and walked over to the door to the kitchen that was being pushed open by the teenaged daughter of the hotel's owner. "Excuse me, honey. I'd like to order my breakfast."

"Do you like griddle cakes?" she asked.

"Fortunately, yes. Especially if the edges are a little crisp."

"There were some partly burnt ones. I'll get them for you."

"I didn't mean burnt. I . . . never mind.

I'd also like some bacon or ham to go with it."

The girl was only a few inches shorter than Whiteoak and had a long, slender frame. Her hair was thick and dark blond, hanging well past her shoulders. The dress she wore was blue and white checked with a dirty apron tied around her waist. She carried a small tray from the kitchen bearing a coffee pot, a jar of jam and a small pitcher of maple syrup. "We don't have any bacon or ham. Just griddle cakes."

"That's it?"

"Yes. That's why I asked if you liked them."

"What if I said no?" Whiteoak inquired.

Her brow took on a severe angle as though the question itself had caused her pain. "Everybody likes griddle cakes."

"Then why ask if I like them?"

"Just sit down and I'll bring you your breakfast. If you don't like it, feed it to the dog. You want coffee or water?"

Whiteoak tensed his jaw and marched to one of the empty tables. "Coffee."

At his table, Corey laughed while picking up a piece of toast from a little plate in front of him.

"How did you get that toast?" Whiteoak snapped.

Savoring every morsel of his nearly burnt bread, Corey said, "By not being an annoying jackass."

That brought a chorus of laughter from the other occupied table in the room. Two men sat there, both looking as if they'd been coughed up from the mountains surrounding the little town. Their dirty faces were barely visible through thick layers of dirt and sweaty whiskers.

Whiteoak drew a long breath and savored its relative freshness since he knew he wouldn't taste its like again for a while. He headed over to the table inhabited by the filthy men and pulled an empty chair along with him.

"Mind if I join you?" the professor asked.

"Why'd you want to do that?" the larger of the two filthy men replied.

"Because every meal tastes better when it's eaten in good company." Since that didn't bring much of a response, he added, "I'd also be willing to pay for the entire meal at whatever table I happen to occupy."

"You'll pay for our grub?" the smaller man asked.

"In the spirit of friendship to a fellow traveler, of course!"

The two men looked at each other for a few seconds. One shrugged and the other nodded. It was the larger man who shrugged again before saying, "Long as you wanna pay, you can sit here. We're almost through, anyways."

"Excellent." Whiteoak placed his chair at an empty spot at the table and began the lengthy ritual of preparing himself for a formal meal. It involved the flapping of a napkin before setting it on his knee and smoothing it, straightening the front of his shirt, flicking stray crumbs from the table directly in front of him, cleaning the crumbs from his hands, arranging his silverware in neatly perpendicular lines and then straightening his shirt yet again for good measure. When he was finished, he announced, "I am Professor Henry Whiteoak."

The larger man grunted, "I'm Owen and that's my brother, Sam."

To that, Sam looked up and burped loudly.

Smiling as though the gaseous exhale had been a cheerful song, Whiteoak asked, "Owen and Sam . . . what?"

"Menlo," Owen said. "Anything else you wanna ask or are you gonna let us eat in peace?"

"Just passing time until my food arrives. I've heard that name before somewhere, haven't I?"

"Maybe. We got plenty of kin in these parts."

"Do any of you get to Split Knee very often?"

Both of the Menlo brothers looked at Whiteoak intently. "Why'd you ask that?" Sam grunted through a mouthful of griddle cakes.

Whiteoak shrugged his shoulders. "Just making conversation. I recently had business there with a man named Parsons. Ever hear of him?"

"Sure we have," Owen said. "He's a rich man who throws plenty of weight around. What business did you have with him?"

"I'm a sporting man, among other things. We engaged in a game of poker that's sure to be legendary in a short amount of time. I wouldn't be surprised if you'd already heard tell of him being taken to the cleaners by a handsome, impeccably dressed stranger."

"Can't say that we have."

Sam shook his head as well.

"What was your business with Mister Parsons, if you don't mind me asking?" Whiteoak inquired.

"I do mind," Owen said as he shoved away from the table. "Thanks for the grub." He and his brother stood up, jerked the napkins from where they'd been tucked into their collars and tossed the soiled linen on top of their plates. They walked away, making sure to fix a challenging glare onto Corey as they left the dining room.

The girl who'd served everyone their meals hurried from the kitchen carrying Whiteoak's breakfast. "Where are they going? They didn't pay!"

"Bring those griddle cakes here," Whiteoak said as he waved to her. "Along with the bill for those gentlemen's breakfast."

Although slightly confused by the arrangement, the girl was relieved that someone would be settling the account. She set the plate in front of Whiteoak and returned to the kitchen to retrieve some more syrup and butter.

"Always making new friends," Corey chuckled. "You're a real charmer."

"It's a gift," Whiteoak sighed.

Now that the dining room was empty, the men could speak to each other as easily as if they were still sharing a table.

After taking another bite and swallowing it, Corey said, "You already knew those two."

"What makes you say that?"

"Because you didn't try to sell them anything."

"They didn't give me a chance," Whiteoak replied.

"You don't need much of a chance. Besides, you've had your sights on them since you walked in this room." Noticing the vaguely stunned air that had settled around the professor, Corey added, "You ain't the only one who notices things."

"I suppose not."

"So what's so special about them two idiots?"

Whiteoak took his fork in one hand and a knife in the other, digging into his breakfast with vigor.

CHAPTER THIRTY-TWO

Whiteoak didn't answer Corey's question during breakfast and didn't broach the subject when they saddled their horses and rode out of Westchester. The town was barely behind them when they spotted a small cart being driven by one man who sat hunched in his seat with his reins in tired hands. The cart's single horse plodded toward Westchester, acknowledging Corey and Whiteoak with a subtle nod. The driver glanced up at them in a similar fashion, focusing on the professor only slightly more than the man who rode beside him.

That lingering glance was enough to put both men on edge. As the cart continued toward town, Corey's hand drifted to his holster and stayed there. Whiteoak's muscled tightened and he shifted in his saddle so he could feel the brush of his .38 against his frame. A few seconds passed quietly and Whiteoak let out a relieved breath.

A few seconds after that, a rough voice called back to them. "Hey!" it said.

While Corey wrapped his fingers around the grip of his firearm, Whiteoak waved lazily over his shoulder and replied, "Hey right back to you, good sir!"

"Hey, I says," the driver of the cart shouted as its wheels ground to a halt.

"Shit," Corey grunted under his breath as both he and Whiteoak turned to face the cart.

The driver was already climbing down, huffing with the effort it took for his boots to reach the ground. He was an older fellow with a mane of gray hair and a weathered face. As soon as he was down, he said, "You're Henry Whiteoak."

"Umm . . . yes," Whiteoak replied.

"Professor Henry Whiteoak."

"Again, yes."

"I've got something for you." The driver reached into his cart. When he brought his hands out again, he was holding two bundles. One was wrapped in canvas and the other was a rumpled water skin. He was so perturbed that he barely flinched when he saw that Corey had already drawn his pistol. "Oh, I see. First you cheat me and then you have your hired gun hand kill me?"

"Corey, lower your weapon. I think I

recognize this man."

"You do?" Corey asked, his pistol remaining where it was.

"Yes," Whiteoak said. "He's Daniel Brock. A business associate of mine."

"It's *David* Brock," the driver roared while stomping toward Whiteoak. "And I am hardly an associate of yours! I bought a bunch of that swill you brewed up!"

Chuckling while holstering his pistol, Corey said, "You're gonna have to be more specific."

"The Fresh and White!" Brock said.

Whiteoak's eyes widened. "Oh, right! You bought a good amount of it. Enough to earn a generous discount, I believe."

"Here," Brock grunted while extending the hand that was carrying the bundle wrapped in canvas. He'd gotten close enough to Penelope to reach Whiteoak, but the professor didn't make a move to take what he was being offered.

"What is this?" Whiteoak asked.

"What's left of that shit you sold to me. It's no good."

"Pardon me?"

"I'm not about to sell it to no one if I can't even repackage it!" Brock roared. "I want my damn money back."

"Repackage?" Corey asked.

Whiteoak sighed. "He bought my tooth cleanser in bulk so he could sell it to his own customers. Asking for a refund in this circumstance is highly unusual."

"Know what else is unusual?" Brock growled. "This!" He raised his other hand which was indeed gripping a water skin. When he relaxed a few of his fingers, the skin unfurled to show several holes clustered around the bottom.

"You should try using a canteen," Whiteoak offered. "Much sturdier."

"No, you asshole," Brock said. "These holes were burned in when that swill of yours burned *through*!"

"You stored my Fresh and White in that?" Whiteoak said. "After I specifically told you to keep it in glass vials?"

"I am a healer," Brock said in a voice that was trembling with rage. "A true medicine man taught by the eldest of the tribes in this great land."

Scowling distastefully, Whiteoak said, "Spare me the sales pitch, Dave. You may bill yourself as an Indian shaman of some sort, but I know better."

"Indian?" Corey scoffed. "He's about as Indian as my Uncle Seefus."

"When I deliver my medicines," Brock continued while shaking the damaged skin, "my customers expect them to be in packages like this, not your damn doctor's vials. Those sorts of things frighten away them folks who don't want to deal with doctors and such. They want to deal with men of nature like me."

"Men of nature who purchase their wares from someone like myself and pass them off as their own," Whiteoak said.

"I mean to help my customers, not burn their guts out."

"My Fresh and White won't burn anyone's innards, just as long as you dilute it and serve it in the proper measurements," Whiteoak told him. "I explained this already. What I gave you should have lasted you for months! You stored it in a leather pouch, so what did you expect would happen?"

Lifting the perforated water skin even higher, Brock said, "Not *this*! Gimme my money back."

"I don't have it on me."

Brock threw the bundle of vials to Whiteoak. By the time the professor caught the vials, Brock had filled that hand with a pistol that had been tucked under his belt beneath his shirt. "Money. Now."

"It's in my wagon and my wagon isn't here."

"Well, you'd better figure something out."

Sighing, Whiteoak patted his pockets. He eventually came up with a small wad of folded bills. "Here. This is all I have on me," he said while tossing the money to Brock.

The disgruntled shaman flipped through the money and grunted, "Ain't enough."

"Corey, are you going to let him point that weapon at me?"

"I reckon so," Corey chuckled. "Seems like you deserve it. Especially for selling acid to folks and letting them drink it."

"It's only mildly corrosive and that's only in larger . . . you know what?" Whiteoak snapped as he stuffed the vials into one of his saddlebags, "I've got business to attend to. I can meet you at a later date to repay you once I have my wagon again. If you want your money now, then he's the one you need to speak to," Whiteoak said while waving a finger at Corey. "Good day to both of you."

As the professor snapped his reins, Brock pointed his gun at Corey.

"Aw fer shit's sake," Corey growled. He dug into a pocket for some wadded cash. "Here," he said while tossing it at Brock. "Take it. That's all I'm giving you."

"Ain't enough," Brock said without bothering to pick up the money.

Drawing his pistol in a smooth, fluid motion, Corey thumbed back his hammer and said, "All right, I'll give you something else. You sure you want it?"

The gun in Brock's hand began to tremble and the anger in his face melted away. Conceding the battle of wills to the man who was much likelier to pull his trigger, Brock stuck his gun under his belt and nodded. "That'll be enough, I guess. But if it ain't, I'll come after that asshole friend of yours to get the rest. If he tries putting me off again, I'll put a real hurting on him."

"And I'll be there to help you do it," Corey said while flicking his reins.

Having dealt with his share of salesmen, Corey wasn't worried about Brock taking a shot at him. The other fellow was too busy scrambling to pick up his money to do much of anything else. Before too long, he caught up with Whiteoak.

"What was the meaning of all that?" Corey asked.

"You were listening," the professor replied. "It seemed pretty self-explanatory to me."

"Tell me that tooth stuff of yours ain't poison."

"It's not. Alcohol and even sarsaparilla can have dangerous effects when used incorrectly, so I won't be judged for another man's ignorance."

"And what about the money?"

"I'll pay him when I see him again," Whiteoak grunted.

"No. My money. What about that? I had to pay that idiot out of my own pocket."

Whiteoak grinned. "If you wanted to save money, you should've shot him."

They climbed at that same angle for the better portion of the day. With every step the horses took, the air around them became thinner and cooler. When they stopped at a stream to fill their canteens, the water stabbed their chests like icy blades, making every subsequent breath a little harder to draw. The spot where they chose to make camp was enclosed on all sides by trees. Below them was a hard plate of stone. Above their heads was such a wide open sky filled with so many stars that it was more than a little disorienting to stare directly up into the sparkling abyss.

Dinner was a quiet affair consisting of a pan of baked beans and some biscuits that were only slightly easier to chew than the stones surrounding their crackling campfire. Amid the grinding of teeth against coarse and mushy foods, Corey said, "You got a hell of a way with partners."

"What's that?"

"How many partners have you had over the years?"

"Enough to know how to keep them alive. Of course," Whiteoak added, "the tricky part in keeping them from trying to kill me."

"That's because you don't tell 'em everything they need to know. After a while, it becomes easier to cut ties and move along."

Setting down his tin plate, Whiteoak said, "All right. Let's start with this business venture that Parsons told you about. Why didn't you tell me all I needed to know where that was concerned?"

Corey sighed. "Honestly. . . ."

"No," the professor said in a droll monotone. "Lie to me."

"I didn't know much about it apart from the fact that it was up in the mountains and it had something to do with a still. There was talk about it being some sort of moonshine, but that it turned into something more like a miracle cure. I didn't know how much of it to believe myself."

Leaning forward, Whiteoak asked, "A cure for what?"

"Hell if I know. I thought it was a bunch'a bullshit, but Parsons and a few others seemed to think it was valuable enough to wager on in that card game. There was also some talk about a group of claim jumpers wanting to take the still by force. They were never heard from again, supposedly."

"Supposedly?"

"Could've been rumors and tall tales. I thought that's what most of it was, anyway. When I hear someone talk about miracle tonics and elixirs, I tend to assume the worst."

"Why would you do that?" Whiteoak asked earnestly. Less than a second later, he nodded. "Ah, I see."

"You gotta admit, Henry. Spending time with you is enough to make anyone suspicious of their fellow man."

"But you must have figured that if anyone would believe those stories, it would be me."

"That's right," Corey said. "I knew you'd eat it up like cake covered in sweet frosting. My first thought was to make certain you didn't hear anything about it since you'd sink your teeth into it and never let it go."

"But then you found a spot where you could use what you knew to your advantage. My hat's off to you, sir."

"It wasn't like that."

"And I wasn't being facetious," Whiteoak said. "There aren't many men out there who could manipulate me so well. A few women come to mind, but that's a whole other set of talents."

Corey shook his head and prodded at the base of the campfire. "I wanted to protect you."

"Protect *me*?"

"From the one person that's bound to get you killed and it ain't no woman."

Stretching his legs out, Whiteoak set his plate aside and laid back so he could gaze directly up at the stars. His face tensed for a moment before he adjusted to the overpowering majesty of the night sky. "Protecting me from myself, eh? Very noble."

"I wouldn't say it was noble. Looking out for my interests is more like it. You're one hell of a gold mine, Whiteoak. That is, when you get an idea in your head that ain't complete horse manure."

Both men chuckled for a few moments as light from the fire dimmed to a soft glow. "This sort of thing," Corey continued. "The business about that tonic or elixir or whatever it is up in these mountains. It's not something you could refuse."

"I am a learned man. I am well above the pulls of base instinct and greed."

"What about curiosity? Or that itch that you feel that makes you think you can do what nobody else can and not only succeed at it, but improve it."

"To what, exactly, are you referring?"

Whiteoak asked.

"Does it matter?"

After a lengthy pause, Whiteoak replied, "I suppose not."

"After that scrape you had in Kansas," Corey said, "both of us had killers after us for one reason or another. This elixir rumor would have made you go off half-cocked at the worst time. At the worst, it could have been used to bait you into a trap."

"Such is the life for a man who chooses to play against the odds. The risk far exceeds the chances for reward and there's no guarantee for one ounce of happiness at the end of it all. On the other hand, there's always the chance that things might work out."

Corey continued in what was clearly an effort to keep from getting too frustrated with his distracted audience. "Most likely, the still in the mountains was some sort of con meant to fleece Parsons of a chunk of his money. The nature of it, though, would be perfect to interest someone like you as well."

Since Corey was having some difficulty, Whiteoak offered, "And when you were the one who needed to point me in a certain direction, you decided to be the one to dangle that business venture in front of me."

"I ain't exactly proud of it."

Whiteoak shrugged as best he could while lying flat on his back. "It wasn't exactly a Machiavellian machination, Corey. Also, I've been a thief long enough, spent enough time among others of my ilk, to know when something is just too damn good. You were anxious to come out here, but dodgy when explaining why."

"There was the bounties," Corey said. "They were real."

"Oh, certainly. No doubt about that. But still . . ." Whiteoak waved his hand in front of him as if he was clearing away chalk words on the great blackboard above the trees. "Having folks want to harm you is the price of conducting our business. If it wasn't for men like those, I wouldn't need to ruin the line of my suit by stuffing pistols under my arms and up my sleeves. By the way, how much was Parsons offering to have me killed?"

"Not Parsons. It was those men from Kansas. The business tycoons representing a group of banks or rich bank owners or . . . aw, I don't know what the hell their business is. All I do know is that they were offering a small fortune to have your carcass brought back to Kansas in a pine box."

Whiteoak laughed. "That's not bad. There

was a fellow in New York City, owner of a string of brothels, I believe. He wanted my head and balls brought to him in a hat box."

"A hat box?"

"Yes, sir."

"Why?"

"I believe it had something to do with a pile of money that I convinced him to hand over to me," Whiteoak explained. "But his threats became truly colorful when he found out what I'd convinced his daughter to do."

"No, no," Corey said. "I mean . . . why a hat box?"

"Oh. I've wondered about that myself more than once. In the end, I chalk it up to one of those things that can't be explained. You just have to wait for a solution to present itself."

"And if one doesn't?" Corey asked.

"Then make up a solution for yourself."

"When all else fails . . . lie," Corey chuckled.

"Children lie to their parents to get toys and candy. Young men lie to young women to get a different sort of candy. Wives lie to their husbands to get peace of mind. The list is endless."

"Every player is a cheater, huh?"

"Only the players who want to win," Whiteoak said. "The true test of character is how far someone is willing to go. When you take into account that cheating is on the table," Whiteoak said, "it becomes part of the game."

"Wait a minute. Were you lying to me about what Parsons told you in regard to that still?"

"Don't be so fidgety," Whiteoak said as though Corey's inquiries were part of the noisy rustle of the wilderness surrounding them. "There's something to that still, even if it's just a little kernel of something, it's truly valuable. Otherwise, it wouldn't have been mentioned at all by the likes of Jacob Parsons or anyone with whom he does business."

"It could be bullshit," Corey grumbled. "All of it. Just a yarn that was spun as part of a con or the wishful thinking of a miner who also believes he'll someday find a piece of gold in his tin pan the size of his fist."

"And if there was such a treasure, wouldn't you want to hide it?" Whiteoak asked. "And if you wanted to hide something, where would be the best place? Whether it's a still or not, Parsons was protecting something of value. And since there must be something valuable hidden out here, we have only one option."

"Ride out of these damn mountains before

we get killed?" Corey offered.

"We find what's at the source of all this commotion and wring every bit of profit there is to be had!" Having spoken his piece, Whiteoak clasped his hands on top of his chest and closed his eyes.

CHAPTER THIRTY-THREE

"We should go back," Corey warned.

Whiteoak rode ahead, but only by a few paces since the path through the trees and brush wouldn't allow both horses to ride side by side. "Why?" he asked without taking his eyes from the path in front of him. "Lost your nerve already? Or did you find a spider crawling into your boot?"

"Mock all you want, asshole. You know I'm right."

"There's no other way," Whiteoak replied. "This trail split off from the other one exactly where it should if we want to find that still. Anyone with a set of eyes can see the terrain only gets rougher if we stayed on the Square Mountain Trail any longer."

"The Square Mountain Trail ain't too rough at all. I've ridden it more times than I can count."

"Not when we head north!" Whiteoak said as he stretched out his arm to point straight ahead. "We need to head north because that's where the still is! I've ridden the Square Mountain Trail as well and can tell you that the terrain north of it only gets worse the farther along we would've gone!"

The professor's voice hung in the air without traveling far. There were simply too many branches and sloping hills on either side of the path for anything to go much further than a few yards. Even the horses weren't having an easy time of it. Just when they found a good walking pace, something sharp would snag their legs or an uneven stone would catch a hoof.

After less than another minute passed, Corey said, "I've heard stories."

"Oh, good. Let's hear some of them to pass the time."

"Men have ridden up this way and weren't seen again."

"Such a pleasant yarn," Whiteoak sighed. "Let's hear another."

"There are lunatics living out here."

"There are lunatics living everywhere, my friend. Just one of the perils of sharing space with your fellow man. In fact, my chosen profession reaps many benefits from the lunacy that lurks within us all."

"Will you stop talking about yourself for one goddamn minute?" Corey growled.

"You're the one who broached the subject."

"The hell I did! I said we needed to turn back because there's crazies lurking in these mountains and you started going on about how you make money."

Whiteoak mulled that over for a short while before shrugging his shoulders. "Perhaps you're right. You know, someone once told me that my verbal acumen is sharp enough to be considered a weapon. The person who spoke those words also happened to be a very beautiful young woman with hair like —"

"Quiet!"

Whiteoak obeyed that command for about twenty-two seconds. Twisting around in his saddle, the professor asked, "What is it?"

"Something's moving behind us," Corey whispered.

"Something? You are aware that there are plenty of wild animals moving about." Whiteoak had more to say, but was cut short by a sharp gesture from Corey.

"Stay here," Corey said before drawing his pistol and turning his horse all the way around to face the opposite direction.

Whiteoak drew his pistol as well. "Where are you going?"

"Something's back there. I aim to find out what."

"It's probably just a small animal."

"Listen to that."

It didn't take long for the sounds of rustling leaves and snapping branches to reach both men's ears.

"Could be a large animal," Whiteoak offered.

"And if it eats us, it'll be on your head. I wanted to abandon this goddamn venture of yours from the start."

The professor's brow furrowed, twisting his features into an angry scowl. "Then go on and leave! You're intrigued by the profit that lies ahead just as much as I am! Don't try to pass yourself off as a saint!"

Corey was almost out of sight, swallowed up by the dense greenery encroaching upon the path from nearly every side. Before taking another step, he pivoted around to fix his eyes on the professor. There was enough venom in that stare to quiet the other man for a short while. Satisfied with his small victory, Corey continued onward.

The snapping he'd heard before was still present. Now that there were no words spewing from his mouth, Whiteoak could narrow down his options as far as where those sounds were originating. While some of them could have come from his left, most of the rustling was directly behind him. "Ungrateful jackass," he muttered under his breath. "Always talking as if I'm the devil and he's some kind of saint."

More rustling came from the left. This time, Whiteoak was certain it was low and close to the ground. Shifting his aim in that direction, he pointed his gun at a tangled mess of bushes filled with stubby thorns and withered berries. "I've a mind to rid myself of his bellyaching and continue on my own. Wouldn't be the first time I've ridden alone. Won't be the last."

A twig snapped as a cluster of leaves shook nearby. Whiteoak steadied his hand and placed his thumb upon the hammer of his pistol. His eyes became intense slits, blocking out anything that he couldn't shoot with the twitch of a single finger. The muscles in his thumb tensed, reluctant to make any more noise than was absolutely necessary.

When the next rustle came, the entire bush shook, prompting Whiteoak to snap back his hammer. He didn't pull his trigger, however. The sound may have startled him, but it was still not enough of a jolt to waste a bullet. His hesitance proved to be justified when a mangy dog emerged from the tangled bushes. That dog was followed by another before the leaves of that bush stopped shaking. More rustling could be heard not too far away. Whiteoak turned to look, only to find a family of small rodents darting from one partially buried stone to scurry behind another.

"In a bit of a hurry," Whiteoak mused. Instead of looking toward the other critters that were scampering into sight, the professor sampled the air around him with a few sharp sniffs. It smelled like autumn and left the interior of his head prickling with sharp stinging pain. Something was burning.

The next footsteps Whiteoak heard were large and stomping straight toward him. "Go!" Corey hollered before exploding from the encroaching foliage.

"What's the matter?"

"Go, dammit! Just go!"

Corey's horse stomped the ground with anxious hooves. Whiteoak's mare was uneasy as well. The next breath Whiteoak took felt like he'd inhaled a scoop of hot embers and it filled him with the acrid stench of crackling destruction. Smoke seeped between the trees behind them, followed by flames that crept forward while reaching out with flickering claws.

"What did you do?" Whiteoak yelped.

"Move that blasted animal before I shoot

it and ride over both of yer bodies!"

Snapping his reins, Whiteoak turned to face forward while hunkering down and clamping his legs around the horse's sides. Penelope might have broken into a gallop if there was more room to run. Within the confines of the cluttered trail, the mare trotted at first and then eventually sped to a run.

Corey was right behind them, breathing in short, choppy gasps while swearing with every exhale. The fire was growing into an inferno in his wake, devouring anything it could touch and sending creatures of all sizes running.

CHAPTER THIRTY-FOUR

The trail narrowed as it cut through some bushes that had grown together to form a thorny green wall. Whiteoak burst through it snapping his reins and hanging on with a grip strong enough to turn his hands white. His eyes were glued to the trail directly in front of him and his ears took in nothing but the growing roar of fire behind. The ground shook with the impact of hooves and when the stench of smoke became more powerful in his nostrils, the professor urged his horse to move faster.

And then he spotted one piece of wood that wasn't sprouting from the ground. Instead, it was a single plank with planed edges that had been exposed to the elements long enough to rot and droop down toward the trail. Most of the wooden surface was covered by leaves and branches that had snaked around it over time but when Whiteoak found that first piece of lumber, he spotted another.

"Whoa!" Whiteoak shouted as he pulled back on his reins.

"Are you out of your damn mind?" Corey shouted.

"There's something . . . *Jesus Christ!*"

Whiteoak had been heading toward a patch of open sky and sunshine that could be seen through a break in the trees hanging overhead like a ceiling. Every instinct in him told him to get to that light as quickly as possible. His nose could already smell air that wasn't tainted by smoke and his mind raced with all the possible reasons for those flames to have sprouted. Thanks to the professor's hungry senses and racing thoughts, he was able to spot the end of the trail no more than five or six yards ahead of him.

For a horse that was panicked by the scent of smoke and ridden by a man who was equally disturbed, ten yards wasn't a long way to travel. Penelope might have covered that distance in less than a few seconds and skidded right over the steep drop-off to whatever grisly fate awaited below. Instead, she was snapped from her tunnel vision by the sharp pull of leather straps in the guiding hands of her rider.

Whiteoak's entire body was filled with the

sensation of falling even though he'd managed to bring his horse to a stop several inches shy of doing so. He steered the mare to the right, clearing some space for Corey to emerge from the trees and look at the drop-off for himself.

"Watch yourself," Whiteoak warned sharply.

Corey looked toward the sound of Whiteoak's voice as his horse reflexively veered to avoid the steep incline. Once he got a look at the drop-off, Corey shifted his weight to keep from falling from his saddle while his horse slowed to a stop.

Behind the two men, the fire still ate away the trees and bushes encasing the trail. Now that there was some distance between him and the fire, Whiteoak could see that it wasn't so much of an inferno as it was a healthy blaze. The flames were already dwindling and wouldn't pose much of a threat after a short while.

"Looks like the trees have enough moisture in them to prevent the fire from spreading," Whiteoak said.

Still breathing heavily, his face covered in black smudges, Corey said, "I suppose you saw that in the couple of seconds it took for us to clear out of that death trap?"

"No. That's something I'm only now

noticing. You're right about the death trap, though. It's clear that we were meant to be panicked by the flames and driven over the edge of that cliff," the professor explained as he pointed toward the drop-off.

Like the fire, the incline wasn't a lot to look at once their hearts had stopped hammering against their ribs. While it was far from a cliff, the incline was more than steep enough to cause a horse to break its legs if it slid over the side in a rush. A man could very well find himself in a dire predicament if he wasn't careful. The slope was solid rock covered in a thin layer of ivy and thorny growth. At the bottom were several large boulders that could easily split the skulls of man or beast.

"I happened to spot a trellis of some kind," Whiteoak explained.

Still catching his breath, Corey gulped, "A trellis?"

"Yes. A structure upon which several branches had either grown or were attached somehow. Presumably, it was to create the distressingly cramped space or some sort of tunnel."

"Between that damn fire and the smoke, we're lucky to have made it out. That trellis would've led us straight to our deaths!"

Beaming proudly, Whiteoak nodded and

said, "Exactly! A very impressive use of the natural surroundings. Now, if only I could figure out what kind of device was used to start the fire. I'm guessing it was some sort of spring-loaded trap that was set off when we passed over a triggering mechanism of some kind."

"Like a torch?"

"Probably, but something a bit more complex I would imagine."

"It was a torch," Corey said as he climbed down from his horse and thumbed back the hammer of his pistol. "A torch thrown by some little asshole who looks like a rat."

Whiteoak craned his neck to look back at the trees where more smoke was drifting out than fire. He stood up in his stirrups for a better look and immediately sat back down again. "Someone's coming. He's got a rifle!"

"Let me guess, he's a short little prick who looks like a rat."

"Well . . . yes."

Both men opened fire on the trees, sending chunks of bark and clumps of dirt flying to create almost as much of a cloud as the smoke that was still seeping out from the trail they'd left behind. The skinny figure Whiteoak had spotted was nowhere to be found. He wondered if one of their bullets had found its mark before the distinct crack of a Winchester split the air. Hot lead whipped past Whiteoak's head. It wasn't close enough to spill any blood, but it did a good job of taking the fight out of him.

"We've got to move!" Whiteoak said.

"That's what I wanted to do when the fire was burning," Corey replied. "Now, it's too late."

Another rifle shot was fired, sending a round at Corey this time. Corey dropped to the ground while his pistol spat its last rounds into the nearby trees. As soon as his cylinder was emptied, he rolled toward a rock and began plucking fresh bullets from his belt.

Whiteoak rode along the edge of the drop-off for several paces. As much as he wanted to keep going, he stopped once Penelope was out of immediate danger and climbed down from his saddle. "Corey! Hurry up and get over here! I'll cover you." Once that was said, Whiteoak opened fire on anything that wasn't his partner.

Corey moved quickly, his feet deftly avoiding the edge of the drop-off while his eyes avoided looking at the rocks below. Since he was no longer looking at the trees, he finished reloading his pistol using fresh rounds from his gun belt.

The Winchester fired a few more rounds at them. The first few sailed wide and high, but the ones following that slowly began to hone in on their target. Despite all his squinting efforts, Whiteoak couldn't make out more than a few indistinct shapes in the trees. Rather than strain his eyes any further, he waited for the flash from a muzzle and aimed at that. After his third shot, the Winchester fell silent.

"I think I got one of them!" Whiteoak proudly announced.

"You want a party in your honor?" Corey huffed. "Just keep moving. There ain't enough room on this ledge for me to get around you."

Whiteoak put his back to the trees and led his horse away. The ground beneath his feet sloped gently toward the ledge and his boots skidded a bit upon loose gravel and dirt. It took most of his faculties to keep from tripping as he struggled to hasten his steps. "I think this path widens up ahead," he told Corey.

"Let's just get there."

"The shooting's stopped."

"That's just because they're circling around to cut us off," Corey said.

"How do you know?"

"Because that's what makes the most sense."

Whiteoak wanted to argue on the side of optimism but couldn't dredge up enough enthusiasm. "All right," he said. "I say we run straight at them. It'll rattle those bush-whackers enough that they probably won't be able to shoot straight."

"Probably?"

"Any better suggestions?"

"Yeah. We stop running before we get killed."

"What kind of suggestion is that?" Whiteoak bellowed. Then he saw what Corey had seen. Two men, covered in dirt, standing with rifles pointed squarely at Whiteoak's and Corey's heads.

"Ah," the professor said as he holstered his pistol and lifted his hands above his head. "Perhaps that suggestion has some merit after all."

CHAPTER THIRTY-FIVE

Even after being captured, Whiteoak still managed to stay in his saddle. His wrists were tied together behind his back and his guns had been taken from him but at least he still had Penelope. Corey was nearby as well. So near, in fact, that Whiteoak could hear every word that his partner grunted under his breath.

"Goddamn yellow-bellied son of a bitch," Corey rasped.

"Pardon me?"

"We still could've fought."

"It was your suggestion to surrender," Whiteoak reminded him.

"Sure, but only after it was too late to do anything else. You were the one who turned tail and ran!"

Turning to get a look over one shoulder, Whiteoak said, "This isn't nearly as bad as it seems."

"Oh, isn't it?" Corey replied. His hands

were tied as well and he'd been placed on Penelope's back behind Whiteoak while his own horse was being led by one of his captors. While the professor was sitting in his familiar saddle, Cory had the added task of trying to keep his balance on the mare's back end without the use of his hands or any proper gear. "Why don't you tell me how all of this was part of some harebrained plan?"

"Well, not all of it. A good deal of it fell together for anyone with a finely-honed set of insight, intuition and instincts."

"Can one of you boys just shoot me now and get it over with?"

The men Corey saw as he turned his head from side to side were the same ones who'd cut him and Whiteoak off before they could make good on their escape. Their faces were caked in dirt and their long whiskers contained a sampling of everything that was strewn across the nearby ground. They wore simple clothes made from pieces of heavy fabric that had been stitched together crudely from several other sets of clothes. The only things that didn't look like they would rot off of them were the weapons they carried.

Besides the rifles in their hands, all of the dirty men wore multiple gun belts slung around their waists and shoulders. At first glance, several smaller pistols could be seen tucked under their waistbands. There were two of them. One stayed close to Corey and Whiteoak while another kept his distance where he could watch prisoners and take a clear shot at them if they stepped out of line. None of them seemed inclined to oblige Corey's morbid request.

Dropping his voice to a harsh whisper, Corey asked, "Do any of these men look familiar to you?"

"We had breakfast with them just the other day. Remember they were in the hotel restaurant?"

"I saw plenty of folks over the last few days," Corey muttered. "Can't remember them all."

"Be that as it may, I'd wager these men are also the ones we'd been hoping to find out here in all this filth and treacherous terrain."

"They're called mountains, idiot. And what makes you think these men aren't just a bunch of robbers looking to clean us out and leave us for dead?"

"Because that section of trail that was set alight was a trap, as I've already explained."

Corey sighed, knowing his partner wouldn't need any prodding to continue with his lecture.

"The boards I spotted," Whiteoak said, "formed a crude wall or trellis meant to create the tunnel in which we found ourselves. The fire that was started was no doubt set to steer down that tunnel as hastily as possible so we'd stumble over that steep ledge where we would presumably break our necks or other important body parts in the fall."

Corey glanced around until he spotted one of the dirty faces. When he'd scouted back along the trail earlier, it was that grimy face that he'd seen in the flickering light of a torch the other man had been holding. A smile had shown through the mud caked around that man's face as he touched the flaming end of his torch to a pile of dry kindling. The fire burst to life and spread along a path from the man toward Corey's end of the trail. At the time, he wasn't in any condition to stop and think why those events had happened or what was behind them. Whiteoak, on the other hand, didn't do anything but think about every little thing. The only thing worse than the professor's incessant chin wagging was when he was right. Because of that, Corey kept his mouth shut as all of the things Whiteoak were saying made more and more sense.

"And," the professor continued, unaware that most of his audience was barely paying him any mind, "if they were robbers, they would have robbed us, wouldn't they? At the very least, they would have tried to kill us. Instead, they proceed through an elaborate ruse to herd us in a certain direction so that if we weren't killed, we'd certainly ride away as quickly as possible."

"Do you ever shut up?" Corey grunted, even though he already knew the answer to his question.

"I was about to ask the same thing," said one of the men from behind Penelope. He was a bit shorter than Corey and had dark hair that was cut an inch or so higher than shoulder length. The ends of his shaggy mane were curled a bit and every strand on top of his head was so greasy that it looked as if he'd just come in from the rain. A spotty beard covered a good portion of his face while leaving irregular patches bare. Set above a crooked nose was a pair of squinting eyes making him look as though he was trying to translate a foreign language. In his hands was the same Winchester that had been pointed at Whiteoak and Corey to convince them to come along with him.

"I'm right, though," Whiteoak said as he twisted around for a better look at the fellow with the greasy hair. "Aren't I?"

"In figuring out that was a trap back there?" the greasy man asked.

"Yes."

"Sure you was right. Real stroke of brilliance to guess that much after the trap's been sprung and you already been caught in it."

Corey laughed. "He's got you there, Henry."

"So he does," Whiteoak conceded. "But if I hadn't figured it out beforehand, we would have both been in much worse condition after riding over the edge of that cliff."

The stranger who rode behind the prisoners but not as far back as his greasy partner was a large man with a round head covered in a much thicker set of whiskers than the greasy fellow's. His bulbous nose gave his face a more amicable appearance and his voice had something of a lazy wheezing quality when he said, "One, that weren't no cliff. If'n you thought that was a cliff, then you ain't been very high up in these mountains."

After a short stretch of silence, Whiteoak asked, "What's two?"

"Huh?" the bigger fellow asked.

"You began your last statement with the

word one, so there must be a two. What is it?"

"Oh yeah," the larger man said as he calmly drew a pistol from his holster. "Two, shut yer damn mouth."

Whiteoak stayed quiet.

CHAPTER THIRTY-SIX

They rode for just under an hour. By White-oak's estimation, they didn't travel a long distance but the ground they covered was rocky and treacherous. Before long, he was shown plenty of examples of what his scruffy hosts truly meant when they referred to a cliff. Some of the drop-offs were so steep that the simple act of looking over them put a swirl in the professor's stomach. Whenever a strong wind blew, Whiteoak held on to Penelope's back with every asset at his disposal.

The trail eventually curved away from the perilous edge, but not for very long before it came to an end. Nestled in between a rock wall and a thick stand of trees was a trio of log cabins. The largest of the three was a modest dwelling with a brick chimney supporting one end. There was a small porch attached to that cabin where an old man sat upon a chair with his feet propped on the rail in front of him. Rocking back on the rear legs of his chair, the old man whittled a stick down to a point with a blade that was nearly as wide as his arm.

"You made good time," the old man said.

"Didn't take long to round 'em up," the fellow with the round face replied. "And they didn't put up much of a fight, neither."

Whiteoak wanted to say something to that, but managed to hold his tongue. The effort it took, however, was great enough for Corey to feel it.

The old man eased his chair down to all four legs and then stood up to give his skinny appendages a stretch. Despite looking thin enough to be blown over by the breeze created by an opening door, he carried himself with a quiet confidence of someone who'd learned a thing or two in the years it had taken to acquire so many wrinkles on his face. Approaching the horses with a good amount of steam in his stride, the old man scratched at the bristly gray whiskers sprouting from his chin and smiled up at Whiteoak. "You're a finely dressed fella."

"Why, thank you," Whiteoak replied.

"What brings you up into these here mountains?"

"They're after the still, Chuck," said the

man with the greasy hair. He and the larger rider were both dismounting their horses so they could approach Penelope and drag both men off of her back.

The old man regarded the men in front of him as he might study a neighbor approaching his house for the first time. "You know about my still?" Chuck asked.

"We heard of it," Corey said. "Plenty of folks heard about it. Just like the rest of them folks, though, we don't have the faintest notion as to where it may be."

Whiteoak closed his eyes and pulled in a deep breath. "It's close," he said. "I can smell the chemicals that have been cooking." Opening his eyes, he added, "But there's been no cooking today."

"Where'd you find these two, Owen?" Chuck asked.

"Sam's been tracking them since they left Westchester," the big fellow replied. "They left the Square Mountain Trail and came this way."

"Through the tinder pass?" Chuck asked with a smirk.

"Yep. Damn near got their asses burnt off too."

"I take it you had to scrape them off the rocks."

"Nope."

315

Chuck's brushy eyebrows went up a bit. "No?"

"They stopped short before going over the ledge. That's where we found 'em."

Nodding slowly, Chuck approached Corey and said, "I'd guess it was you who averted that disaster."

"If it was up to me," Corey replied, "we wouldn't have been anywhere near that spot."

Whiteoak spat out a grunting laugh. "He tends to exaggerate. He also gets angry when I prove to him how often it is that I'm right."

"Is that so?" Chuck mused.

Straightening his posture as if he was accepting a medal, Whiteoak said, "It is, indeed. We've come a long way to pay you this visit, sir. Might I ask for a look at the operation you're running here?"

Sam raked his fingers through his greasy hair before drawing the pistol tucked under his belt. "Only thing you're about to see," he said while pointing the gun's barrel at Whiteoak's head, "is the face of God."

"Hold up, now," Chuck said.

Those three simple words were enough to dim the murderous fire in Sam's eyes and lower the pistol in his hand. A certain degree of calm drifted through the air, such as what one might feel after the passing of a bank of storm clouds. Owen marked the occasion by spitting on the ground and rubbing the wet spot into the dirt with the toe of his boot.

Chuck narrowed his eyes as if he could glimpse the juices flowing beneath Whiteoak's skin. "You're a smart one."

"And how astute of you to notice," Whiteoak beamed.

"Come with me and have a drink. Owen, cut his hands loose."

"Does that mean you're not going to shoot them?" Sam asked in a disappointed tone.

Chuck shrugged and turned to amble toward the nearest cabin. "Not right now, anyways."

CHAPTER THIRTY-SEVEN

"Do you know how many men have tried to find me?" Chuck asked as he stepped inside the little cabin.

On the outside, the cabin wasn't much more than a stack of old logs held together by mud and moss. The chimney was well built, but didn't seem strong enough to support the rest of the structure attached to it. Its porch was made from old lumber supported by studs sunken into the ground and felt as solid as the mountain upon which it had been built.

Inside, the cabin was something else entirely. A clean floor was partly covered by a rug splayed in front of a crackling fireplace and a heavy old trunk used for storing rifles. A kitchen area was immaculately kept and every piece of furniture was nicely polished. The air smelled of burnt coffee and tobacco, both of which were sampled by the thin old man who stepped over to the kitchen table.

Chuck picked up a smoking pipe that had been waiting for him there and then reached out for a steaming mug.

"I would imagine there have been quite a few who've tried to find you," Whiteoak said. "As well as a few who've succeeded."

"What makes you think that?"

"Because you're out to make a profit and a man can't do that without attracting a customer or two."

As the old man sipped his coffee, he walked around the kitchen table. With every step, his frame became more rigid and strong. Before he made it all the way around, he barely seemed like the frail scarecrow who'd first greeted the group of horses. Now, he looked like someone who wouldn't hesitate to use the Army model Colt at his side. "You're a businessman too."

"Naturally."

Looking Whiteoak up and down, the old man said, "Chemist, I'd reckon. Probably a snake oil salesman, judging by them fancy clothes. A real man of science don't dress like such a dandy."

"If you like these old rags," Whiteoak said while shooting his cuffs, "then you should see my Sunday best."

"What do you call yourself?"

After a short bit of contemplation, the

professor replied, "Phantasmagorical. I don't know if that's a real word, but one of my first customers referred to me as such and I liked the sound of it. There's also visionary. I like that one too."

Chuck's face turned to a hard scowl.

"Professor Henry Whiteoak, at your service. You'd be one of the storied Menlo family?"

"I'm Chuck Menlo, all right. Do I really want to know the stories you've heard about me?"

"They're mostly hot ash on the wind, but that only means there's a fire to be found. And that fire," Whiteoak added as he pulled one of the chairs out from the table and sat down, "is why I'm here."

Chuck took a seat at the opposite end of the table. "Go on."

"I've been working the Square Mountain Trail for a short bit of time now, selling tonics and medicines of all kind."

"Along with plenty of laudanum, I'm sure."

Whiteoak gave him half a nod. "Some medicines sell better than others. I'm not the only salesman to have passed through here over the last several months and nearly every last one that I've encountered have had something to say about the Menlo clan

320

living in the mountains."

Leaning forward to place his pistol on the table in front of him, Chuck growled, "And what did they have to say?"

"I'm sure I don't have to tell you."

"Oh, really?"

"You must already know," Whiteoak said, deftly ignoring the menace in Chuck's voice. "Any man with a reputation as fearsome and mysterious as yours must have gone through a lot of trouble to build it. From what I've already seen, I would say that your reasons for doing so are twofold. First, to draw customers to the wares you have for sale and second, to discourage unwanted visitors."

"Seems that second reason didn't work out too well," Chuck pointed out.

"Only because I am a kindred spirit, good sir, and refuse to be deterred like the common folk."

"Are you, now?"

"Why yes! And I am also a fellow salesman."

Chuck drew a hunting knife from a scabbard hanging from his belt and used the nine-inch blade to pick a bit of dirt from beneath one of his fingernails. "You truly think I'm some goddamn salesman?"

"Not just some salesman. An extraordi-

321

nary salesmen."

"You don't have the faintest idea what you're saying."

"And I suppose you're not brewing a healing tonic right here on these very premises?" After studying Chuck's face for less than three seconds, Whiteoak snapped his fingers and declared, "A-ha! I knew it!"

"I brew my own shine, if that's what you mean."

"No manner of liquor requires the chemicals I smelled outside. I've heard from some very reputable sources that you are concocting a mixture that is a true miracle cure. Something like that could be worth several fortunes."

"And who are your reputable sources?" Chuck asked.

"Jacob Parsons."

The faintest amount of surprise flickered across Chuck's face. "And here I thought I might have to knock you around some before you told me that. Who else?"

"I'm a man in the trade," Whiteoak said as he leaned back and swung his legs up to rest his feet on the edge of the table. "It's in my best interests to listen for anything that might point me in the direction of what folks want or who else might be providing for them. Previously, I spent some time in

Kansas. I had to leave under rather extreme circumstances, which meant I had to lay low. While in that position, gleaning information from rumors and gossip was a good way to stay alive without drawing attention."

"Yeah," Chuck grunted. "I know."

"I'll bet you do. That's why you've holed up all the way out here with traps and the high ground working to your advantage."

"You callin' me a coward?"

"Not in the slightest," Whiteoak said with a smile. "You've been playing your game splendidly. I just want to do my part."

"Which is?"

"Why don't you tell me? After all, there must be a reason why you've kept me alive this long."

Chuck tightened his grip on his knife and scratched the tip of its blade against the table. "You'd best hope there is."

CHAPTER THIRTY-EIGHT

After a few minutes inside the cabin, White-oak and Chuck Menlo stepped outside. Corey watched from where he sat with his back against a post and his arms tied behind it. His body ached from the ride, the awkward position in which he sat, and the stray punches he'd been given by the men who'd tied him up. Mostly, the punches had come from Sam.

Like most men who were shorter than those around him, Sam lived to prove that he could look down on them all. It was a strange and hopeless battle which left those short men angry and flustered. Hoping to goad Sam into making a mistake, Corey taunted and teased Sam while he was being led away from the horses. Sam had been all too willing to swallow the bait and laid into Corey pretty good. As Sam was about to make a move that would allow Corey to snatch a gun away from him, Owen had stepped in to put a stop to it. The big man's fist thumped first into Corey's gut and then into Sam's, leaving both men gasping for their next breath.

"Don't be stupid," Owen warned.

The fight was over and no amount of barbed comments from Corey was going to start it again. Just when he was about to run out of steam, Corey heard the cabin's door open and Chuck and Whiteoak emerged. Instead of being led outside like a dog on a leash, the professor strode onto the porch with a mug of coffee in his hand and an easy smile on his face.

"What did you do?" Corey snarled.

Whiteoak replied by raising his coffee in a silent toast.

Corey scrambled to get his feet under him, but was tied too tightly to the post to do any more than kick up a bunch of dust. "What did you tell him?"

Chuck stepped onto the porch as well, talking to Whiteoak in a casual tone that was difficult for Corey to hear. When the old man placed a friendly hand on Whiteoak's shoulder, Corey felt enough rage to rip the post against his back completely from the ground.

There were a few heavy footsteps behind

Corey and then a dull thump against his head.

"Was that truly necessary?" Whiteoak asked.

Corey slumped sideways against the post. The only thing keeping him from laying on the ground was the rope binding his wrists. Blood trickled from the fresh scalp wound and a string of drool hung from one corner of his mouth.

"He'll be fine," Chuck said dismissively. "See to it, Sam."

"If you want him to be fine," Owen said as he stood his ground behind Corey, "then you should let me watch him."

"Just keep him breathing for now. When he wakes up, make him tell you anything he can about this dandy partner of his."

"If you're looking for insults about the way I talk and dress," Whiteoak said cheerily, "then Corey's the man to ask."

Chuck slapped his hand onto the professor's shoulder with decidedly more force than he had before. "I'll be after anything and everything he wants to tell me. And if he tells me enough that don't line up with what you tell me, you're both dead."

"I wouldn't worry about that, my good man."

Showing no reaction to Whiteoak's soothing voice or disarming nature, Chuck added, "And I don't mean just dead. I mean screaming, crying, begging, wriggling around in pain for a few hours first. Then dead. Got me?"

Whiteoak didn't bother trying to gussy up his words when a simple nod and, "Yes, sir" was more than enough to get the job done.

"Good. Now let's give you a look at that still." Chuck shoved Whiteoak ahead, keeping the professor in front of him as they both made their way to one of the smaller cabins. "You see, I've heard a few things about you as well."

"Really?"

"Yep. Professor Henry Whiteoak, the medicine man from Kansas, Leadville, even as far south as New Orleans."

"I wouldn't believe everything you heard about my time in Leadville," Whiteoak said. "Much of that has become wildly overblown."

"More than a few men I trust say you know your way around a tonic," Chuck said. "You can brew up a few drops of chemical water that'll put a man flat on his back for hours at a time. Even sniffing the cork in a bottle of your potion can set a man's head to spinning."

"Who . . . uhhh . . . told you about that?"

"Doesn't matter. What does matter is this." Having arrived at the smaller cabin, Chuck stepped forward to open its front door. Inside was a small maze of copper tubing, wooden racks, funnels, steaming barrels and crates stacked up to within a few inches of the ceiling. The scent of burning chemicals was enough to drop a mule. Chuck shoved Whiteoak through the doorway and watched him carefully.

Whiteoak staggered for a step or two before digging into one of his pockets for a small white handkerchief. Placing the clean linen over his mouth and nose, Whiteoak coughed a few times before lowering the handkerchief and waving it in front of his face. "This is an impressive setup, Chuck. Although I might have some suggestions regarding proper ventilation."

"Sam and Owen can barely stand it in here. Fumes get to 'em."

"Well they're not chemists, are they?"

"No. They're not. I brought you in here to see how well you know your way around this sort of equipment and if you're any better than they are."

Tucking the kerchief back into his pocket, Whiteoak said, "I suppose by standing in here for this long is a way to pass your first test. Do you trust that I've brewed more than my share of chemicals now?"

"Yep. You know what they say about rumors, Henry. They can paint an unfair picture. I had to be certain you were truly the chemist that I heard you were."

"What's the next test? Want me to mix up something to clear up that skin condition of yours?"

Touching a hand to the withered patch covering most of his right cheek, the old man replied, "No. I want you to keep my miracle cure tonic from killing anyone."

Whiteoak grinned. "That's the real trick, isn't it?"

Chuck wasn't grinning when he said, "I killed a dozen men in the Dakota territories with my first batch and even the folks who knew about it were begging for more. Just imagine if I could keep a few of them from dying off. They'd sign over everything they own for another taste."

"What, exactly, are you curing?"

"Anything. Nothing. It don't make a damn bit of difference just so long as they pay for another sip. I figure if'n I keep them from dyin' right away, they'll sell their mommas, daughters and souls to me just to keep the tonic comin'. That kind of desperation," Chuck said with a glint in his eye, "is a beautiful thing."

Chapter Thirty-Nine

Once he'd been allowed to see the setup used to brew the Menlos' tonic, Whiteoak wasn't allowed to see much else. The next couple of hours were filled with glass tubes containing noxious liquids and a still that spat foul steam whenever it was heated. The heating fire would turn different colors whenever some of the chemical sprayed or dripped down into it. Professor Whiteoak rolled up his sleeves to mix the different ingredients while breathing through a bandanna he'd tied around the lower portion of his face to cover his mouth and nose. Chuck Menlo stood nearby, always watchful but never within arm's reach.

"I'm surprised you're allowing me to work so freely," Whiteoak said.

"Why?"

"Because this is your still, your product. A man's product is his livelihood."

Chuck scratched his bristly chin. "I know

this still better than I know the faces of my kin. I'll know the instant you do a thing to her that might hurt her. As for my product, I can mix up more of it any time I please."

"Naturally," Whiteoak said as he scooped out some yellow powder from one of the many jars lining a shelf built into one of the cabin's walls.

"That bein' said," Chuck added, "if'n I see you trying to ruin what I made, I'll chop off yer hands and make you watch 'em burn in that there fire."

The flames were the colors one might expect from any fire, but Whiteoak regarded them with extra interest. He swallowed hard and forced a smile onto his face as he carefully sprinkled some of the yellow powder into a sample of tonic in front of him. "Yes, well no need for that."

"Yeah?"

"I think I've discovered what made your mixture so embracing."

Chuck had been leaning casually against the doorframe, but took a half-step forward. "What's that supposed to mean?"

"Embracing," Whiteoak repeated. "Similar to what you mentioned earlier about how some customers will do anything to get another taste. Certain chemicals embrace a person, takes hold of them, and makes it

331

next to impossible for them to give it up. You can commonly see such a thing where liquor is concerned but when you start dealing with chemicals like laudanum and opium or even peyote, people can be embraced to an even greater extent."

"Good Lord almighty," Chuck growled. "Do you always use twenty words when three will do?"

"How about these words? Your tonic's better."

"Better?"

"Yes," Whiteoak declared. "Thanks to me, of course. By thinning out some of the compounds you already use, I've managed to decrease the potential dangers that might be faced by anyone who ingests this tonic of yours."

"What about the other effects? That tonic ain't no good to me if it's diluted down to practically nothing."

"Don't worry about that. Your customers should still see a good amount of delirium and euphoria after a few sips."

"A good amount?"

"Yes. That was the point, right? To decrease the tonic's potential dangers while retaining the more desirable side effects?"

Stalking forward with his hand resting upon the grip of his pistol, Chuck said,

"Don't talk to me like I got sand in my head. Tell me how risky it still is and how much of the original formula is preserved. I want percentages."

"That's hard to say without proper testing," Whiteoak explained. "I'd say the risk to your customers has dropped by at least thirty percent, however."

"To what end?"

The proud gleam in Whiteoak's eye faded as his hopeful expression drooped into something more serious and businesslike. "To the end of not killing your customers."

"I don't give a wet pig's ass about my customers just so long as they live long enough to pay me more than once."

"Men in our line of work thrive on our reputations. What will become of your reputation once people die after they drink your tonics?"

"Does anyone give a shit when a drunk drinks himself into a hole in the ground? Does anyone think twice when they see a couple of Chinese dragging a corpse from one of their opium dens?"

"I suppose not."

"And the people who die will only do it after they've paid me. So long as they pay me more than once, I can sleep fine with it."

"That's not the typical view of a healer," Whiteoak pointed out.

Surging forward a couple of steps, Chuck was able to root Whiteoak to his spot using nothing more than the ferocity in his glare when he said, "We ain't healers. We're salesmen. There's a hell of a difference between the two. You know what the difference is between a town's drunk and some rich bastard smoking opium through a brass pipe?"

"The size of their fortunes?"

"Exactly! You see? We ain't so different, you and I. Both of us are in the same business and both of us want to do better than we have been. You got your wagon and I've got my still. We both brew something to sell that puts a smile on our customers' faces. The fact that it kills them ain't important. Whiskey can kill a man. So can bullets, but that don't stop the distillers and gunsmiths from making 'em."

Whiteoak reluctantly nodded.

"You know what I hear when folks drink my tonic?"

"What?" the professor asked.

"I hear that them same folks have been healed. They been healed of everything from a sniffle to consumption. They feel like they could win a fistfight with the devil himself!"

"And what about after?" Whiteoak asked cautiously.

"After," Chuck replied, "when it wears off . . . they want more. They want to feel that same thing again and nobody gives a shit whether the strength they felt before was real or not. They just want more." Smirking and studying Whiteoak through narrowed eyes, Chuck added, "You know that look in another man's eyes. That look that tells you they're ready to pay any price for what you got."

"Yes. I do."

"Imagine that look with double the fire. Triple the intent! They're feeling better than any woman could ever make them feel and it's because of that," Chuck said while stabbing a finger at the barrel that collected liquid from the still. "They feel better. When you think about the never-ending string of horse shit that all of us gotta deal with day in and out, is that kind of relief such a bad thing?"

"Not at all."

"Hell, some of them miserable bastards are such sorrowful messes that they don't even mind dyin' if they can feel that good before the reaper comes!"

"That is true, sir."

"So get to work," Chuck said enthusiastically, "and we'll both be rich men."

CHAPTER FORTY

When the sun dipped too low to cast its light upon the mountains, a chill seeped into the air that soaked all the way down to the rocks in the soil. The wind now had sharp teeth that gnawed through clothing and flesh to touch the blood inside a man's veins. The Menlos hardly seemed to notice the shift in the air and Whiteoak did his best to keep his teeth from chattering as he was led away from the still and to the cabin directly beside it.

Looking inside once the door was open, Whiteoak asked, "Where's Corey? If he's been harmed . . ."

"Don't get your britches in a twist," Owen said. "He's tucked in with the horses over there."

"Then that's where I wish to go."

"Suit yourself."

The grip on Whiteoak's shoulder tightened and the professor was roughly pointed

337

toward the small stable. Even though its walls looked less sturdy than the leaning slips of paper that formed a house of cards, it only gave the slightest creak as another powerful gust blew in from the north. Inside the stable, at least one lantern was lit because a trickle of light could be seen through the cracks in the wall. Large shapes blocked the light every now and then, moving even more once the smallest door was yanked open.

"Here you go," Owen said while shoving Whiteoak into the stable. "Rest up. We'll see you in the morning."

"What time will breakfast be served?" Whiteoak hollered after he'd staggered forward a couple of steps.

Owen slammed the door shut.

There wasn't much to see inside the stable. Four horses stood in stalls lining one side of the enclosed space and two more occupied the stalls along the opposite wall. That left two stalls open, one of which proved to be occupied as well. Corey grabbed hold of the low dividing wall between stalls and used it to haul himself up to his feet. "Looks like they got sick of your mouth, huh?" he said.

"Hardly," Whiteoak replied. "It was my idea that I share accommodations with my partner." In a whisper, he added, "I think they trust me enough to give us the leeway needed to make an escape. All we need to do is wait for our moment and . . ."

The professor stopped talking when he heard the metallic clang of a hammer striking the flat back of a nail. One after another, the little spikes were driven home, each one of them poking through the wood surrounding the door through which Whiteoak had made his undignified entrance.

The last nail was being driven home as Whiteoak approached the door and pounded on it. "That is not a wise idea! What if there's a fire?"

"Then I might let you out," Owen said through the door.

"What if I have to . . . use the outhouse?"

After a few seconds, a single pistol shot exploded through the old wood of the door. Splinters flew through the air, joining the dust kicked up by Whiteoak's feet as he hurried backward away from that side of the stable.

"Here," Owen said as he inserted the barrel of his pistol through the bullet hole. "You can piss through that. Happy?"

"Yes," Whiteoak squeaked. "Quite."

"Good. See ya in the mornin'."

Turning away from the door, Whiteoak

waved wildly at the freshly made hole and said, "Those men are insane!"

"I'll be damned," Corey said. "You really are smart."

"For your information, I could've had much better lodgings for the night if I hadn't insisted on checking in on you."

"And why would you do that? Seems to me that we don't have much time left on this earth. Might as well get a good night's sleep while you still can."

Whiteoak approached the stall where Corey had been sitting. When he attempted to move closer to his partner, Corey shot him a look that was almost as scathing as the hot lead that had punctured the door not so long ago. Rather than try to douse that fire just yet, Whiteoak stepped into another empty stall and pressed his back against the wall. "I may have made a mistake in coming here," he said while sliding down to a seated position.

"And once again the mighty professor proves his worth!"

"Enough, already. I get it."

The stable fell silent.

Soon, the horses in with the two men became restless and began scraping at the ground with their hooves. Once they found a more comfortable spot in which to stand, however, they settled down once again.

"Are you all right?" Whiteoak asked tentatively.

"Yeah," Corey grunted. "Just got a little knocked around is all. Nothin' I ain't used to after riding with you for this long."

"It hasn't been too long."

"I know, which makes it even more sad how I've gotten used to being knocked around while in your company."

Whiteoak chuckled at that, his laughter soon to be muffled when he lowered his head to rest upon his arms which were now crossed over his bent knees. Soon, Corey joined him as a tired laugh escaped from his cold body as he dropped back down to a seated position.

"Honestly, though," Whiteoak said. "These men are insane."

"Not Owen. He seems like a decent enough fella. And Sam too. He may be an asshole, but he's not crazy."

"Chuck Menlo is out of his mind. Not in the sense of a babbling lunatic, but he honestly doesn't care about leaving a trail of dead bodies in his wake."

"There's plenty of killers like that around, Henry. Or have you forgotten?"

"I haven't forgotten," Whiteoak sighed. "Those killers are crazy as well. Some men have good reason to kill. Others have justifications that make at least some kind of sense. Chuck isn't either of those. He's the worst kind of killer. He kills the way another man might scratch an itch or slam a door instead of easing it closed."

"What, exactly, were you hoping to find?"

"Here, you mean?"

"Yes, goddammit," Corey snapped. "When you came all this way and dragged me along, what the hell else did you expect to find? Sane men don't usually live out in the mountains brewing miracle toxins."

"I thought I could find some bit of profit," Whiteoak said. "Like I explained on the way here."

"And you didn't think it'd be guarded?"

"That's something we could handle. Another job, another payday, another bunch of animals bearing guns who the world is better off without."

"And you figured on using me as cannon fodder."

"Will you stop whining?" Whiteoak said. "It doesn't become you. If you were so opposed to the way I do things, you wouldn't have done them by my side for this long. Funny how you never seem to complain when I'm handing you your share of the money after one of these jobs."

After a heavy silence, Corey said, "I suppose not. You know what the problem is, Henry?"

"What?"

"You're too damn good at lying. After a while, it's hard to tell when you're making something up and when you ain't."

"Have I ever lied to you?"

"Yes," Corey said.

Whiteoak's head snapped up. "When?"

"A couple days into the first job we pulled together back in Arkansas."

"Ah, yes. I remember. Can I ask you something?"

"When have I ever been able to do anything to stop you from talking?" Corey chuckled.

"Do you think I'm a bad person?"

"Huh?"

"You heard me," Whiteoak replied.

"There's plenty that you and I have both done that keeps us from being considered good folk in the strictest sense of the word. I mean, it ain't like we can walk into church and sing a hymn knowing we're pure and good. But at the core of it . . . I've seen a whole lot worse. Why?"

"Because Chuck wants to tear lives apart for the sake of earning money," Whiteoak said. "He doesn't mind ending those lives just so long as he gets a few more dollars while he can. And when he told me about this, he talked as if to a kindred spirit."

"He was just tryin' to make you do whatever he wanted to do. It's an old trick, Henry. Convince a man you're both on the same side and it gets easier to point him in the right direction. We've both done that."

"I know, which is how I can spot it when that trick is being played on me. I don't think Chuck was feeding me a lie, though. He thinks we're both in the same business of peddling death and sorrow in a bottle." Whiteoak gazed forward, his brows furrowed in concentration. "That's not what I do. Is it?"

There was some rustling in the next stall as Corey got to his feet and leaned his elbows on the dividing wall. Looking over at the professor, he said, "I've seen you pull some underhanded tricks in the name of profit. I've also seen you rein yourself in when you could've gone a lot further. Tell me, with that business in Kansas, wouldn't it have been easier for you to feed all them folks a lethal poison so you could take all the time in the world to get at that bank?"

"Yes, but —"

"There you have it. You're a lot of things, but a cold-blooded killer ain't one of them.

You got a conscience. Might not be much of one, but it's in there somewhere."

A tired smile drifted across Whiteoak's face. "So I'm a good person?"

"That's a stretch. Now what do you say about getting us out of here?"

"We can't just leave. Not without putting that still out of commission. The tonic that Menlo is making is as deadly as it is desirable. Men will clamor for it even if they know it's harmful."

"That's nothing new. We can't exactly purge the world of things that are bad for you."

"No, but we can't leave something in it knowing how much death it can cause. At least, I can't."

"So, what do you propose?"

"All it will take," Whiteoak said, "is the right medicine for the job."

CHAPTER FORTY-ONE

None of the Menlos made their presence known until several hours later. When one of them did announce himself, it was with a couple hard thumps against the livery's door. "You ready to get to work?" Sam asked.

"Yes!" Whiteoak replied. Once the door was opened, the professor rolled up his sleeves and asked, "What took you so long?"

"Chuck wants to make sure you're in."

"If you mean in for the proposed job of —"

"Yes or no," Sam snapped.

"Oh, well, yes."

"Then get moving." Sam's pistol was in one hand and a torch was in the other. He stepped back out of Whiteoak's reach.

After a few steps toward the cabin containing the still, Whiteoak stopped and said, "I need something from my saddlebag."

It was well past midnight and the darkness was thicker than wet tar, which was how Chuck Menlo could remain hidden until he stepped closer to the single torch set outside the still's cabin. "Anything you need, I got in there," he said while hooking a thumb back toward the cabin.

"Nearly everything," Whiteoak corrected. "I was doing some thinking about the problem you've been having with your elixir."

"You mean tonic."

"Actually, an elixir contains more of an intoxicating effect and is meant to soothe while a tonic is meant to cure."

Wincing as though he'd just bitten into a rotten piece of chicken, Chuck said, "Is that what some fancy doctor told you or somethin'?"

"Actually, it's more of my own personal definition, but it's suitable for this occasion."

"What the hell do you need from your goddamn saddlebag?"

"A vial of sodium trichlorinate."

"Huh?"

"It's not readily available in this area, but it's basically a purifying agent. You see, the main problem with your elixir is that it's contaminated by elements that render it more dangerous to your customers."

"I boil that stuff within an inch of its life," Chuck said. "And then I strain it to keep the flakes of rust and such out. It's plenty clean."

"I'm referring to toxins that aren't so easily seen. Once they're gone, however, you will most definitely notice."

"Bullshit. Just do what I asked you to do."

"I'm trying, sir. Allow me to show you what I'm talking about."

Chuck let out a tired sigh and motioned to Sam. "Let him at his saddlebags. If he touches anything other than a vial, you shoot him through the skull."

Sam grinned and shoved Whiteoak around to the back side of the stable. There, both sets of saddlebags taken by the Menlo clan were piled like so much firewood.

"Mine are the bags with the fringe and finely crafted leatherworking around the edges," Whiteoak explained.

"Yeah," Sam grunted. "The ones that look like they belong on a lady's horse. That's what I figured." Taking hold of the fancy set of bags as though it was about to infect him, Sam dragged them a few inches away from the other set and dropped them beside Whiteoak's feet. "Get what you need and be quick about it."

The professor hunkered down and opened

the bags, only to be stopped by the sound of the cocking of a pistol's hammer.

"Slow," Sam warned.

"Of course. I know exactly what I'm after. See?" Whiteoak said as he eased his hand from the bag.

The vial Whiteoak held was as wide as his thumb and as long as his middle finger. It was about three quarters full and sealed with a cork stopper. Sam took it from him and said, "Step back."

Whiteoak raised his hands and stepped away from the bags. "Of course. As you can see, it's nothing harmful."

"You think I'm stupid? You're a medicine man. This could be poison."

"What would I gain from poisoning you? Your two compatriots would only kill me straight away."

Sam shrugged, taking obvious comfort from the weapon in his hand that could be fired by the twitch of a finger. "You're damn right about that."

"Besides," Whiteoak added, "that elixir your father is making is already poison. That's the problem, isn't it?"

"Chuck ain't my pa. He's my uncle."

"I haven't had much in the way of family for quite a while. Must be nice to be so close to yours."

Sam lifted the vial to his nose and sniffed the corked end. Surprise showed on his face and he smelled it again tentatively. "Don't seem like any poison I ever smelled." He grinned. "I know one way for you to show you ain't lyin'."

"Do you have a bible for me to swear upon?"

"Nah," Sam grunted as he stretched out his hand toward the professor. "Drink some."

"This isn't meant to be drank. At least, not without being diluted or mixed into something."

Sam's other hand inched forward slightly, enough to put the barrel of his pistol that much closer to its intended target. "Drink it, I says."

Whiteoak took the vial from Sam while stammering on the beginning of his next flippant comment. After removing the cork, he lifted it to the black sky as though that might help him examine the contents while he wiggled the glass container in a tight circular pattern.

"Drink," Sam insisted.

Bringing the vial closer to his lips, Whiteoak paused and then lowered it. "Honestly, this isn't some kind of sarsaparilla or sugar water. It's supposed to be —"

The barrel of Sam's gun tapped against Whiteoak's forehead as Sam glared directly into the other man's eyes.

"Fine," Whiteoak said. "I'll drink. But if I get sick and can't work, you'll be the one to blame." Since Sam didn't seem overly concerned about that, Whiteoak brought the vial to his lips and took a little sip.

"More," Sam said. "You barely got a taste."

"This is all I have. I can't waste it."

"You got more. I know because I looked in them saddlebags myself."

Whiteoak sighed and then drank a bit under a quarter of what was in the vial. "There," Whiteoak said through a forced nonchalance. "Harmless. Just like I told you."

After watching him for a few seconds, Sam backed up a step and shoved Whiteoak in the direction of the cabin where Chuck and his still were waiting. When they got there, Chuck was already inside the cabin and smoke was drifting up from the ventilation pipes attached to the ceiling.

"What's he got?" Chuck asked as he emerged from within the cabin.

"One of them vials we found when we searched the saddlebags," Sam reported.

"Did he try anything stupid?"

"Nah. Some whining was all."

Chuck nodded. "Seems you're pretty smart after all, medicine man."

"I prefer to be called Professor," Whiteoak said.

"You'd rather be called dead man?" Chuck asked.

"No."

"Good. Keep doing the right thing and minding what I say and we'll get along fine, Professor."

That small concession was enough to bring a grin to Whiteoak's face. After Sam handed over the vial, Chuck took it and swirled its contents around. He then looked to Sam and raised an expectant eyebrow.

"It ain't poison," Sam said. "Least it ain't the kind that'd kill you right away."

"You could say the same about whiskey, am I right?" Whiteoak said.

Chuck slapped the professor on the back and led him into the cabin. "You sure could! Sam, do me a favor and bring the rest of them vials from those saddlebags over to me. There's still plenty of work to be done."

CHAPTER FORTY-TWO

Hours ticked by.

Eventually, sunlight broke the darkness.

Through most of this time, there was little movement in the small Menlo compound. Eventually, however, the door to the still's cabin opened and Chuck stepped outside and stretched his legs. He remained outside, but close enough to see in through the door which he kept propped open using the heel of one foot. The old man rubbed his eyes, stretched his back and smoked most of one cigarette before going back inside where the professor diligently worked.

"I'm about ready to take you away from here," Chuck sighed.

Hunched over a small table that was blackened and stained by his efforts and experimentations, Whiteoak didn't even bother looking toward the older man when he replied, "Why would you do that?"

"Because I think you're wasting my time,

that's why!"

"You've watched me through every step of the process, haven't you?"

"Yes," Chuck said. "And if you think you're buying time for your friend to get the drop on one of my nephews, then you're dead wrong. From the looks of it, that slug ain't been doing anything but resting his eyes in that livery."

"My time has not been wasted," Whiteoak announced as he straightened his posture and held a glass jar in front of him. "I believe I've created a masterpiece."

Squinting at the liquid in the jar, Chuck approached cautiously. "What'd you do to my elixir?"

"Exactly what I promised. I've purified it of most, if not all, toxins and rendered it safer for consumption. Here," the professor added while offering the jar to Chuck. "Try it and see for yourself."

"You think I'm an idiot? Shut up and take a drink."

"What?"

"Go on and test that almighty concoction of yours," Chuck demanded.

Whiteoak chuckled once and held the jar up to the light of one of the lanterns hanging from one of the cabin's beams. "This is hardly my concoction. You are the man who invented it. I merely perfected it."

"And you've also been adding to it and mixing it into something else. Take a drink."

"Must we do this every time?"

"Yeah."

Seeing he wasn't making any progress, Whiteoak raised the jar in a silent toast and took a sip. Smacking his lips, he said, "Quite good, although it could use a bit more fermentation."

"How do you feel?"

"Slightly lightheaded. Perhaps a bit dizzy, but nothing more than I would've gotten from a few shots of brandy. I also feel strong. I can definitely see why your customers find this so appealing."

Chuck took the jar from Whiteoak's hand, sniffed its contents and then took a careful fraction of a sip himself. His lips opened and shut in a fast series of motions that sounded like a mouse nibbling at a piece of bread. "Tastes like my elixir," he said as his tongue flicked out to lick his lips. Closing his eyes, he smirked and said, "Ahhh. Feels like it too. Except, there's something else. Something . . ."

"Better?" Whiteoak offered.

Eyeing the professor, Chuck said, "I wouldn't go that far, but there may be something to whatever you did to it. I don't feel the same spinning in my head that I felt before and my stomach don't feel so hot after drinking this stuff."

"Yes, well, that's because of the impurities that have been removed."

"I filtered that elixir plenty. That's what those are for over there!" Chuck said as he motioned toward a set of narrow copper tubes that curled in and around themselves like a poorly made intestinal tract.

"But you didn't get the same results as I did. That's incontrovertible."

Chuck didn't have anything to say to that.

"Thanks to you allowing me to work in your still," Whiteoak said, "I was able to put my considerable expertise to good use."

"Will that stuff of yours work on a bigger batch of elixir?"

"Add it and see for yourself."

Chuck's eyes narrowed into what had become a familiar scowl. As with most of the other times Whiteoak had seen that expression, Chuck drew his pistol and pointed it at the professor. "Hand over the rest of that purifying juice."

"Gladly. Take it and I'll escort my friend away from here."

"Not just yet. First I gotta see if it works like you promised. For all I know, this here is just one good jar of elixir and your talk of purifying the rest is nothin' but bullshit."

"Add it to as much as you want. It'll need to go through the works, however," White-oak said while nodding toward the larger contraption running throughout much of the cabin that was powered by the fire sputtering and flaring whenever some of the fluid dripped into the flames.

"Why?"

"Because the main problem you have is with your tubes and pipes. They're dirty."

"I can change them whenever I like."

"You're not understanding me. My mixture isn't just something that's stirred into your elixir like a spoonful of sugar. It coats the interior of the tubing of that smaller still you've allowed me to use for my experiments. It cleans the tubing and bonds with the liquid that passes through them to not only filter impurities but burn away the elements that have been harming your customers."

Chuck glanced back and forth between the larger still and a miniature setup he occasionally used as a backup in case something busted within his main apparatus. Since the smaller still was separate from the larger one, he hadn't objected when White-oak asked to use it. Glaring at it and the professor with equal suspicion, Chuck approached the small still and yanked one of the main copper tubes from the burner that kept the fluid hot and moving through the tubes. Keeping his eyes on the professor, Chuck sniffed the end of the tube and touched the tip of his tongue to it.

After spitting on the floor, Chuck said, "Smells like the stuff from your saddlebags. Tastes like it too."

"Of course it does. While you could use that smaller still to produce your elixir, it would take considerably longer to —"

"How do I treat the big still with that stuff?"

"I've got to be the one to —"

"No," Chuck said as he took aim with his pistol. "Tell me and I'll do it. I won't have you tampering with my livelihood."

Staring down the cold black eye of tempered iron, Whiteoak nervously used the back of his hand to dab a bead of sweat that had formed at his hairline. "It would be much more beneficial if I was the one to make the adjustments. After all, I am the expert and creator of the purifying solution."

"And I'm the one holding the gun," Chuck said. "Now unless you want me to ditch the whole notion of a partnership, I'll end you right here and now. Or, you can tell me what I need to know."

"And . . . after that?"

"After that, you'll get to draw another breath or two. Sound fair?"

Whiteoak cleared his throat. "Quite."

CHAPTER FORTY-THREE

Whiteoak was tossed into the livery and immediately scrambled back to his feet. He barely seemed to notice the door was being nailed shut behind him when he rushed over to where Corey was sitting. "What have you done while I was away?" Whiteoak asked in an urgent whisper.

Corey stretched his arms and scratched his groin. "Got some sleep."

"It's all right. You can talk to me in earnest. The Menlos are quite busy at the moment. What have you done in regard to our escape?"

"I got some sleep. If they aim to send us to hell, I'd rather be awake enough to enjoy it."

Whiteoak blinked at him and gaped in open astonishment. "After all I went through to buy you some time, you don't even get anything done?"

"What was I supposed to do, Henry?

Build a rifle out of straw?"

"You could have at least encouraged one of the horses to kick out a wall or something. For God's sake, use your brain!"

"Kick out a wall and ride straight into gunfire, huh? Good plan, especially when at least one of them Menlo boys proved to be pretty handy with taking long shots with his Winchester. I would've been picked off of that horse before I reached the trail. And even if I did get away, I'd be wandering around this mountain that these assholes know like the back of their hands!"

Clearing his throat, Whiteoak said, "Good. I see you've been using your brain after all." He leaned in closer to the other man and said, "Fortunately for both of us, Chuck Menlo is extremely single minded and his two nephews are blind followers. We'll be out of here in no time."

"How do you figure?"

"I've already given you part of the plan, if you recall me suggesting you to use the horses to break out of here."

Cocking his head to one side as if he was working out a particularly annoying kink, Corey said, "You got that from me. Or don't you recall I was the one with you when we were tossed into that barn in Nebraska?"

"Oh, right. We have had some good times,

Corey. In time, this will be another one to add to the list. Get those horses ready to go and I'll gather any materials that may be of use. I've gotten a look at where they're keeping our gear and after we pick it up, we'll be on our way back to Hannigan's Folly. I believe that's the closest town from here."

Corey drew a deep breath and let it out in a measured flow. "All right, Henry. I'll admit that we may be able to get away from these idiots, but only if we get an opening pretty damn quick. We need to throw them out of sorts in a big way," Corey said. "Busting out of this stable won't be enough. They're ready for that. We may get the jump on one of them or maybe two, but it'll be messy and that leaves the third man to gun us down."

"We've faced worse odds in a fight," Whiteoak pointed out.

"But this isn't just a fight. These men took us down, brought us in and held us prisoner and they wouldn't have if they weren't sure they could hold us once we were here. At the least, we can be sure they're killers and won't hesitate to spill more blood when the time is right."

Whiteoak listened intently, nodding and practically beaming with anticipation.

"What's got you so wound up and eager?" Corey asked. "You look ready to burst into song."

"I was hoping you'd be ready to go and you didn't disappoint. I've already set a plan into motion that should lead us to our emancipation from this place."

"What plan?"

"With a good enough distraction, we should be able to get some weapons and burn straight through these animals."

"You call that a plan?" Corey scoffed. "It's the inkling of a plan, at best."

"Don't be crass."

Ignoring the professor's scolding tone, Corey said, "And don't think that any of these men will go down easy in a fight. Just because you've survived with that mouth of yours for so long, don't think you can lock horns with a real killer on your own and walk away unscathed."

"I can handle myself in a fight," Whiteoak said intently. "All I need is the proper circumstances in which to strike. After that, I am deadlier than a cobra, my friend."

"Jesus Christ."

Something thumped loudly outside, sounding like the muffled footstep of a giant. That was followed by a flat explosion accented by the clatter of thin metal slapping against wooden walls.

"What the hell was that?" Corey exclaimed.

Whiteoak was already opening the door to Penelope's stall. "That," he said, "was the best circumstance we could have wished for."

CHAPTER FORTY-FOUR

"What are you waiting for?" Whiteoak shouted.

The shock Corey had felt from the explosion was still rushing through his body, but his survival instincts were sharp as ever. He rushed over to the stall where a horse fretted nervously. Rather than try to soothe the animal, Corey yelped and slapped its hind quarter to whip it into something close to a frenzy. Keeping behind the horse and to one side, Corey knocked against the back wall of the stall before giving the horse one more sharp slap on the rump. Between the explosion, the growing amount of noise outside and the confusion inside the stall, the horse started to buck. It wasn't long before its powerful back legs cracked against the wall, splintering several planks of wood.

"That's it," Corey urged. "One more!"

The horse kicked again, but wasn't quite wild enough to finish the job. When Corey hopped around to upset the horse by yelling in its face, he instead calmed the animal by giving it a glimpse of the human it knew best.

"Seems you're a bit too good with animals," Whiteoak said.

Frustrated by the horse's lack of enthusiasm, Corey turned his sights toward the damaged wood at the back of the stall. Several of the planks had been cracked and the wall itself bowed slightly outward. "Aw, to hell with it," Corey grunted. Before he could think any better of his idea, he charged at the wall and hit it with his shoulder.

Eyes widening at the sight of his partner crashing through the wall amid a cloud of dusty splinters, Whiteoak grabbed the first thing he could find that might be used as a weapon and followed Corey. Two of the three Menlos could be seen near the cabin containing the still, but were preoccupied by the fire which now consumed that structure. Whiteoak rushed to Corey's side, who was on one knee and pressing both hands to his head.

"Come on," Whiteoak said. "We need our guns."

"I think I busted somethin'," Corey moaned.

"You certainly did. Excellent job!"

"No. In me. I think I busted something in me."

Without a thought to the words, Whiteoak slapped his friend on the back and said, "No time for coddling. We need to move before one of them sees us."

Whiteoak took the lead by dragging Corey toward the spot where their saddlebags had been piled. Before he could make it halfway there, Whiteoak was stopped by a shot that blasted through the air to send a bullet hissing past him. Turning toward the source of the shot, he saw Owen running straight at him. The professor took a few steps toward the bigger man and then swung the jagged chunk of wood he'd picked up back at the stable.

Owen's finger tightened around his trigger one more time, but not before his wrist was struck by the piece of lumber. The pistol barked as it was knocked aside, spitting its round into the black Montana sky. When Owen tried to bring the gun back, Whiteoak slapped it from his hand. He started to swing the chunk of wood at Owen's head, but was hit by a meaty fist that stopped him in mid-swing.

"What did you do?" Owen snarled as he punched Whiteoak in the stomach. "What did you do, you son of a bitch?"

Coughing up a dry heave, Whiteoak backed away to avoid being hit again. The tactic bought him a few seconds which he used to catch his breath. In that short amount of time, Corey also got some wind in his sails and used it to drive forward into another charge. Instead of ramming into a wall, he pounded his shoulder into Owen's midsection while wrapping his arms around the large man's waist.

Although Owen was taken aback for a moment, he remained upright. Having absorbed Corey's assault, Owen grabbed hold of the other man and lifted him off his feet. With one hand gripping Corey's belt and the other Corey's shoulder, Owen swung him to the side like a sack of grain and brought him crashing straight down again. From there, he started slamming his boot against Corey's body.

With the big man distracted, Whiteoak took a look around. One cabin was still on fire and the other two Menlos were trying to put it out. The flames were dying already, meaning that Whiteoak had precious little time to take advantage of the opening he'd been given. If he and Corey were going to escape, it would be within the next couple of minutes. After that, their lives would surely be forfeit.

The professor gripped his makeshift club with both hands and took a deep breath. Letting the breath out in a feral battle cry, he ran at Owen while cocking both arms near his right ear. He didn't stop when he reached Owen. In fact, Whiteoak swung the broken plank so the strength from his arms was added to the power of his body's momentum to hit Owen squarely in the jaw. Before he could celebrate a resounding victory over his burly opponent, Whiteoak had to turn back around to finish him off.

"Here!" Corey said while extending one hand toward his partner. "Hand it over."

Whiteoak tossed the plank toward Corey without sticking around long enough to see if it was caught.

Not surprised to see the professor bolt when he had a chance, Corey snatched the plank from the air and swung it with everything he had. It wasn't enough. The piece of wood clipped Owen's shoulder and head, splitting in half on impact to leave Corey with a shortened stump.

"You'll need more'n that, asshole," Owen sneered.

Shifting his grip on the plank, Corey held it like he would a knife with the jagged, freshly broken end acting as the blade.

When he attacked Owen again, it was with vicious stabbing motions instead of swings. Although he had to be considerably closer to the big man, he was doing more damage every time wood connected with flesh.

Even as blood poured from the spots where the broken plank had torn open his skin, Owen swung his fists at Corey. Most of his punches glanced off rather than landing solidly due to Corey's erratic movements. The smaller man bobbed like a cork on rough water, thumping an empty fist against Owen's ribs before using his other hand to carve a fresh, bloody gash. His feet kept him circling around to one side, backing off and pressing forward yet again.

At first, it didn't seem as though he'd be able to do anything to hurt the angry Menlo. After a few more seconds, however, Corey managed to work his way back to the spot where he'd started and land a blow that sounded wetter than the ones before. The instant his knuckles hit the bloody flesh in Owen's side, Corey knew he'd struck pay dirt.

"Didn't like that too much, did ya?" Corey taunted.

Owen bared his teeth in a ferocious snarl, but the pain was visible in his eyes.

A few more steps put him in a spot where

he could see a good portion of the damage he'd done to Owen's sides and chest. Parts of the bigger man's shirt were shredded away as if by a raging animal and the edges of the gaping holes in the fabric were soaked with blood.

Enraged by the pain he was feeling and to avoid taking any more punishment, Owen grabbed hold of Corey. He took equal portions of skin and shirt within his grip, lifting Corey to his tip toes. From there, Owen snapped his head forward to crack it against Corey's skull. Owen tossed Corey aside and started looking for the pistol that had been knocked from his grasp earlier in the fight.

Corey barely realized he'd hit the ground. His head was still spinning from the knock and his rough landing blended in seamlessly with everything else that was teetering within his brain. After taking a few seconds to reorient himself, Corey clutched the only weapon he had and got his feet beneath him. Owen already had his gun in hand and wouldn't wait long before putting it to use. Running on nothing but pain and inner fire, Corey launched himself at the bigger man for one more attack.

Instead of using his body as a battering ram, Corey leapt up to wrap his left arm around the big man's neck. His right arm swung down and around to drive the jagged end of the broken plank into a bloody section of Owen's side. The meat there had already been tenderized and ripped open by previous attacks, allowing this blow to dig straight into tender flesh.

Owen howled in pain and dropped to one knee. He was in too much agony to think straight. His body was no longer obeying the simplest command, allowing the pistol to slip from his trembling fingers. Corey leaned back to pull Owen's head at an angle to expose the big man's throat. Within seconds, Owen's screams were reduced to a wet gurgle.

CHAPTER FORTY-FIVE

Whiteoak knew he didn't have to worry about Corey. If that one couldn't take advantage of a good chance when it presented itself, he would've been dead a long time ago. Instead, the professor headed straight to the largest cabin and kicked in the door that was already ajar. His eyes darted back and forth to pick out the most likely spots where he might find what he was after. The first place he went was a trunk resting against one wall. After flinging it open, all he found was stacks of neatly folded coats and heavy wool shirts. His next destination was a long crate that had most likely been used to ship an assortment of rifles.

"Damn it," he growled as he removed the crate's lid.

With the fire crackling nearby and the scuffle just ending between Corey and Owen, it was easy for Whiteoak to miss the sound of footsteps clomping against the boards of the cabin's small porch until they echoed within the cabin itself. Whiteoak turned to see a wiry figure framed in the doorway. The man standing there held a gun in his hand, which immediately spurred Whiteoak into motion. Unfortunately, his first motion caused a foot to catch on the edge of the rifle crate. As the professor fell and rolled clumsily onto his side, the man in the doorway fired a shot that drilled a hole into the wall behind him.

"What'd you do?" Sam hollered as he stomped forward. "How'd you get your hands on dynamite to cause that explosion?"

Despite laying on the floor and cocking his head at an awkward angle, Whiteoak could see a hunting rifle propped against the wall nearby. As he scrambled toward the rifle, his foot knocked once more against the side of the rifle box. Instead of kicking the box aside, however, his wild movement wasn't able to move the crate as much as an inch. Pain jolted up through his leg, urging him onward.

"I was almost killed!" Sam shouted while firing again.

Now that he'd heard the younger man's quaking voice and seen how unsteady his aim was, Whiteoak was certain that Sam had been closer to the blaze than he'd originally guessed. Probably dizzy and partly blinded, Sam was most likely partially deaf as well but that wouldn't last for much longer. The professor got to his feet and ran across the room to pick up the rifle. Several shots were fired at him along the way, none of them coming close enough to make Whiteoak abandon his mission.

Sam continued to pull his trigger until the hammer of his pistol slapped against empty brass. He chucked the pistol away and grabbed another one stashed under his belt. Instead of again firing away, he squinted over the top of the barrel to take better aim.

By now, Whiteoak had gotten to the rifle. He picked it up, brought it to his shoulder, and fired. Sam took his shot as well, but his aim was knocked to one side when Whiteoak's bullet tore through his upper chest and sent him spiraling backward. On his way down, another bullet erupted from the rifle in Whiteoak's hands, drilling a messy hole through Sam's forehead.

Lowering the rifle, Whiteoak said, "A fine weapon."

"All right!" Chuck shouted from outside. "You killed two of mine, so I kill one of yours!"

As much as Whiteoak wanted to rush to the door, common sense led him to a window instead. The moment he peeked outside, a shot was fired through the glass a couple of inches from Whiteoak's head. That split-second glimpse was enough for Whiteoak to see Chuck standing over Corey and the prone remains of Owen.

Positioning himself beneath the window with his back against the wall, Whiteoak took a more cautious look through one corner of the pane. Sure enough, the situation was as he'd first surmised. Owen was dead and Corey was being held at gunpoint by the last remaining Menlo. "We can make a bargain, you and I," Whiteoak shouted.

"Sure," Chuck replied. "Come on out and we'll bargain."

"I want to talk terms first."

"Terms? I got your partner out here and he's about to die. What terms have you got?"

Whiteoak peeked first up from one corner of the window and then from the other. When no return fire came his way, he said, "Why should I care if you kill him? Seems like I'm the one behind cover and you're the one in the open."

Corey's face was a bloody mess and the rest of his body wasn't much better. He struggled some when Chuck pulled him up off his knees, but didn't have the strength to put up much of a fight. "Drop the pistol and come on out of there," Chuck said. "You ain't gonna get me to believe you'll just watch this one die."

"I drop my weapon and then what?" Whiteoak asked. "We resume our partnership? Bygones be bygones. Water under the bridge?"

"There's still money to be made. Besides, after all the blood that's been spilled, it's too late to just walk away. The fight's started. It's gotta be seen through and I won't be on the wrong end of it."

"I'm a businessman," Whiteoak said as he pressed his back against the wall.

"And this one out here's a dead man. You ready to have that on your conscience?"

After a few quiet seconds, Corey shouted, "We can take him! Just shoot, Henry!"

"If'n you truly had ice in your veins," Chuck said, "you'd already be gone instead of staying there talking through that window. And don't think you can sneak up on me. I'll know exactly where you are the moment I hear a twig snap."

Whiteoak leaned out to look through the window. "What do you want from me?"

"Come on out and I'll tell you. Toss that gun and I'll even let your partner go. He can barely walk as it is. Seems my nephew beat him pretty good before he got sliced to death." Growing more frustrated, Chuck jammed his gun barrel against Corey's head with enough force to knock him off-balance. "Show yerself, coward!" he roared. "You two bled my kin and now I'll —"

The cabin containing the still shook as if it had somehow drawn the ire of a fiery god before exploding into a ball of flame. Every plank from every wall flew in different directions, scattering the structure like a mess of dry leaves. The force from the blast hit Chuck and Corey and sent them both staggering toward the larger cabin.

Having pulled himself away from the window just before the glass was blown out of its frame, Whiteoak stepped around to point the barrel of his commandeered rifle outside. His sharp eye found Chuck and his steady finger calmly squeezed the trigger. The rifle barked one time to blast a hole straight through Chuck's left eye and out the back of his head.

Corey stood in his spot, mouth agape and hands open wide. The more he tried to take in what had just happened, the less he seemed to grasp it. Finally, he managed to get a few words out.

"What . . . huh?"

Whiteoak smirked. "Our saddlebags are right over there," he said, pointing to the spot where the gear had been stowed. "We're going to need them."

"What about our guns?"

"I suppose you can get those too, but I doubt they'll be as useful."

CHAPTER FORTY-SIX

When Corey saw Whiteoak again, the professor was in the main cabin kneeling on the floor next to the long rifle crate. Carrying a saddlebag over each shoulder and a pistol in each hand, Corey asked, "What the hell are you doing now?"

"I'm getting what I came for," Whiteoak replied.

"You're getting us both killed? Seems to me that's what you've been after most of the time."

"Don't be so dramatic. Just give me a hand lifting this damned crate."

Although Corey dropped the saddlebags, he wasn't about to relinquish his weapons so easily. He kept one gun in his left hand and tucked the other under his belt. "There's only a few more rifles in there. Why don't we just take them out instead of moving the whole crate?"

"Because I'm not after the rifles," Whiteoak explained.

With one concentrated effort, they hefted the crate only to find that it was attached to the floor. It, along with a section of the wooden planks beneath it, swung upward on a well-oiled hinge to reveal a square hole beneath it framed by dusty cobwebs. The professor reached into it and gleefully pulled out a small burlap sack. Without hesitation, he turned the sack upside down and spilled several bundles of cash onto the floor.

"How do you always know where to find the hidden money?" Corey sighed.

"It's my talent. One of many." Reaching back into the dark hiding space, Whiteoak added, "Seems that sack was one of many as well."

Corey dropped to one knee so he could help stuff the money into their saddlebags as it was brought into the open. "Honestly, how did you know this was here?"

"As I mentioned while we rode here," Whiteoak replied. "It was obvious that the Menlo family was into some kind of lucrative endeavor, which means they were pulling in some degree of income. That's just basic logic. I surmised upon arrival that Charles Menlo was the man in charge and he struck me as the sort who would want to keep his money close at hand, which meant it would be stored in this cabin above the others."

"You had a nose for that, did you?"

"Any salesman worth his salt needs to have a nose for things like that."

"And that exact hiding place?" Corey asked.

"I found it on accident. This crate didn't budge when I tripped over it after Sam started shooting at me. It seemed to be attached to the floor and there's not many reasons for that unless it's to hide something underneath. Seeing as how there were no other hiding spots to be found in here, I deduced this was where Chuck Menlo was keeping his profits."

"I'm surprised you didn't claim to sniff that out through sheer smarts."

"I considered it," Whiteoak admitted. "But didn't think you'd buy it."

"How right you are. Now what the hell happened with those explosions? You rigged them stills to blow, right?"

Whiteoak straightened up so his smug grin could be seen. "You might say that."

"And you used that stuff you sold in Hannigan's Folly that was supposed to clean folks' teeth."

The professor's self-satisfaction quickly gave way to shock when he said, "How could you know that?"

"Because the smoke comin' from them fires smelled like mint leaf. You mean to tell me that the same junk you sold for people to use in their mouths is explosive? That's low, Henry. Even for you."

"It's not explosive. It is, however, mildly corrosive. That's how it burns away the yellow from an old fellow's teeth."

"But that wouldn't start a fire," Corey pointed out.

"No, but in larger concentrations it can eat through an old length of tubing. All I had to do was convince Chuck that adding it to his elixir was a good idea. My Fresh and White product already had the necessary ingredients to make the swill being sold by the Menlos seem a thousand times more agreeable. I adjusted the formula a bit to make it more corrosive than before. Once the lines were eaten through, Menlo's elixir was exposed to an open flame which caused the fireworks. The smaller still blew up fairly quickly. In time, the larger explosion would happen and to get to that point, I needed to keep Chuck Menlo talking."

"Talking ain't never much of a chore for you," Corey said. "But how'd you get Menlo to agree to use that potion of yours, anyhow?"

"He made me taste it first and I did. That seemed to be enough."

Corey's brow furrowed. "You drank that stuff straight from the bottle? I thought it had to be diluted."

"For the common person, yes," Whiteoak replied. "But I am far from common. I cannot even begin to list the number of chemical concoctions I've tasted, smelled, inhaled, smoked, injected, or otherwise consumed in my career. Builds up quite a tolerance, you see. I even survived small doses of cyanide once."

"Bullshit."

"Not at all. Tastes like almonds. Very nice."

Whiteoak lay down on his side to reach as far as possible into the narrow space beneath the floorboards. "You didn't really think I intended on joining forces with Menlo, did you? All that chatter while you were being held at gunpoint was just that. Simply talk to buy time until the tubes were ruptured and the elixir was dumped into the fires heating the stills. And when they did," he added while sitting up to show Corey the last money bag he'd found, "the real fireworks started. Not a bad haul, eh?"

"Did you stop to think before you did all of this?"

Still holding some of the money, Whiteoak

lowered his hands a bit and replied, "Of course I did. I knew there would be a stash of money here."

"Since this Menlo fella ain't much more than a huckster like you and all of you hucksters have a stash of money."

"I wouldn't say he's anywhere in my league, but I also knew it wouldn't be too difficult to win his confidence and figure a way to get the better of him."

Corey was almost finished loading the money into the saddlebags. "That's not what I meant, though. Did you think about what would happen *after* you got the best of these Menlos?"

"We spend their money!" Whiteoak laughed.

"Obviously the Menlos have friends all through these mountains. Friends with pull like Jacob Parsons and any other thieves or killers who work to sell that elixir. Obviously, plenty of it's been sold and it don't seem likely that the three of these men could have done it all. What do you think will happen when those men find out their gravy train has been derailed?"

"I won't tell them. Will you?"

"They always find out, Henry. You're smart enough to know that."

Whiteoak let out a tired sigh. "That elixir

Chuck Menlo was making was worse than opium. It was delicious poison that men craved. Having something like that out on the open market just makes it more difficult for those of us in the trade. Customers tend to get skittish."

"It also makes them dead," Corey added.

"Exactly!"

"Wanna know what I think?"

"That we need to load up our horses while the getting is good?"

"I think," Corey said as he hefted one of the saddlebags onto his shoulder, "that you've got more of a conscience than you let on. You knew how much money was being made with this poison and you could have easily talked your way into being Menlo's partner."

"It wouldn't have been easy to wrangle a fair cut from that one."

"But you could've done it," Corey said. "Instead, you not only settle for whatever scraps of money you can find, but you destroy the stuff that made all that money. It ain't like you."

"These Menlos were savages," Whiteoak said. "Putting them down was a public service, not to mention profitable."

"These men will be missed and when word gets around of what happened to them, their friends, partners or kin will want to know what happened and who was the last one to pay these fellas a visit."

Whiteoak glanced nervously about. "You think there are more Menlos?"

"Since when do idiots like these come from small families?"

"Good point."

"And once all that commotion starts," Corey said, "it'll eventually find us. And when that commotion finds us, it'll make it that much easier for bounty hunters to find us."

Whiteoak nodded and looked around as if taking some last bit of comfort from the chaos of his surroundings. Once his eyes settled on the mountains just beyond the clearing, he said, "Time to move on, is it?"

"Yep."

CHAPTER FORTY-SEVEN

Professor Henry Whiteoak was no stranger to putting towns behind him under cover of darkness. With precious little fanfare, he returned to civilization just long enough to retrieve his wagon, settle his accounts and catch a few hours of sleep in a small rented room. Before the sun crested the horizon the following morning, he was gone.

Sometime later, having taken the Square Mountain Trail to its southernmost limit, Whiteoak was joined by another man who rode up alongside his slowly moving wagon.

"So, that's it, then?" Corey asked after a few silent moments.

Without looking over to the other man, Whiteoak replied, "And here it comes. When I try to partake in a new enterprise, you call me a fool and a thief. When I opt for the quiet exit, you show up to call me a coward who tucks his tail and runs when things get difficult."

"I never called you a coward."

"Not yet, but I'm sure it's coming."

"I just thought you'd stick around Split Knee or Hannigan's Folly for a while and try to sell that elixir you got from Chuck Menlo."

Now Whiteoak looked over at him. "And when did I have time to steal that elixir before blowing it to hell?"

"You wouldn't need to steal a drop," Corey replied. "You saw more than enough to be able to make it yourself."

Whiteoak shrugged and gave his reins a lazy flick. "I might have picked up a thing or two."

"More than that, I'd say. You're a smart fella."

"Now that must have been painful to say," Whiteoak scoffed.

"Stop being so sore. You're just pissed because you're leaving. You always get that way when you have to pull up stakes and move on before wringing every last penny from a place."

Wistfully, the professor mused, "And there was still so much to be wrung from those four little towns."

"You could still be there."

"So could those bounty hunters. I doubt anyone in these mountains has enough authority to counter whatever offer is being made by my estranged acquaintances from Kansas."

"True," Corey said, "but this isn't the first time you've had someone after you. I think there's another reason you decided to move on just like there's another reason you blew up that still."

"Since you're obviously setting up your grand reveal, just get on with it."

"You've grown a conscience," Corey said with a smirk.

"Back to that old chestnut? Just because I decided to put a stop to the Menlo clan creating a bunch of glassy-eyed drunks craving that foul serum of his doesn't make me a saint. Although," Whiteoak added as he glanced upward, "such a title would make an excellent addition to the side of my wagon. It would help win over the Bible thumping crowd who berate me on Sunday afternoons."

Corey shook his head. "Conscience or not, Henry. This whole mess has made it too risky to ride with you any longer. Folks like those Menlos and the rich men you crossed along the Square Mountain Trail won't forget you just because you're out of their sight."

"That's why I thought we should —"

"No," Corey snapped. "No *we*. Not no more. I go my way and you go yours."

Whiteoak pulled back on his reins to bring his two-horse team to a halt. Turning to face Corey directly, he studied the other man for all of two seconds before extending his hand. "I can see you've made up your mind. Where might you be headed?"

"That way," Corey replied while nodding toward the east. "I've got a hunch of where the next bunch of bounty hunters might be coming and there's a good chance I can throw them off our trail. You still intend on riding south?"

"Yes, and I hope to meet up with you again before too much time passes."

"Me too, Professor," Corey said while shaking Whiteoak's hand.

Whiteoak snapped his reins and got the wagon rolling again. Before he'd travelled more than ten yards, he heard Corey shout, "Henry, where's my cut of that cash you took from the Menlos? Or did you think I forgot?"

Letting out a defeated sigh, Whiteoak grunted, "Dammit."

ABOUT THE AUTHOR

Marcus Galloway is the author of several novels and short stories in the western genre. His previous series includes the *Man From Boot Hill* (HarperCollins), *The Accomplice* (Berkley) *Sathow's Sinners* (Berkley) and *Easy Pickin's* (Five Star). He currently resides in a small West Virginia town with one perfect dog and a whole lot of books.

The employees of Thorndike Press hope you have enjoyed this Large Print book. All our Thorndike, Wheeler, and Kennebec Large Print titles are designed for easy reading, and all our books are made to last. Other Thorndike Press Large Print books are available at your library, through selected bookstores, or directly from us.

For information about titles, please call:
(800) 223-1244

or visit our Web site at:
http://gale.cengage.com/thorndike

To share your comments, please write:
Publisher
Thorndike Press
10 Water St., Suite 310
Waterville, ME 04901